Since Forever

Cass Michaels

ISBN: 979-8-89034-720-6

To my beautiful mom:

You always believed in my passion and supported my dreams.
Thank you for being my biggest cheerleader...

This is the story you always said I should write-

I'm sad you aren't here to read it

I miss you every day

Prologue

Sitting on the couch, Andi snuggles deeper into the cushions, losing herself in the story. She reads contentedly, enjoying the peace and quiet of the old home. It's some time before she feels piercing eyes watching her.

"I thought you guys were going to collaborate and work on college applications? Aren't they due at the end of the month?" Rayaan Collins asks.

"Mine are all completed; I've already been accepted at two of my choices. I was just trying to get him motivated." She rolls her eyes. "Besides, Jenny called and asked him to work on their science research."

"Jenny? Isn't she his new flavor of the week?"

Not wanting her face to betray her true feelings, she doesn't look up. She flips the page in her book. "I guess so."

"Why sit here and put yourself through that punishment?" He moves into the room, the fluid movements of a swimmer, and leans against the shelf, folding his arms over his college sweatshirt.

Wanting to change the subject, Andi lifts the book from her lap. "Your dad always has good books."

"That's mine."

She turns the cover over, looking at the dinosaur, and

shrugs. "It's really awesome. Some of the science is fascinating."

He nods, his dark brown eyes watching her. "I was going to recommend it to you."

"I like it." She blushes, stamping down the butterflies in her stomach. "It's a great escape."

He's silent for a moment, his features full of concern. "Why do you keep doing this to yourself?"

Closing the book, Andi bites back the desire to sigh. All she's wanted for the last three years is for his brother to pay attention to her. Instead, it's like a revolving door of popular girls coming in and out of the Collins' house. And she has a front row seat to watch it because she's the girl next door. But maybe, just maybe, one day Arin will see her for who she truly is, and not what's on the surface. Not that she's holding her breath for that moment.

She swings her legs to the floor. "I know he's never going to pick me. I know I'm the one who watches from the corner while everyone else gets picked for the dance." She pulls her shirt down over her plump belly. "I know what I look like."

Rayaan's lip curls into a smile. "Do you really, Red?"

"Chubby, with unruly hair. I read. I know girls like me don't get the guy."

"Beautiful and brilliant-"

"-You're just saying that to make me feel better." She

stands. "You're the older brother, deflecting his shitty behavior." Andi tucks the book to her chest. "I'm taking your book and going home."

"Andrea, wait-" Rayaan pleads, but she doesn't turn around as she leaves the room.

Chapter One

"Come on, Andi. It's an easy story."

"No, Janessa, I told you I didn't want to cover anyone who is a 'social media influencer.'" Andrea Jennings dramatically air quotes. "It's all make-believe bullshit."

"And interviewing actresses to find out their fitness routines isn't?" Janessa Flannigan asks.

Andi lowers her eyes, glaring at her friend and boss. "Low blow. You're the damn editor of the magazine. If you don't want our advertisers influencing the types of questions we ask, tell them 'no.'" She flicks her hair over her shoulder. "Believe me, I don't give a fuck what Brooklyn Nash eats, or how she stays fit. But I gotta ask the questions to pay the bills." She rolls her eyes, tossing the latest copy of the women's magazine on the table. "I'd rather have had the Peterson interview. That was a huge Senate scandal, and I should have had it."

Janessa nods, rocking back in her chair. "Hey, I'm trying to get you in the door here. I had to give the story to Henley because of seniority. My hands were tied." She flails her arm behind her, acknowledging a photo with some of the main shareholders in the company and shrugs her shoulders. "With your background in finance and politics, it should only be a matter of time before I can get you writing more hard-hitting stuff. But for now, this is what I have." Janessa points at the frozen image on her computer screen. "He's going somewhere."

Ignoring the photo, Andi turns her hand to examine her nails. When was the last time she'd had a manicure? "Can't you find me something better to write? I don't want to write a fluff piece on the internet's boyfriend."

Janessa leans forward across the desk, making her last pitch. "He lives in your hometown. You can take a paid vacation. Write the story quickly and take some time off."

Andi can't remember the last time she'd really relaxed. Her last vacation, so to speak, had consisted of finding a new job and moving to a new city. The view from her friend's office window tells her the company can definitely foot the bill. And it's not like anyone else is pounding on her door for time or attention. Eyes calculating and growling deep in her throat, Andi huffs. "Fine. I'll do it."

Janessa hardly hides her smile. "There's my girl. I knew you'd see it my way."

"You don't play fair. When do I leave?"

"Martha has the tickets reserved, she simply needs to verify some of your information on your way out," Janessa spins back in her chair, pleased with the outcome.

Rising up, Andi reaches to the table beside her for her

laptop bag and bulky winter coat.

Janessa lifts her chin. "Cheer up, it's not like you have to stay here and endure another winter storm. You'll be in the sun, having fun."

Andi presses her lips together. "Can Martha set me up in a hotel? Something nice? If I'm doing this, I'm totally making a vacation of it. Room service and everything."

"Sure," Janessa nods, eyeing her computer, ready to shift back into work mode. "Ask Martha for the materials you need to take too."

Walking backwards to the door, Andi says, "Let me guess, testing out some product for an advertiser."

Janessa tilts her head. "Some lighting and sound equipment, as a gift to him, hoping he'll use it as product placement."

Banging her head back against the door, Andi sighs, "When did the job become about all this shit, Janessa? Why can't we just investigate and report on things like we used to?"

"Higher paychecks now, darling. Bigger headaches, more shit," Janessa chuckles. "Have fun. Tell your parents I said 'hi.'"

Opening the door, Andi throws a kiss over her shoulder. She decides to test her luck one more time. "Can you bring me some sample clothes so I can pack my bags?"

Reaching for a pen, Janessa makes a quick note. "Sure, I'll drop them off on my way home from Turner's house. Love you."

"Love you too, babe. By the way, what did you say his name is?"

"Arin Collins."

In the elevator, Andi rests her forehead against the wall. "Why me? Why me?" she sighs out.

The box of gadgets Martha gave her sits at her feet. She knows she won't be able to carry it home on the El, so she arranges an Uber. Going through the list of things before she leaves town in less than 36 hours, she thumps the research packet against the wall. "My hotel better have poolside service and all-day drinks, that's all I can say."

Arriving in the lobby, she exits the elevator, nearly forgetting the box. The doorman rushes over to help her and she asks him to put it on the bench. Sitting down next to it, Andi reaches in the outer pocket of her sturdy leather bag and pulls out her phone. The battered case has seen better days. She warily eyes the new update, sitting on top of the supplies Martha handed her. Thirty-six hours to learn new technology. Fabulous. She can't wait to get started.

Blinking rapidly, she hits the little image of her mother's

face on her screen. She waits. One. Two. Three. Four. Her mother always picks up after the fourth ring. "Hey, Mom. What's new?"

Andi listens while her mother regals her with stories from the morning fitness group. Her mother has been teaching aerobics to older women for so many years, she's now old enough to be her own client. "That's great, Mom. Tell Belinda I'm sorry about her broken leg and hope she gets back to class soon. Are there exercises you can adapt for her?"

"Mmhmm," Sarah Jennings hums. "I can do that. But this isn't why you called, dear daughter. What's afoot?"

Andi laughs at her mother's strange turn of phrase. There's so much to tell her, but she doesn't even know where to start. She shrugs. "How can you hear that through the phone?" She's amazed at her mother's wisdom, even from so far away.

"Are you prepared for the snowstorm later this week? I hear it's supposed to get bad by Friday."

Watching the traffic out the lobby windows, Andi replies. "It won't matter. I'm getting on a plane Wednesday afternoon. I'm coming home. I have to interview," she chokes on her words, "Arin Collins."

Her mother gasps. "Oh, I love him! His videos are so funny and relatable. Your father and I haven't seen him in ages. You should bring him over for dinner."

"I shouldn't be surprised. Of course, you've seen his videos."

"Honey, I think every woman in America has seen his videos. I saw one of his recent posts on one of the morning shows."

That's how Andi ended up with the story. One of the press directors had also seen the segment and wanted to make sure he was featured in their magazine before anyone else could get him. Arin Collins. Her childhood next door neighbor- her high school frenemy.

Her college sweetheart.

Andi had learned from Martha he was contracted for the interview and was paid a hefty sum not to talk to any other publications for the foreseeable future. This knowledge simply added to Andi's dislike of social media entrepreneurs, and him in general.

"He's so talented," her mother continues. "I think his mother said he's trying to get into acting and-"

"Isn't everyone on the coast?" Andi scoffs.

"Apparently not everyone. Some of them want to find the truth, rather than play a scripted role."

Sighing, Andi turns away from her reflection in the elevator doors across the lobby. Her mother never understood her fascination for reporting and politics.

"There's more to life than a pretty face. Isn't that what you always taught me?"

"Well, yes. But that was before you were professionally single."

Andi's bark of laughter echoes off the marble tiles in the waiting area. "Being single is a full-time job, and I'm good at it." She inhales. Thinking about giving up her independence at this stage in life makes her skin itch. She's very set in her ways and hasn't found a man yet who makes her want to change them. "Mom, I have to go. My ride's almost here. Just know I'm coming to the house for dinner Wednesday night, okay? Alone. Nothing too leafy. I like a little more protein, especially after the flight."

"Greens won't kill you- Aren't you going to stay with your father and me?"

Shaking her head 'no' even though her mother can't see her, Andi says, "No. The company is putting me up in a hotel, giving me new equipment, and even sending over some clothes. I'm trying to think of it as a vacation, instead of an assignment. But I'll be in town several days, to get the story the editors want, and I'll see you as much as I can. I promise."

Hanging up the phone, she realizes this assignment won't be too awful if it means getting to spend a few extra days with her parents.

Chapter Two

The next day and a half was a total blur. Packing, getting her hair and nails done, arranging a sitter for Luna, her three-year-old tabby cat. And watching videos. Hours of them, all in short, two-minute segments social media sites seem to crave. Andi has to admit, some make her laugh- not that she'd share that with him. Mostly she wants to strangle his neck. Arin's observations are too accurate, and the suave moves he displays on film are fodder for the romance seekers.

And she still has more to watch on the three-hour trip home. Tucking the notes from her research back into her bag, she readies to board her flight when her section number is called.

A voice inside says, 'no more.' She mutes the phone, his face still moving on her screen. Resting her head against her travel pillow, Andi sighs. Of all people she was being sent to interview, why him?

When Andi was in 6th grade, the Collins' moved into the empty house next door. Two more boys for the neighborhood was disappointing. Andi had been tired of being the last one chosen for streetball teams every time, and had really been hoping a family with girls would move in. The older brother was already driving, and didn't have much time for fun, it seemed. The younger boy, Arin, instantly became her competitor at school, defeating her in all the things she was best at- she hated him.

Over time, the parents became friends, the dads sharing lawn equipment and the mothers organizing potluck dinners. With heavy reluctance, Andi and Arin learned to be civil with one another, and eventually grew to have a wary friendship.

The summer before they started high school, the boys and their mother left to visit family in India when their grandfather passed away. They were gone so long; Andi had begun to wonder if they were coming back.

She was sitting on her front porch swing, reading, the evening they returned. As they climbed out of the car, she'd felt her stomach flip in an unfamiliar way. These were no longer the boys she had grown up with... Rayaan had filled out, his shoulders more broad, his hair flopping in his face. Was that stubble on his chin? He'd finished his freshman year in college shortly before they left. Andi missed talking with him about books and their shared interests in swimming and history. When she turned her attention to Arin, he was almost unrecognizable. Was it possible to grow a foot taller in two months? His skin was darker, kissed by the sun. She couldn't take her eyes off the way his muscles moved, shown off in a blue tank top and board shorts, as he helped his mother unload the car.

An unknown force had pulled her from the swing. Prisha Collins was struggling to balance two bags, and Andi rushed over to help. "Welcome back!"

The woman enveloped her in a motherly hug. "Oh, I've missed you, *beti*. All this time with these boys?" She'd rolled her eyes. "Your mother and I need to take you for a girl's day before school starts."

Prisha Collins had always wanted a daughter, and Andi was hers by proxy. Any time there was anything remotely feminine needing to be done, Sarah Jennings always invited Prisha to join them.

"Wait until you see the gifts I bought for you and your mother!"

With a smile, Andi grabbed the suitcase and said she couldn't wait to see them and tell Prisha all she'd missed over the summer. Carrying the bag inside the house, she'd blushed when the boys greeted her. "Looking good, Red," Rayaan teased.

Catching her reflection in the plane window, she's happy with the ginger-red now. "Red." She scoffs at the old

17

nickname the Collins' boys used for her. Her wavy red hair never did anything back then. It wasn't sleek, like Julia's, the girl Arin dated freshman year, or curly, like Samantha's or Tarin's, the girls he dated sophomore year. It just was, and hung loosely at her shoulders, often a tangled mess by the end of the day. But the boys next door delighted in teasing her about the color of her hair.

Lifting her hand to brush it back, she's managed to tame the waves, twisting small tendrils around her face. Gone are the giant glasses and the colorful make-up of her youth. Muted, soft tones highlight her skin, coordinating with her earth tone outfits. Through the years, Andi's learned to style her clothing to accentuate her full, curvy figure, rather than to hide it.

A tiny part of her can't help but wonder what the Collins' boys- men- would think of her now.

The wobbly wheel on the bottom of Andi's carry-on bag drags through the terminal. Her skin feels tight and itchy from the pressurized air. She stops her march, apologizing to the family behind her for stopping in the path. Digging in her travel bag, she finds a little jar of moisturizer and dabs a spot on each cheek, rubbing it in. Reaching for her lip gloss, she looks up in time to see an older gentleman walking towards the baggage claim. She giggles, shaking her head. Without hesitation, she crows like a bird, passengers moving away from her, to avoid her craziness.

The man crows in return, a family tradition for finding one another in crowded spaces, spinning on his heels to face her. "My girl!" he calls out.

Dropping the lip gloss back in her bag, she drags the wobbly bag to him. "Dad! I told Mom you didn't have to come!"

Stephen Jennings embraces her in a tight hug. "I wasn't about to miss the chance to see my little girl without your mother asking her probing questions and butting in." He knocks her on the chin affectionately. "Bless her."

Andi smiles widely. "She can't help it. I have to keep reminding myself she means well. And if it weren't for her probing questions, challenging me to always get to the truth, I wouldn't be at the top of my career now."

He nods, taking the bag handle from her and pulls it up to the barrier wall. "You wait here. Does your suitcase still have the bright purple buckle on it?"

She nods, remembering when they bought the attachment for her senior trip to Mexico. He'd told her she always needed something when traveling to make it easy to find in a sea of black cases. "The bag is school-bus yellow, too. You can't miss it."

"That's my girl! See, I told you it was good advice. Always make it easy to spot- ah, see, there it is."

He jogs off to get her luggage from the carousel and quickly returns to her, while other passengers wait to determine which bag is theirs.

"We'll be back on the freeway before most of them even get to the parking lot!" He laughs.

Chapter Three

Watching the lanes behind him in the rearview mirror, Stephen clears his throat. "You know your mother has lots of questions?"

She points to a silver car changing lanes ahead. Andi aims to keep her voice steady. "And you know I don't want to talk about it. It's only an interview. For work. Nothing more."

"He broke your heart-"

"Dad!" Andi drops her arm, hitting it against the window.

"I'm sorry, was I not supposed to know?" He swivels his head to take a brief look at his daughter before returning his focus on the road. "Your mother told me years ago- it was the reason you quit coming home as much."

Andi huffs. "Yeah. Okay. He did. But let's face it, we all knew he would. Can we let it go now? I have."

Stephen flips on his turn signal. "Your tone doesn't indicate-"

"Dad! I swear, I will fling open this door, and jump out of this car!" Andi places her hand on the door latch. Her tone is light and teasing, but she feels some truth to the words. She doesn't want to think back to Arin leaving her but especially not less than twenty-four hours before she has to interview the bastard and act like she's interested in his life and career.

Taking his hands off the wheel, Stephen puts them up in mock surrender. "Good. You're ready for your mother then. I'll just make sure there are no sharp utensils on the dinner table."

"I don't want to interview him, you know. I begged for another assignment. But Janessa can only throw me so many bones." She tugs at the seatbelt, trying to keep it from scratching her collarbone. "She's still getting on her feet as the new editor at the magazine."

Taking in her words, Stephen thumps the steering wheel with his thumb. "Are you sorry you left DC?"

Andi chuckles softly. "Goodness, no. It was a cesspool even in the good times, and there was no way I was covering his presidency." She can't even bring herself to name the new leader of the nation. She shudders. "I stayed long enough. I have good contacts- I just need to be able to use them."

"Kinda hard when you're interviewing fashion models and social media stars."

"Thanks, Dad, for that vote of confidence."

He guffaws, a deep, comforting sound. "I am confident you will find what you want. You know with all your experience as a White House correspondent all those years, I can get you a job at the university."

Stephen was proud of his work in the classroom at the local college. He was always trying to get Andi to join the staff, to teach journalism, government, or history.

"I know, but I'm not ready to come home. I'm too old to come home." She adjusts her skirt. "I'm making new friends in Chicago, really starting to make it mine. I can do this."

He nods. "I know you can. I'm proud of you." He signals to turn off the exit ramp. "Are you sure you're ready to see Arin?"

Andi smiles, seeing her distorted view in the side mirror. "I saw him every day, next door, for how many years when we hated each other as kids? I think I can handle two days for this interview."

Stephen pats her hand, resting on the center console. "Hopefully he's as mature about it as you are."

"Highly unlikely, but it is what it is."

Pulling down the quiet suburban street, Andi hopes the Collins's aren't out in their yard. She isn't ready to see Prisha or Neal yet. She feels it's inevitable but would like to spend time with her mother first.

Sarah Jennings bounds down the steps to greet the car with a youthful vibrancy. Her appearance belies her years. Despite a few gray hairs, she looks young enough to be Andi's sister. Even her curls bounce with excitement as she waits for her daughter to exit the car. "You're home!" She cries out, throwing her arms open for a wide hug.

Andi slides into her mother's embrace. "You look so good! I missed you!"

"I love what you've done with your hair!" They both exclaim at the same time, dissolving into giggles and holding each other tightly again.

"You both go on inside. I'll get the bags."

Sarah nods, tugging her daughter's arm. "Tell me everything. What's your new office like?"

Andi calls over her shoulder, "Dad, I just need the backpack. It has the Chicago-mix popcorn Mom wanted." She freezes momentarily, seeing the curtains move in the house next door. "Everything else goes to the hotel." She swallows hard, forcing her eyes forward, careful not to trip on the uneven pavers of the sidewalk, as her mother pulls her into the house.

Nothing has changed. It's been nearly two years since her last visit. Sarah and Stephen prefer to visit her, wherever she's living, using the time away as an excuse for a vacation. The paint on the walls seems a little more crisp, clean. Maybe that's been updated, but everything else is the same. She looks to the house next door once more before fully stepping inside and closing the door behind her.

"They don't live there anymore, remember?" Sarah says quietly, squeezing her shoulder. "When Prisha broke her leg skiing last winter, they decided they didn't need such a big house for the two of them."

Andi vaguely remembers that from one of her mother's rambling calls. She sets her purse on the stairs. "It must be weird not having them next door."

Over the years, the families had become very connected. The parents had taken to claiming the other children as their own, and the kids referred to the opposite sets of parents as 'aunt' and 'uncle.' With everyone grown now, Sarah was known to brag about her three handsome sons, and Prisha was excited about the grandmotherly status she had with her brother's son.

Sarah nods. "Prisha and I have coffee several times a week. Your father and Neal play golf, and we have our weekly dinners together. They hate the condo." She begins to walk to the kitchen. "She's even joked when the house goes up for sale again, they'd like to buy it back."

"It is a lovely home." Andi had always loved to be at the house. Her older brother and his friends always made so much noise, with their garage band, that she always felt the Collins' house was quieter. She knew every little nook and cranny of the neighbor's home. She'd spent many hours reading and studying in Neal Collins's library. Following her mother into the open room, she says, "I hope the new owners appreciate those bookshelves."

"Oh, Neal took the ones he could! Not all of them were built in. And he gave two of them to us, and plenty of books to fill them. They're downstairs in the family room." Sarah opens the fridge and takes out a bowl of lettuce. "The lasagna will be ready in about twenty minutes."

Andi eyes the basement door. She'd love to go see the books Neal had left behind.

Reading her daughter's mind, Sarah chuckles, "After dinner. Help me get the tomatoes cut."

Andi washes her hands, and the two women prepare the meal together, working in a comfortable silence.

"It's good to have you home," Sarah says, as the oven beeps. Stephen comes in behind her, grabbing the oven mitts to take out the pan of lasagna. Resting it on the counter, the cheese still bubbles and sizzles, the aroma making Andi's mouth water.

Handing over a stack of plates, Sarah nods to the table. Andi begins to set out the dishes. "So tell us about this interview. What's going to be your focus?"

Taking napkins from the buffet, Andi hides her scowl from her mother. "My angle? I don't care about the damn fluff piece. Maybe I should expose," she air quotes, "'the hopeless romantic' as a lying womanizer."

"Come now, Andrea," Sarah appeals, putting the hot pan on the table. "It's been nearly ten years. That's a little harsh, don't you think?"

"I don't care. I'm an investigative reporter." Andi pulls out a stately oak chair and sits down. "I'm not going to go easy just because he's my old…" She pauses looking for the right word. Neighbor, rival, heartbreaking crush all come to mind, but she says what feels most right. "Friend. Do you know how many sponsors he's getting, for advertisements? All because they think he's the perfect boyfriend? It's a total scam."

Sarah scoops out a hefty serving and plops it on her husband's plate. "His videos are really insightful. He's perfected the art of appealing to the female gaze- what? He's handsome!" She explains when Stephen's glares.

He drops his fork and unbuttons his shirt sleeve. He slowly rolls it up. "Anyone can do this. Is it that appealing?"

Sarah can't take her eyes off his arms.

"Dad, stop, before she has a stroke," Andi laughs. "Yes, it's very attractive when men do that-"

She swallows, remembering how hot the video of Arin leaning against the wall and rolling his sleeves made her. The two actions. At the same time.

Asshole.

"- And you're totally a silver fox, honey-"

"Mom, I'm eating." Andi continues, grinning at her parents. "Arin's good at picking up on social cues, observing

27

dynamics between men and women. Eighty percent of his videos are tropes. Big deal, so he can lean on a counter, dance, and tie a Windsor knot."

"-It took Neal a week to teach him that-" Stephen interjected. "It was for the debate in Philadelphia, right? The big one, when the team qualified for that competition-"

"- My point is, social media is ridiculous. Did you know to gain followers, an influencer has to post four or five videos a day? Add in all the time to create the script, to edit the damn two-minute clip, when the hell can they find time to do anything else? How is he paying for a roof over his head?"

"Prisha says he still runs all his stock investments, and he only started doing this for entertainment, and discovered he was good at it." Sarah adds dressing to her salad. "Two hundred thousand followers can't be wrong."

"Try three hundred thousand, and growing. It's ridiculous. People have time to sit and watch videos all day. It's such a waste of time."

"Everyone needs an escape, Andi," Sarah says. "Watching the videos, and making them. Not everything has to be factual and serious. He's looking to bring a little joy and humor to the world. There's nothing wrong with that."

Suddenly losing her appetite, Andi pushes her chair back. "I didn't say it was wrong, just there's more to life than letting social media and streaming videos suck away all the real

28

enjoyment."

"Sweetie, are you nervous about seeing him again? Is that what this animosity is about?" Stephen asks gently.

Looking out the window to the house across the way, Andi can't help but wonder if her father is right.

Chapter Four

Tapping her finger against her empty breakfast plate, Andi's mood flips from annoyed to relieved. Honestly, she's not surprised by Martha's call, letting her know Arin needs to reschedule their interview time. 'That something came up.'

He works from home. What the hell could have come up?

She smiles at the waitress returning her credit card and looks through the doorway of the hotel restaurant. Andi watches the people milling around the lobby, getting ready for important meetings, or families heading out for a day of sightseeing. The sunlight bounces off the highly polished floors, calling her out for her own adventure.

With her appointment to meet Arin rescheduled, she sees no need to go back upstairs and change her clothes. Her fashionable workout clothes will do for a drive out to the lake. Maybe she can call and make plans with her mom for lunch while her dad's at work?

Grabbing her wallet from the table she makes her exit, striding confidently out into the lobby. Andi nods to the vendor setting out a table in front of one of the boutique shops the hotel is known for. She gawks at the items in the window, and silently vows to return later to check out the pretty earrings on display. She walks to the queue formed at the valet parking station. Waiting in line, Andi absently looks through her phone, adding a heart to a photo her sister-in-law posted of her nephew. She can't help but feel a little relieved the meeting was canceled. Always the professional, she fears she won't be able to complete the job with the level of steadiness and sophistication she is known for in the industry.

Smiling at the picture her mother shared of the three of them after dinner, Andi feels more calm. She's had more difficult assignments before. She's handled them, and she can totally handle this one.

One second, she's feeling centered, and the next Andi's totally thrown off balance when someone brusquely walks into her.

The culprit was too busy talking into his phone to notice the long line of people waiting for their cars.

Regaining her footing, Andi looks up, directly into the eyes of Arin Collins.

The handsome man squeezes her arm. "Are you okay? Sorry to bump into- Ands? Is that you?" His eyebrow furrows in confusion.

Hearing his nickname for her, all the air feels sucked from her lungs. She swallows. "Arin," she says, just as shocked as he. She knew she'd be seeing him again, yet she realizes now she wasn't prepared. How can he get better looking? But, this isn't where she was supposed to meet him? She blows out her breath, frowning. "How did you know I was staying here?"

He speaks into the phone. "I'm gonna have to call you back." The flustered look on his face grows. "I didn't." Arin's hand slides down her arm, to take her hand in his. He holds it tightly, stepping closer and pressing his lips to her cheek. She hates to admit his cologne smells like heaven. "You look amazing; you've hardly aged. You still look like the girl, sitting on my swing set, reading a book." Andi blushes as his eyes search her face, his crinkling at the corners from his wide smile. "What are you doing here?"

Giving his hand a squeeze, Andi steps back. "I could ask you the same thing. I had a message you had to cancel- we're supposed to meet down on the waterfront. How did you know I was here?" She asks again more emphatically, hoping her office wasn't giving out such personal information.

"I had no idea you were in town, Ands. Or staying here."

His eyes quickly scan the lobby, and she casts a glance over her shoulder for a look too.

"Are you searching for someone?" Andi asks.

"Yeah, something like that," Arin says quietly. He tucks an unruly curl behind his ear.

Watching his movement, she says, "I guess some things never change. Still in need of a haircut." Andi looks ahead, wondering what's the hold up with the cars. Wanting to escape this scene, she feels less than confident in her outfit

32

now and tugs down on the bright blue top.

"Wait-" Arin reaches out to touch her again but drops his hand awkwardly. "What do you mean I canceled on you?"

The line advances and he steps forward with her. "I'm in town to interview you for *The Edge*." She feels like she's explaining this to a toddler. "We were supposed to meet for brunch, but I had a call from the office secretary; you had to reschedule?"

Andi finally takes in his appearance. A rumpled shirt, and a jacket thrown over his arm. Wrinkled pants. A scuff on the top of his dress shoes. Is that a lipstick smudge on his neck?

She fights to control the eye roll. She drops her voice, and asks, "Is this a walk of shame?"

Now it's his turn to blush, but he doesn't acknowledge her comment. "They said they were sending their best journalist. I had no idea it was you."

They step forward again.

Andi fidgets with the valet tag in her hand. "Your agent didn't tell you my name, or I mean, the name of the person interviewing you?"

"My agent." His voice sounds concerned, and Arin's eyes scan the lobby again. He shakes his head. "No. I was just told the meeting was for later this morning. That the interviewer might request another follow up session, if necessary. I don't know. I'm new to this fame and publicity thing. Am I supposed to ask who will be conducting the interview?"

Andi shifts her weight over to the other foot. "No, I guess not-"

"- But you knew you'd be seeing me? Doesn't that seem like an unfair advantage?"

Andi tilts her head. "How so?"

At the front of the line, Arin takes the tag from her hand and passes it to the attendant. He watches as the man types in some information before sending a driver to her car. "You've had time to think about seeing me again, what you'd want to say. I haven't had that luxury…" He steps closer, and whispers in her ear. "Well, maybe the three or four daydreams I have every week of seeing you again."

Flustered by his comment, she steps away from him, following the direction of the attendant pointing her outside to the line of cars pulling up. She wants distance between them; hating how he can still get a reaction out of her with just the quiet purr of his voice.

Arin follows her out onto the sidewalk. He reaches for her elbow. "I think about you all the time, Ands. The one who grew up next to me, who knew everything about me- and still loved me. The one who got away."

Andi's mind swirls and bitterness fills her. "'Got away?' You left me. You didn't show up and didn't return my phone calls for weeks! When I finally heard from you again, you actually told me to forget about you. And stop calling me 'Ands.'" Her stomach lurches.

"You didn't though," he says with a confident arrogance, ignoring her anger. "Not like I could forget about you either." Arin caresses his hand over the expensive coat on his arm, a small smile on his face. He leans forward, like he's telling her a secret. "I never forgot your bright eyes, or your red curls; how it felt to twirl them around my fingers."

"Arin, I'm in town for work, an interview. Not a walk down memory lane-"

"-Do you remember our first kiss?"

Her eyes pop open, in shock at the memory he's chosen to relive. She dashes towards her rental car as it pulls into view. "Let's not do this-"

"You trembled in my arms, and your hair smelled like apples." Arin steps up behind her. "I was so afraid my braces would cut your lips-"

"Arin, I don't wanna talk about something that happened when we were sixteen. We need to focus on the interview-"

"- I always thought it was so sweet, innocent, that I was your first kiss, at sixteen. Like you'd been waiting for me to see you."

The valet looks at them with interest, lurking to listen to the drama. He sulks away, disappointed after Andi hands him a tip.

"I did wait for you, you fucker." She reaches for the door frame. "I waited five hours that night, in that dress, and you didn't even have the guts to call me. You had Rayaan do your dirty work." She shakes her head, pushing out the vision trying to run across her brain of that horrible night. "I knew this was a bad idea. Instead of me writing an article about the image you portray in your reels, what if I portrayed you as the ass you are?" Yanking the door open she climbs into the seat. "I'm here for the story, not so you can tear me down again. If you can behave like an adult, and you want to be paid for the interview, call my secretary when you can be civilized, and we can reschedule."

Slamming the door closed, she drives off in a huff, her nerves bracing every move.

Driving almost blindly from indignation and tears, she's not surprised to find herself at the old boat dock on the lake. Rote memory brought her here. It was where she always went when she was a teen and had needed to think. Putting the car in park, she hits her hand on the steering wheel. "Shit. How did that happen?"

Still numb, her mind races through images of Arin in her memories. Running like an old VCR tape in fast forward, moments flit through her head. Arin and Rayaan moving in next door. Playing basketball with her brother and the boys at the end of the cul de sac. Neighborhood picnics. Family dinners. Board game nights in front of the fireplace in Neal Collins's library. Her mother's homemade ice cream in summer. Camping. Debate competitions. Swim meets. Graduation. Going off to college. Every memory, with Arin at her side.

The tape rewinds to the boat dock in front of her and she sighs deeply.

The memory is put on hold when her phone rings through the dash of the rental car. She taps the green circle. "Hello?"

"What's up, lady?" Janessa's voice sounds like it's coming through a tin can. "Martha informed me the internet guy needs to reschedule for tomorrow? He said he'd meet you at the same place and time. What happened?"

Andi snorts. "A trainwreck happened." She starts to relay the story to Janessa and then realizes she left out a key detail.

"*WHAT?*" Janessa's polished voice blasts through the stereo. "You didn't tell me you know this guy?"

"It never actually came up when you gave the assignment. I didn't know I knew him until it was too late."

"You dated?"

Andi drops the seat back and stares up through the closed sunroof. "Yes. No. Kinda. I don't know. It's complicated. He was the boy next door. Arin was just always there."

Janessa coughs, the sound like static on the speakers. "Are you telling me Arin is one of the infamous handsome brothers who grew up in the house next to you? Holy shit. Are you okay? Which brother?"

Pushing her hair out of her face, then resting her hands over her plump belly, Andi gets an image of lying on a therapist's couch. "The younger one."

"Oh." Janessa stretches out the word. "Oh crap, does he know?"

"No, of course not. Like I'm gonna tell him I was planning to lose my virginity to him that night he stood me up." Andi rolls her eyes. "It didn't really come up when I ran into him in the lobby of the hotel where he'd obviously spent the night with some woman."

"Holy shit; is that why he canceled?"

Andi scoffs. "Ya know, I ask a lot of delicate questions to get a story, but that's just not one I felt I needed to ask."

"Damn. The interview. Right. The whole reason you're there. Can you do this? I can make other arrangements for it."

Andi is offended by the question. As much as she'd love to write an expose and show the world who the true Arin is, she also knows there's more to him than that. He's smart and funny, and volunteers at a center for kids in trouble. Or at least the old Arin did.

She owes it to the dreams she once had of their future together to find out if he's still that man.

Janessa misinterprets her silence. "Oh honey, I'm sorry I put you through that." She sighs. "I'll just set up a phone interview and let someone else do it."

Andy watches a little bird hop across the sunroof, its tiny claws clicking the glass. "No. I'm here. I'm going to do it." She pops the seat up, and the little bird flies away from the sudden movement. "I can't cry over what happened. It's long over. He called to reschedule, so I'll go."

"That's my girl! Wear the green dress I sent with the clothes. The designer one? That'll stop him in his tracks. Make him sorry he ever left you."

Andi chuckles. "He can't be sorry for something he never knew he missed."

"So tell him…" Janessa's voice is encouraging. "Oh, listen. I gotta go. Jacob's here for approval on the layout for next month's magazine. We're saving three pages for you."

"Great." She has no idea how she's going to fill the space. "Love you, bye."

The line goes dead, the connection to her friend ended.

Andi exits the car and walks out on the dock. The water rocks under her feet, in a forgotten way, and she hopes she doesn't get motion sickness. The sun feels good on her skin, after a long, cold Chicago winter. She eases down on the wooden planks, closest to the water, and sits cross-legged. Many hours of her youth were spent like this, when she had a problem, or was lonely. For a brief moment she wonders if Arin would come look for her here but realizes it's probably not as memorable for him as he claims.

The blue car comes to a halt on the hill, hidden by the trees. Arin recognizes the rental car parked further down the hill. He leans sideways in his seat to get a better view of the dock. He inches the car forward some more, stopping when he sees the back of the familiar redhead.

They'd shared their first kiss on that dock. The two families had planned to celebrate the end of a busy school year with a long weekend in the campground. Instead, they'd spent it locked up in the rented campers, hiding from the rain. They'd worn a mud path between the two doorways, running back and forth, as the fathers met up to watch a baseball game on TV, and the mothers prepared dinners. The kids were left to themselves. Her older brother was excused from the family trip, as he was starting a new summer job. His older brother, Rayaan was huddled over the table in the camper kitchen, prepping for a summer internship at a law firm.

Arin never minded hanging out with Andrea Jennings.

They liked the same movies, she was a worthy opponent on the debate team, and she always let him have the pickles off her hamburgers. She laughed at his jokes and told him he was funny and smart. She wasn't like the other girls, who were always fawning over him because he was on the football team or telling him he was handsome.

She was simply Andi. The girl next door. His friend.

He'd tired of being indoors and decided to go bother her. When Arin stepped outside, he was glad to see the rain had stopped, though it was still overcast. Andi didn't want to go for a walk. She'd already started on her summer reading list and didn't want to leave her book. Something with a military tank on the front. He'd remembered the title from the list the teacher had passed out on the last day of school. His copy of the list went straight into the trash. Bored, he'd pulled the book from her hands and told her the war could wait.

On their walk, she told him about all the things she was learning in the historical book. He added in details he'd seen from a documentary. Why did he need a book list? Talking was easy and relaxed. It always was with Andi. Gathering stones, they walked out on the boat dock, and skipped them across the cove. The little dock was further back, not really meant for boats, although they'd sometimes used it for kayaks. He pointed out the blue herons to her, watching them from the other side of the shore.

Something in her gray eyes, matching the clouds rolling by, spoke to him. Without a word, he grabbed her by the arm, and twirled her to him.

Arin had been just as surprised as she was!

Arin wasn't lying when he said Andi'd trembled in his arms. At the time, he'd thought it was just excitement, and he'd kissed her a little harder, her lips soft under his. His large hand had clutched her hip as he pulled her close, and she'd whimpered softly as he kissed her again. She broke the spell, pointing out the heron diving into the water, to catch his dinner.

They'd spent the weekend kissing, hiding from their families. He'd been so surprised when she laid with him on his bed in the camper, letting him feel her up. Her hands were timid, touching him lightly, yet gripping his arms each time he kissed her more deeply.

Things were getting a little heated, their legs rubbing against one another as they rolled around on the bed. When there was a knock on the door, Andi flew away from him, grabbing the closest thing to her, and pretended to read.

Rayaan, his older brother, barged in, breaking the mood.

"I'm going to town. Why don't you two ride with me, so you don't cause any trouble." He paused, eyeing Andi, the magazine, and her flushed face. "Didn't know you were into fly fishing- come on, your mom already said it was okay."

Andi had pulled up the hood on her sweatshirt, hiding from his prying eyes. She was out the door first, and in the back seat of the Jeep before they could catch up.

"She's not like other girls," Rayaan had said quietly.

Arin remembered rolling his eyes. "Yeah, which is exactly why I like her. Mind your own fuckin' business."

On the ride into town, they'd held hands. Rayaan's watchful eye kept turning to them at stoplights. He tried to engage them in conversation, attempted to start a debate on which movie to rent for the evening. At the video store, Rayaan went in alone. Arin had lunged at her again, catching her lip between his teeth. She'd sighed loudly and returned the exchange, tugging his bottom lip between hers. Andi attempted to break apart when the vehicle door opened, but he'd kept kissing her.

His brother never said a word but kept scowling at them in the rearview mirror while they kissed the whole ride back to the campground.

It wasn't until weeks later that Arin found out from her brother it had been Andi's first kiss. He'd been sorry he teased her about it, but appreciated her fighting spirit when she dumped a milkshake over his head, angry he had told Logan about it. He'd deserved that. He knew he did, because he'd spent the afternoon in bed with another girl.

Arin sighs. That's not why she's mad at him now. He knows perfectly well why she's angry, and he doesn't blame her for that either. Shifting the car to drive, he makes a U-turn, leaving without bothering her any more than he already has.

Reaching the highway, he turns his car to the left. He knows he should get back to his studio apartment and catch up on filming for the day. But other thoughts fill his head, so he gets a bucket of chicken at a drive-up window, and heads to the other side of the lake. It's not long before he pulls up to his parents' condo and parks in the guest lot. Taking the stairs to their unit on the fifth floor, he thinks about how much he hates this place. He hates they sold the house and wishes they'd bought a smaller house on the waterfront, rather than a spot in this cold, impersonal building.

The glass door is open, and he can see his mom at the kitchen table. She jumps up in surprise when she sees him, and waves him in. Entering the space, the door bangs on the back of his heel as he calls out his hello. He slides off his shoes, leaving them on the mat by the door, padding over to his mother in his bare feet.

"Oh, what a nice surprise!" Prisha Collins exclaims. "I

wasn't expecting this."

Hugging her tightly, he stretches one arm out to put the chicken on the table. "Brought dinner too," he chuckles.

Prisha leans back, putting her hand under his chin. "Your father will be happy; we haven't eaten from there in ages." She moves his chin from side to side, admiring his face. "When did you get to be so handsome?"

"Ma, I've looked the same since I was seventeen years old," he chuckles. "I look just like *Nana*, or at least that's what you always tell me."

Prisha nods, the memory of her father bringing a small smile to her lips. "That's right. You always have." She steps away, her voice thoughtful. "Why don't you go out onto the balcony and get your father. Tell him it's time to come in and eat. I'll get salads ready."

His feet hit the cold tiles and he feels like a teenager again. He slides open the patio door and steps onto the colorful outdoor rug.

His father is on a phone call, so Arin walks to the railing overlooking the water five stories below. It's not warm enough yet for a swim, but a family is heading down the sidewalk, ready for an evening boat ride. He breathes in the fresh air and tries to clear his mind.

Neal Collins steps up behind him, patting his son on the back. "And to what do we owe this pleasure, son? Or were we expecting you, and your mother forgot to tell me?"

Arin chuckles, turning away from the water. "I haven't been over in a while. Is it a crime to visit one's parents? I brought a bucket of chicken. Ma's getting salads. She said to come in."

The two men head to the door, wiping their feet before entering the house. Neal whistles at his wife. "Hey, gorgeous!"

"Oh, please," she giggles. "You saw me not twenty minutes ago, when you were refilling your drink!"

Arin hates the condo, but he must admit, he likes the open space concept of the dining- kitchen- living room. Watching his parents together has always been his favorite hobby. He's spent his life searching for a love as easy and balanced as theirs but keeps falling short. He can't help but wonder if he's being given a second chance to right a wrong?

As if his father can read his mind, which Arin's sure he has that talent, Neal exclaims, "Son, when are you going to get yourself a woman like that? Pretty, funny, smart, and she cooks!"

Prisha rolls her eyes. "It's chicken in a cardboard bucket, dear." Carrying the salad bowl to the long table, she tilts her head to the counter. "You two get the plates, and some dressing from the fridge."

Moments later, the table is set, and the family gathers at

the table. Prisha nods, signaling it's time to eat. Neal reaches in the bucket and pulls out a thigh and drumstick. "You didn't just turn up here, Arin. What's on your mind?"

"Oh, wait! Was the interview today? How did it go?" Prisha questions, adding some vinaigrette to her salad.

Arin places his napkin in his lap, avoiding his mother's knowing gaze. "It had to be rescheduled." He takes the bucket when his mother hands it to him. "I had another thing come up and was downtown. You'll never believe who I ran into?"

His father shakes his head, not knowing.

"Andrea Jennings."

"Oh, my! What's she doing in town? How is she? Wait, is she the journalist for the interview?" Prisha asks, one question running into the other. "You didn't know?"

"Is that a thing? Am I supposed to ask the name of the person who is interviewing me?" Arin tears the crunchy skin off his chicken, popping a bite in his mouth.

"Did Sarah say anything to you?" Neal asks his wife.

Prisha shakes her head no. "Did it not go well?" She leads. "When was the last time you saw her?"

Arin looks at his mother pointedly. She knows damn well when he last saw her. "It went about as well as you'd think... I wasn't at my best. I was shocked to see her- we were in the lobby at the Regency." He doesn't miss his mother's raised eyebrow. "I turned up the charm too much, trying to hide my own feelings about seeing her again, I suppose."

Neal looks to his wife, and back at his son. "Too much charm? You?"

"I was a total ass. If she completely trashes me after the interview, I'll deserve it. For more than one reason."

Neal scratches his forehead. "I've never known her to be a vindictive person. She's so poised and professional; I can't imagine she'd do that. Did you reschedule?"

Arin runs the back of his hand across his bottom lip. He groans. "Yeah. I've called my manager, and set up another time for tomorrow, to meet with her again."

Prisha pauses, fork halfway to her mouth. She lowers it. "I don't know how that will be any better."

"Tell me about it," Arin sighs, reaching for his beer bottle.

Chapter Five

Andi is determined to stay on course for the interview- to not allow her memories and emotions to detract her from the job at hand. She arrives at the restaurant early, requesting a table on the outside patio. She promises to mention the business in the story in a favorable way, and the staff is happy to accommodate her. A few tables are moved, and some of the lighting and camera equipment is set up. She discusses the camera angles with the local photographer hired to do the shoot, requesting candid and posed photos.

With her file in hand, questions ready, she is armed and dangerous. The feeling reminds her of debate preparations when they were in high school together. Arin could charm a crowd, but she always had the facts.

The hostess notifies her he is on his way in, and she stands at the ready. Her heart is pounding under her green dress, but she knows she looks good. She's swept her hair back in a braid, to keep from fidgeting with it. Her silver pendant necklace hangs low, but not enough to draw attention to her cleavage. Other than a silver ring she's worn since college, she's kept jewelry to a minimum. It's distracting in an interview, and bracelets banging against a table while she jots notes can get annoying.

She swallows hard when she sees him. His gray suit, the one he always wears in his videos. It's cut perfectly for him, and the pink shirt adds a warmth to his olive skin tone. He raises his eyebrows at the set up, and she nods curtly.

"Good to see you again, Arin." She's grateful he's wearing only the suit coat, and not the vest as well. That would be too much for her to resist.

"You too, Ands." He ignores her scowl. "It feels just like yesterday!" He laughs. As he did the day before, he steps close, placing a kiss on her cheek. He whispers, "Don't worry. I'll play nice."

She waves her hand to the seat angled towards her. The set up is less of a lunch, with only a small table to hold glasses of water. "I hope you don't mind, I thought we could forgo lunch today. Just the interview, some photos." She indicates the cameras, and the photographer snapping a few pictures.

Arin cocks his head, considering her words. "I'm fine with that," he nods in agreement, "as long as one of the cameras can be set to video, so I can edit a few pieces for my blog."

Andi hides her surprise. Despite her past work experience, she hates being on camera. Caught off guard, she falters for a moment. "Sure, I don't see why not. That's what made you famous, right?" She indicates to the young woman which camera to use, choosing one which will feature her in the best light. She is thoughtful for a moment. "As long as I have final approval of whatever you edit and decide to use."

"Fair enough." He waves to the notepad resting in her lap. "Any other rules?"

She smiles wryly. "It's just like Mr. B's journalism class," she remembers, mentioning their favorite teacher. "Answer the question as directly as possible. If you don't understand the question, let me know. Try to avoid yes or no answers. And I'd like to keep this professional, not personal, if you understand." She looks around the room, slightly confused. "Where's your manager? Does he or she have anything to add?"

Arin sighs, looking at his phone. He tightens his lips. "Running late, as always, but this time, he has a good reason."

Andi is curious about his comment, but let it slide. She leans forward on the arm of her chair, reaching for her pen. She can feel his eyes on her, staring down her dress. Righting herself, she runs her tongue over her teeth, disdainfully. "Do you always act like a hormonal teenager?"

He chuckles. "Is that an actual question? Because the answer is yes. I can't help it. You look stunning in that dress and I'm a guy." He leans back in his seat, his eyes looking her over from head to toe. He looks back to her face and smiles crookedly. "You have my attention."

"That. We're not doing that," she says. "I asked you to keep this professional."

"What? You put on a tight dress, and I can see the cute freckles on your chest, and I'm not allowed to look and tell you you're beautiful?"

Taking a deep breath, Andi changes tactics. "That's part of your charm online, isn't it? Using the female gaze and tropes to your advantage to win over women?"

Arin bites in his lip, fighting back a small smirk. "I observe people, relationships. I watch my parents, hell, I watch your parents. I see how much in love they are, after all their years together. I see the little, silly things they do. How they keep each other entertained and interested. It's really like a big social experiment."

Jotting a few notes, she looks up. "Is this a joke to you, something to make people laugh?"

He shakes his head. "No. I mean, I'm glad they laugh, because people connect to it. When I put on the ridiculous pink wig, and act out both roles, people see themselves in each place. And at the end of the day, I'm simply hoping I find that someday."

"You're using this platform to date?"

Shrugging, Arin bows his head. "My DM box is always full. I've learned to filter out stalkers and attention seekers. I'm a good wedding date, it seems. I get asked to a lot of those," he smiles.

She smiles too, remembering the number of videos he

had, featuring him dancing, or enacting party scenarios between himself and his "soulmate," himself in a bright pink wig, playing the female role.

"Why do you feel like promoting yourself on social media is the way to find a life partner?" Andi reads from her notes. "Readers want to know what your dating life has been like that led you to this point."

"Your readers, huh?" He tugs on his jacket sleeve.

"'Inquiring minds want to know.'" She smiles, repeating the tagline from their youth.

"Thank goodness for the internet. Now our mothers can get Hollywood gossip for free."

Andi nods in agreement, anxiously awaiting his response. She keeps saying she doesn't care where he's been, or what he's done. But when her handsome, old friend is sitting across from her like this, she wants to know more than the little details her mother has told her over the years.

"I guess we can skip over high school, you can write those formative years however you want." He settles back against the chair, crossing his leg over the other, resting his ankle above his knee. He absently runs his finger over the crease of the dress pants on his thigh. "There was a girl, in college, several actually, but one I dated for about two years." Arin's eyes look past her, to the shimmering blue water behind her. "For whatever reason, I don't even remember now, she left school. It was heartbreaking, because I thought we really had something." He pauses for a moment, thinking. He huffs, "I got really depressed. It's really silly, but finding the girl in college was important to me, it's how my parents met, when Mum was studying here on a fellowship." He clears his throat. "I made the mistake of turning to an old friend, someone who cared for me despite my flaws. I know I have flaws," he says emphatically.

His eyes lock on to Andi's. Under his intense gaze, she does her best to lock down any physical reaction to the story he tells. She doesn't want him to know how tightly she's wound; how she's straining to keep it together, so close to him after all this time. Inside, all her nerve synapses are firing, waiting to snap, and she wonders where he plans to take his response.

"I gave into old feelings I'd never acted on, and then I fucked it up. Badly. And I never told her I was sorry or explained anything. And honestly, I've been looking in all the wrong places ever since."

Before she can even process his words- his apology- movement around the corner of the building catches Andi's eye. A man, tall and dark, moves with confidence, coming through a side gate onto the patio. He shouts angrily, "I told you not to say anything until I got here."

Something in the voice stirs Andi, but she can't match the

vision she sees with her memory. Arin stands and turns to face the approaching figure. "I can handle it on my own, I told you, *bhaiya*."

"Rayaan," Andi whispers, standing as well.

Rayaan pushes past his brother and grabs Andi into a warm embrace. "So good to see you, Red," he says, his nose gently brushing her ear. "It's been too long."

She allows him to hold her longer than necessary, as he gently sways her. She inhales his cologne, smelling like forest and saltwater at the same time. Andi blushes against his shoulder, hidden from view, remembering one of the trope videos his younger brother recorded. She's just missing a third scent. Arin had pointed out women always describe men as smelling of three different, opposite things. And it's true. Rayaan smells like opposite parts of the Earth, so different from one another. Looking so different from his former self.

Arin coughs, and the pair break apart.

"What are you doing here?" Andi asks, trying to catch her breath.

Rayaan winks at her. "Wouldn't miss a chance to see my favorite girl." Having pushed his brother aside, he takes that chair, leaving Arin to sit in the third seat in the half-circle arrangement. "And I'm this fool's manager. I had to make sure he didn't step in it and say something stupid."

Andi can see the photographer rushing around to change the camera placement, now that Rayaan Collins seems to have taken center stage. But he deserved it. Aging with perfection, he looks better now than he ever did. Appearing more assured, his lithe swimmer's body was replaced with the stronger, bigger build of an athlete. His hair is long, pulled back into a man bun, with a few curls escaping on the nape of his neck. She never would have imagined that's the look he would adopt. But it defines him. He has a quiet, earthly assured resolve about him. Andi wishes to stare longer, to find the other differences between the boy and the man, but she snaps back to attention. There's a job to be finished.

"Let's go with that. Why exactly would a social media influencer need a manager?" Andi asks, placing her notebook firmly in her lap, using one of her prepared questions.

Rayaan tilts his head, considering her question. His eyes run over her body, much like his brother's had minutes before. His linger at the neckline of her dress, and his tongue darts out involuntarily to lick his lip. Lord help, between the two of them, how is she ever going to survive this interview?

"He's always needed someone to keep him in line." He looks to Arin, and not so playfully punches him in the arm. "Over the years we've been partners in stocks and real estate deals. But entertainment law is my specialty. So when he came up with this idea of making videos, we needed to cover our bases."

Arin butts in. "Making sure we knew fair use rules for using certain movie or music clips, keeping track of public appearances, and contracts for those. Knowing liabilities for presenting characters in certain ways. All the characters, the girlfriend, the nosy neighbor, the dopey best friend, those are all mine, and we needed to protect those ideas too."

Impressed with his answer, Andi uses her own creative shorthand to jot a few things down, surprised by the thoughtfulness behind his venture into being an online video creator.

"Money comes in, from sponsors. We have to track that," Rayaan explains. "Like part of this deal with your magazine included this free equipment, for product placement in the videos. Someone has to organize all of it for him, while he works on the creative side." Rayaan taps the arm of the chair, sunlight bouncing off the silver rings on his fingers. "I gotta hand it to him, I thought he was crazy when he came up with the idea." He looks at his brother and smiles. "But he knows what he's doing. Telling life stories in two-minute segments. He's good at it. Have you seen them?"

He turns his attention back to Andi. She can feel the blush rising up her neck. She clears her throat. "I'm more of a political groupie," she chuckles. "I have to admit, I was unfamiliar with Arin being the internet's boyfriend until

Monday morning." She tips her head to Arin. "Since then, I think I have watched every video, for research. You do capture those moments between a man and a woman really well."

"Do you have a favorite?" Rayaan asks, his eyes still appraising her.

"A favorite?" She bides for time, looking at her notes. Andi knows the answer but hates to say it aloud. She claps her hands together, going for it, and laughs. "I do! There was one that was so spot on, I made a note of it. The man is emptying the dishwasher, and the woman is ready to-" she swallows and censors herself. "She's ready to drag him off to the bedroom." She shrugs.

Cocking his eyebrow, Rayaan says, "You find this to be a common response?"

She laughs. "It's so true. Men will try anything to get us in bed, and all we want is some help around the house. Wash the plates, sweep up the crumbs, put the juice back in the fridge. We'll be yours forever."

"Oh, God, that's so much work," Arin whines.

"Having a good woman is work." Andi smiles, relaxing into the interview now that Rayaan is here to manage the task. "I mean, I'm assuming you want to find a woman who thinks for herself, has her own interests and career. What is Arin Collins, the internet's boyfriend, looking for in a woman?"

Manager and journalist turn to watch Arin. He squirms in his chair a bit. "Like I said, I'm looking for a love like my parents have... Something that lasts. Yes, someone who can think for herself, who can be independent-"

"Who doesn't care if you don't call her back."

"Hey, not cool *bhai*, this is my interview-"

"- And you need to be honest. Right now, you're using it as a way to hook up with women, nothing lasting longer than two weeks. It's like your own personal dating service."

Andi leans forward. "Is that true?"

Arin's head bounces. "Maybe a little." He tries to look offended. "I'm not in an office job anymore, my building has its own gym, I'm really not the guy who goes to the bar every Friday, despite what my videos might show. It's hard to meet women." He tugs the lapel of his jacket. "They send me DMs and photos and ask me out. After chatting a few times, I might say yes."

"And what happens on these dates?" Andi can't help the rise in her voice. She's mad for all womankind at his behavior.

"Usually nothing," Arin stammers. "There's a lot of lonely cat women on the internet. They just want to talk."

Scooting to the edge of her seat, Andi asks, "What's wrong with having a cat?"

"Do you have a cat?" Rayaan asks quietly, his lips twisted into a smile beneath his beard. Andi ignores him.

Arin throws his hands up. "Nothing. Nothing wrong with cats. I love them- put that on the record. Shit. I just meant, a lot of the women in our age group who are still single have cats. And I enjoy talking to those women, finding their perspectives on life and love, having a nice dinner."

"But if you really want something, you answer DMs from younger women," Rayaan provides. "Or older. Whatever you're in the mood for." Catching the gleam in his eyes, Andi can deduce the older brother is enjoying watching his younger sibling squirm under her scrutiny.

"Dammit, you're not helping."

Andi dissolves into a fit of laughter. She throws her hands up, her head back, and full body laughs. When she sits up, both brothers are watching her with interest. "You haven't changed. Either of you. Arin, you still want to be a carefree playboy, and Rayaan, you think you have to protect him from himself." She pauses. "Why is there no older brother character in your videos?"

"Because then he'd have to have a conscience about what he does," Rayaan says wryly, before reaching for a glass of water with a lemon perched on the edge.

From the corner of her eye, Andi watches him squeeze it into his water, licking his fingertip. He doesn't even pucker from the bitterness and takes the unused lemon she left on a napkin and uses it too.

Arin adjusts his suit collar. "Maybe a little of what he said, but the dopey friend kind of pulls that off too, in the innocence his character portrays. A lot of those videos are based on conversations we've," he motions between himself and his brother, "had before, or ones I've had with other guy friends. We're not the saints our mother believes us to be," he smiles, attempting to regain his charm and composure.

"How do your parents feel about your new found fame?" Andi asks, resting comfortably in her chair again.

"I wear nicer suits," he chuckles. "If I get recognized when we go out for dinners, people offer me upgraded tables and free desserts. But I'm not living in the lap of luxury yet. The carry over from my first career, in stocks, pays the bills for now, puts a roof over my head."

"You're not living in their basement, so to speak?"

"No, only one of us has resorted to that for a while, and it wasn't me." Arin looks pointedly at his brother. "I started the videos after I had knee surgery. When I was recovering, I couldn't get out of the house, but needed to fill my time. Reels were just getting started on the platform, and I was playing around for a bit. Then one day, one really took off. It was a video about the types of looks couples give each other in romance movies to communicate without speaking?" Andi

61

knows the video. His assessment was fairly accurate of the silent signals she has used in previous relationships. "The next day, I had hundreds of new followers, and other accounts coming out of the woodwork to offer me advice on how to get more attention online." He pauses to take a drink. "I borrowed some camera and lighting equipment from the studio Dad helped arrange, and it became a full-time job."

Rayaan adds in, "To get a following, and have solid content to keep people coming back, he really needs to post about five times a day. He does all the editing, and sound, but we are slowly working on putting a team together to help with some of that, so Arin can have more time to write."

"All the videos are filmed in my apartment or my car- my neighbors at first thought I was crazy, sitting in the parking lot. And my studio isn't big. People have asked if I'm that poor, in messages I get." Andi smiles, knowing the apartment looks sparse on screen. "But I moved out the bigger table and chair, so I would have more space to move around. I keep the tripods set up, so I can just use my phone wherever I need to-"

"The place looks like it's set up to film porn," Rayaan adds.

"Yeah, I can't really invite women back to my place. It does look bad. There's makeup all over the bathroom, different things I've purchased as props for the 'soulmate' character. It looks like I live with a woman, and that tends to scare off other women."

"Does the 'soulmate' have a name?" Andi questions.

Arin blushes. "For a while, I was calling her Karen in my head, but when that name started getting such a bad rap, I quit using it. I know sometimes the woman I picture having those conversations with, but she's nothing like the bright pink wig."

Not rising to the perceived poke at her personality, or their former relationship, Andi presses on. "You didn't have it in some of the earlier videos-"

"No, I didn't. I hosted a Halloween party, and when everyone cleared out the next day, it was left behind-"

"- God, we were so drunk. Who was wearing that?" Rayaan interrupts, scratching his beard in thought.

Briefly, Andi ponders if it's soft or scratchy. She gives herself a mental shake, refocusing on the task before her.

"I really don't remember. We partied hard after your divorce, bro."

Andi's eyebrows shoot up. How had she forgotten her mother telling her Rayaan and Gemma had divorced? She knows there were details her mother shared with her, but they've escaped her.

She leans to the side in her chair, and pats Rayaan's arm, resting on the arm of his seat. "Mom told me. I'm really sorry about that."

He lays his hand over hers. It feels warm and comfortable. "Don't be. I'm not. I see Elias whenever I want, and he stays with me every other weekend." He shrugs. "I'm happier now. Free. And she's living her life. It happens."

Curious to know more of the story, but knowing now is not the time, Andi looks at her phone. "We've been at this for an hour. I don't know about you boys," she smiles at her old nickname for them, "excuse me, gentlemen, but I could use a break. I'm in town a few more days. Should we pick this up later?" She focuses on Arin. "You could watch back the tape, see if there are specific things you want to discuss. I can go over my notes and adjust a few things?"

Arin shakes his head. "Ma was hoping to see you? Maybe we could do something at their condo?"

Andi grins. "Any excuse to see what your dad is reading? Sure, that sounds great."

"It's a date." After a beat, Rayaan sheepishly dips his head. "I didn't mean it like that."

"If you still feel like he needs supervision, why don't you two decide what works best for you and let me know. I'm staying at the Regency."

Rayaan raises his eyebrow. "The Regency, huh?"

Arin chuckles, hitting his brother's leg. "Fancy digs."

She nods. "It is really nice, and I have no other plans so

I'm flexible." She can feel her cheeks burning.

"Sure you are, Red," Rayaan laughs. "Still can't do a cartwheel, can you?"

Andi laughs, motioning the photographer over. "When in my adult life do I need to do cartwheels?"

Standing up, she quietly chats with her about a few shots of Arin she'd like for the magazine. Agreeing, the young woman offers a few suggestions as well.

She looks back at the brothers, sitting head to head and quietly talking. She directs the photographer to snap the photo. She claps her hands together and the men look up. "Arin, if you'll go with Monica, she can take some photos of you."

Arin rises and walks away, linking arms with the photographer. Andi can hear him ask if she's seen his work.

"Jesus, he's a handful," Rayaan says. His voice is practically in her ear. His heat fills her and she knows he's standing too close.

She looks over her shoulder. "He always was. I guess it's a good thing we kept him in line."

Rayaan places a hand on her hip, turning her slightly to point out some fish jumping in the river, and birds swooping down to catch them. "It wasn't your job. I'm afraid you got burned too many times by him."

The touch is heated. Possessive.

Andi likes how it feels.

She holds her breath a moment, gaining control before turning to face him. His hand stays in place, following her as she turns. "That was a long time ago. I'm over it now."

The restaurant manager calls out to her, and they step apart. The fussy man asks if they're finished, as the afternoon crowds will arrive soon, and they need the seating back in place. Andi bows her head, thanking him profusely for adapting the layout to the needs of the interview. Feeling awful they didn't eat anything, she orders a meal to be delivered to her parents' home, and this seems to satisfy the man.

"Well," she holds out her hands, "unless you have anything else, I guess we're done for the day." She looks down to the riverfront where Arin is having his photograph taken. "He probably has a date with Monica, and I have notes to read over."

Rayaan watches her quietly for a moment as she collects her notes. He looks at the equipment. "Do you know how to take this down?"

"Shit. No. Can you help?"

As they unhook lights and cameras, the staff puts the seating area back in order.

"Where do you want me to put these?" he inquires.

"Actually, those are gifts from the magazine to Arin, so I

guess you could take them?"

He shakes his head, no. "I'm on my bike. Can't really weave around traffic with a lighting system."

"No, I guess not." She looks down to the water again, and sees Arin has his arms around the young woman's shoulder, showing her something on the camera. She huffs. "I guess we just leave him?"

"Were you the rental car I saw in the side lot?" He starts walking to the side gate. "He's a stray puppy. He'll find his way home when he's ready."

She follows, grabbing a small box of cords, thanking the manager again as he meets them at the gate. "More like a cat in heat," she mutters, digging in her bag for the keys.

She sees Rayaan grin at her assessment of his brother, but he says nothing. She clicks the hatch button, and it pops open. His bike is parked across from her. "Nice bike," she compliments as he stretches to put the items in the car. She's reminded of the time the boys returned from India and she watched them unload the car for their mother. His back is broader, filled out, and the muscles are obvious, even under the coat he wears.

Boxes in, he spins and rests on the open ledge. "Gemma called it a mid-life crisis. I'm not mid-life yet." He runs his hand over his beard and reaches for the sunglasses in the pocket of his jacket. "It was something to do, to be away from the house." Andi had never liked Gemma, but now is not the time to say so. She waits to see if he adds anything more. "Sometimes, a person can be so right for you on paper, when you plan it all out. But in practice, it's just wrong. And it takes a long time to figure that out."

She sits down on the ledge of the open hatch, keeping a respectable distance between them. "I've had relationships like that before. It's hard, and I'm sure it was more difficult because of Elias." She remembers the boy had been maybe six the last time she had seen him. "How old is he now?"

"He's nine. He plays a lot of video games, and wants to try out for a summer soccer league this weekend."

"I bet he looks just like you."

"A scrawny, swimmer nerd? Sure." He laughs. "Exactly like me at that age."

"Well, you didn't grow up too bad." Andi blushes.

He bumps her shoulder. "Neither did you, Red."

With his head tilted to the side, he watches as the blush rises over her chest and cheeks. She can feel it, itching at her skin, and she tries to hide her embarrassment. He lifts his hand to the silver pendant and straightens it, the light brush of his fingertips against her skin, hot. Her heart pounds in her ears. She rubs her lips together, wondering what to say.

"You hated that nickname. It wasn't about your hair. It was about how we could make you blush at the littlest thing."

His voice is soft and inviting.

"I seem to recall you didn't like being called 'King,' either." She teases.

Now it's his turn to blush. "I don't even speak much Hindi."

"Your mother told me once, the meaning of your name… 'Little King.' But you were older, so I never used 'little.' It seemed out of place. Arin's name was something about being strong." She tries to remember what Prisha had told her so long ago.

"Bull-headed is more like it."

They watch him cross the parking lot with the young woman. Arin waves goodbye to them and gives the photographer a kiss on the cheek before he climbs in his car and drives away.

"I guess that's that." She stands and addresses the young woman, requesting a look at the unedited photos. They quickly choose a few that would work for the magazine layout. Andi gets the woman's contact information for more photography work if necessary.

"Don't worry, Arin has my number," she says, before heading to her car.

"I'm sure he does," Andi says scornfully.

Rayaan stretches out his legs, still sitting on the back tailgate of her rental. "You can't still be hung up on him?"

Andi rubs her eyebrow. "Of course not, that was over ten years ago." She drops her hands, placing them in the dress pockets. They were the best feature of the dress. Pockets! "But finding out he was my subject for the interview? It brought back a lot of old memories, you know?"

He bobs his head. "I do." He combs down his beard on his cheek. "When he called yesterday and said you were the journalist, I had a moment of shock. I didn't realize you'd left DC until I Googled it last night."

Google. She'd never thought to Google information about his personal life, their lives. Both were successful businessmen. Searching for information seemed too much like work, and she tried to keep her personal time away from work-like tasks. Not one for social media herself, she didn't keep up with her classmates like some people did. Andi only kept one account, just to keep tabs on her parents and brother.

She wondered what Google would have told her about the Collins' boys.

"Your essay on relations in the Middle East was exemplary."

"I learned a lot when I lived in Dubai, covering politics there."

"I'd like to hear more about it. It sounds fascinating."

A car speeds through the lot, honking at Andrea and she

jumps out of the way, practically falling into Rayaan's lap. She rights herself and smooths down her dress. His eyes are drawn to her cleavage again.

"My eyes are up here." She points to her face. "If you want to talk to me about intellectual things, King, quit checking out my rack."

He throws his head back in a laugh and stomps his foot. "Caught, huh?"

"You never fooled me. I'm just more outspoken now to call you on it."

"What do they say? The older you got, the farther apart the letters were on your school t-shirts."

She swats his thigh. It's solid enough that she nearly hurt her damn hand. "That's awful! I was Arin's age!"

He stands up, moving close. "I know. I always had to remind myself of that." His voice is low and gruff. He puts his hands on her shoulders and spins her away from the traffic in the lot, getting busier as afternoon crowds come in for lunch. "But age doesn't matter now? Does it?" He slides his hands down her arms. "It is good to see you again, Andi. I'd forgotten how you could always make me smile." He steps away from her. He points to a small card next to the space where he had been sitting. "There's my business card, if you think of anything else you need, from the interview, or while you're in town." He retreats a few more steps and bows. "Till we meet again, Red."

Without fully standing up, he spins away from her and climbs on his bike. He waves as he rides away, leaving Andi speechless in the parking lot.

Chapter Six

Andi wasn't lying to Janessa when she said she wanted to
spend the time off work by the pool. She laughs at her friend,
sending text messages complaining from the snowstorm back
in Chicago, as she leans back in the chaise lounge. She has a
romance novel she brought from home; there's a mimosa on
a table beside her. And Rayaan's business card, laying on top
of her work notes.

She sighs, unable to focus on her book, when she has her
own love life to contemplate. The Collins brothers are
suddenly back in her life again. Replaying the afternoon,
Andi's pretty sure Rayaan was flirting with her. She had
always felt he sometimes did when they were younger, but
brushed it aside, thinking he was being kind because she was
the neighbor, and Arin's friend. Yet she had the littlest crush
on him, despite their five-year age difference.

Rayaan would share book recommendations with her, and
somehow, they were the ones left to decide what movies to
rent on family movie nights when everyone was together.
Other times, if just the kids were hanging out in the
neighborhood, they might find themselves alone together.
Her brother would sneak off with his girlfriend, and Arin
often got distracted because of his ADHD. Unless he was

really interested in a movie, he would often disappear to do other things as well.

Andi can remember one time when both families were camping, and all the kids were watching a movie together, some type of psychological thriller. Definitely not her type of movie, yet she was still sucked into the story line, and liked the actor in the lead role. Halfway through the movie, she realized she and Rayaan were the only ones in the camper, sitting together on the small couch.

She tilts her head, thinking more on that memory. With her eyes closed, she can see the moment play out in front of her. She had a terrible perm, but was wearing the favorite sweatshirt she had in high school. She had to have been a junior, maybe a senior. Which means Rayaan was too old to be sitting so close to her at the time. She remembers he left to get more popcorn, and she had moved on the couch, so there would be a little more space between them. But in his absence, the boys' dog decided to jump up next to her, leaving a smaller area for Rayaan to sit when he returned. Right next to her.

Opening her eyes, she looks up to the sky, the sun beginning to set. Families at the pool are clearing out, most likely to get ready for dinner. A mother calls to a child who won't exit the water.

Andi sinks back into her memory.

She and Rayaan were sitting side by side on the couch, watching the movie. Andi remembers clutching the popcorn bowl to her, nervously excited to be so close to Rayaan. Even with her crush on Arin, she'd also had feelings for Rayaan. She accepted he just thought of her as the kid next door. He had a girlfriend away at college. Yet she remembers thinking had it been a real date, it would have been a nice one. Simply enjoying a movie together, with someone she liked. When the killer in the movie was revealed, there was a scary chase through dark hallways, and she shrieked and hid her face in Rayaan's shoulder. He'd held her head to him, massaging her scalp, and whispering, "It's only a movie. It's okay."

His voice had been soft, and gentle, and he didn't make fun of her for being frightened. Not like the boy in her class she had dated for a few weeks. Rayaan was kind and considerate. He'd paused the movie and asked her if she wanted to finish it. She'd nodded, and wrapped her arm around his, sitting a little closer as the scary movie came to the finale.

When the movie was over, he'd asked about her classes in school. She remembers they talked about JFK and policies of the early 60s. As a pre-law student, those were interests of his, and maybe became hers too, just so she had things to talk about with him.

Andi had wondered over the years if she had become a

political correspondent because of his influence.

When she was calmed after the movie, and their chat, Rayaan had walked her across the road, to her family's camper. She hugged him and thanked him for not making fun of her for being scared. She remembered he held her tight, exactly like he'd done earlier at the restaurant. He'd given her another quick squeeze, before letting her go, and walked off into the dark night, not returning to his trailer.

In the present, the sun fades over the building, and the night air turns cool. Andi huffs out, exhausted from reliving the memory. She sits up and tosses the romance book in her bag. Sliding on her sandals, she stands, tightening her poolside robe around her waist. She walks around the back of the chair, gathering the notes and camera from the interview. Rayaan's card flutters to the ground. She stoops to pick it up, now slightly soggy from landing in a poolside puddle. Andi wipes it on her sleeve and drops it in her pocket. Scooping up the towel, she heads into the hotel.

At the elevator, she rolls her neck from side to side, feeling the tension of the last few days. She makes a mental note to book a massage at the hotel spa. Her phone begins to ring as she steps into the wooden lined box.

"Andrea!" Her mother shouts into the phone. "I have wonderful news! Since you're home for a few days, your brother has decided to come visit too! Of course, he'll have

Lauren and the baby with him." Before Andi can say anything, Sarah Jennings rushes ahead. "They've rented a house on the lake, and it's so big, Logan invited the Collins's to come along. It'll be just like old times."

Sure. Just like old times. Caught between Arin and Rayaan, at the lake.

Across town, Rayaan sits on the terrace, overlooking the city below. He listens to the cars honking as they zip by on the street. He flips his phone, end to end, letting it hit against his thigh. He contemplates his mother's call, inviting him to join the Jennings family at the offer of his old friend, Logan. They hadn't been in the same grade, but had a few classes together, and were known to cause trouble around the neighborhood.

His thoughts straying, he drops the phone, and leans over to pick it up. Deciding a run will clear his mind, Rayaan enters the condo to change into his running gear.

Lacing up his shoes, he thinks about the afternoon. Andi had looked amazing, like someone from a page in a fashion magazine. He'd lied when he said he didn't know she'd left DC. He followed politics less in her absence from the political scene. Rayaan had seen every press conference, every public appearance, every interview she had ever conducted on

TV news. He was impressed with her style, her ability to find the perfect clothing to fit her full figure. She always looked good.

He groans slightly at his wandering thoughts, rubbing his hands over his face and pulling down at his beard. He can't. He just knows he can't.

With a bolt, he dashes out the door, taking the stairs rather than the elevator. The punch of adrenaline would do him some good.

She's his friend's sister.

His brother's old flame.

Showered after a long run along the riverfront, he's made up his mind not to go for the weekend. He's still contemplating a valid excuse to give to his mother when his phone buzzes.

He looks down to see a message from his brother.

Lake getaway? Andi will be there. May the best man win, bhai

Throwing the phone on the bed, he runs the back of his fist over his mouth. "Fuck," he sighs out. Thinking back to what Andi commented earlier in the day, he says, "The stray puppy's turning into a wolf."

Chapter Seven

The sound of the radio grates on her nerves. Andi reaches over to shut it off, keeping her eyes on the road. The morning massage at the spa helped with some of her stress. After a quick stop at the store, the front seat of the rental car is loaded down with gifts. Her sister-in-law, Lauren, has already texted her three times, telling her to hurry up.

Andi hasn't had the nerve to ask if the brothers have arrived, or even if they plan to attend for the long weekend.

Arin's words from the day before echo in her head. He had come to her broken, the summer before their senior year in college. The breakup with his girlfriend, and struggling to actually choose a career, was weighing heavily on him. Arin had been working towards a business degree, but really had no idea what he wanted to do with his life. They'd spent most of the summer together, too old really to still be camping with their parents on holidays. Family game nights, playing miniature golf, and afternoon boat rides together. As old friends, their easy compatibility and camaraderie slowly developed into a relationship that lasted through the fall and winter. Although attending different schools, the two were only a few hours away from each other. They racked up miles on their cars, much to her father's chagrin.

Lost in memories, Andi smiles. Emails and computer technology were just coming to the forefront of communication, and she and Arin could spend hours chatting online. They messaged about anything- their classes, movies they had seen, gossip of former high school friends. She even tolerated when he would write for hours about sports.

She'd thought it was the beginning of their forever.

When she'd had the opportunity for a job interview at a newspaper office in San Diego, near his college, she booked a hotel. She figured it would be quieter and less stressful than staying in his apartment with his roommates. Arin had texted her that day, wishing her good luck, planning dinner, and making arrangements to meet her when her interview was over. She was thrilled with the opportunity and so impressed with the offices. The interview had gone really well. She couldn't wait to tell him all about it. Andi dressed for dinner, in a beautiful spring dress he'd given her weeks before, for her birthday. She couldn't wait for him to see it on her. Or the surprise she'd purchased just for him that she was wearing underneath.

She had been ready to take the next step. That night was going to be the night she would finally let him do all the things he whispered in her ear.

When he was an hour late, she worried about traffic. When he was two hours late, she worried he'd been in an accident. When he was three hours late, she called "Auntie" Prisha, with the pretense she was calling to tell all about her interview, but really just to see if his mother knew where he was. Four hours passed, and his roommates didn't know where he was. Rounding on the fifth hour, the phone rang in her hotel room.

Rayaan made little excuse for his brother. His voice was gruff, and angry- not his usual self. "Forget about him, Andrea. He's not coming."

With the use of her full name, she knew it was true. Knew it was final.

Tears sting at her eyes. Nearing the lake, she maneuvers the car over to a convenience store. In the parking lot, she allows herself a good cry. Letting go once and for all the pain Arin Collins had caused in her life.

Wiping her face, she whispers, "I'm here for the story. He wants the paycheck just as badly as I do." Banging her head against the back of the seat, she just needs to finish the interview later in the evening and get back to her hotel.

After regaining her composure, she drives back onto the road, making the last of the trip in good time. Driving through the small vacation town, the stores and sidewalks are crawling with people. Chuckling, Andi remembers in some parts of the world, spring comes early, unlike Chicago. Continuing on the main road, she drives past the turn for her boat dock, and continues a few more miles before turning left. Following the winding and curving road down the hill, she can see the lake through the trees, and finally arrives at the turn into the rental house.

So many cars are parked out front, and she doesn't recognize any of them. Andi can hear boats on the water, and aches to get close to it as soon as possible. The lake was always home to her, her place to rejuvenate and come alive again. Forgoing unloading anything, she reaches for her pool bag, and the few gifts in the front seat. She hears laughter coming from the back of the house but can't make out any of the voices.

"Ands! Here, let me help you with that!"

Arin appears from nowhere and takes the gift bags from her full hands. She keeps the flowers for his mother tucked under her arm as he gives her a hug and a quick kiss on the cheek. "I was beginning to think you weren't going to come."

"Stop calling me that," she warns. The cute little nickname he had for her now just feels like barbed wire, poking her brain. "Please," she says, a little more politely. "Of course I came. We have to finish the interview,"

He shrugs, most likely already forgetting her request. "That's not what I meant. No, I was worried I wouldn't get to spend time with you. Really talk to you." He tilts his head, pointing his chin to the flowers. "Ma's favorite. She'll love them. She's been talking about you all morning."

Andi follows Arin up the stairs of the wide porch. "When did everyone get in?"

He holds the door for her, and she steps into the grand entryway. "I guess your family arrived last night." They slip off their shoes, leaving them at the doorway. "My parents were here before me this morning. I stopped at the store to pick up some things." He stops walking, and so does she. "I got your favorite ice cream. It's in the freezer. There's a home theater and I thought we could watch a movie tonight."

She pulls her lips over her teeth, keeping quiet for a moment. "Arin, I'm not staying tonight. I want us to finish the interview this afternoon."

He looks defeated. "Oh, so I guess you don't need me to show you to your room?"

"No. Just a place to set my things down, and I need to take those items to the kitchen." She points at the bags he is holding.

"Sure I can't convince you to stay?"

"Not even threats from my mother will change my mind."

Two hours later, her mother has threatened imminent

death if she leaves the property. Arin has not left her side, and she's spent the afternoon catching up with her mother, Lauren, and Prisha, while the baby naps.

With the interview postponed till later, she tries to excuse herself for a rest. Arin bumps her arm. "Come on. We can sit poolside. It's still too cold for lake water, unless you want to jump in, like that one February weekend."

Andi shivers at the thought. "That was just damn stupid. What were we thinking?"

Prisha laughs. "*Bachche,* if truth is told, I think there might have been some alcohol involved."

Putting her hands up, Andi says, "I can neither confirm nor deny that underage drinking was ever involved in any of our crazy schemes."

"Ah, *beti,* it was more like two boys trying to impress a pretty girl, and you always just went along with it!"

Andi acts shocked. "I have no idea what you are talking about!"

"If Logan was involved, there was drinking, and maybe a car taken without permission," Sarah interjects.

"That, that may be true," Arin confesses. He waves goodbye to Lauren, who is silently signaling she needs to check on the baby. "The pool is heated, Red. Let's go."

Andi sighs, admitting defeat- at his use of another nickname, and at being forced to stay against her will.

"Alright, alright." She stands up. "I'll need to bring in some clothes later, but my suit is in my beach bag. Where's my room?"

Sarah begins to explain, but Arin interrupts. "It's near mine, Sarah. I can show her the way."

The view from her room is blocked due to blooming spring trees, but she can see the lake through a break in the branches. Laughter and splashing echoes around the side of the house, and it sounds like the fathers, her brother included, are having a wonderful time.

Andi's very cautious of Arin's attention. Hanging her beach towel over her arm, she carries her sandals in her hand and Arin guides her down the steps carefully, taking a back stairway leading directly to the swim deck.

"Arin, I'm fine. I'm not as clumsy as I used to be. I'm not going to fall."

At the bottom of the stairwell, he puts his hand over hers. "That's not why I wanted to help. I want to be near you, to feel you close. I want you to depend on me, like when we were younger."

He moves closer to her, and Andi dodges the other way, pushing the door to the patio open. "I'm not a naive teenager anymore. I don't depend on anybody."

Her heart pounds, trying to keep up her icy facade. Still undecided about her feelings towards him all these years later, she keeps up her guard. However, his hold on her is warm, and comforting. Familiar.

Taking her sunglasses from her hair, she puts them on her face and steps out of the shadows. She walks to the nearest lounge chair. He follows. Speaking quietly, Arin says, "I didn't mean it like that. Of course, we're older, hopefully wiser," he chuckles. "I want to get to know who you are now."

As he speaks, Andi's attention is over his shoulder. Attracted by the splashing of a volleyball rolling to her feet, she watches Rayaan emerge from the pool. He places his palms on the stone ledge and hoists himself up. The water sluices off him, forming rivulets over his tight chest, glistening off the tattoo on his right pec and shoulder. Andi grabs the top of the chair to keep from swaying. She feels warm, inside, in a way she hasn't felt in a long time. She blinks, and sadly he's out of the pool before she can memorize the event in slow motion.

Andi's fearful she's drooling as she admires him walking towards them. She doesn't even register Arin standing by her side, talking to her. This isn't the same Rayaan she knew. This is a man. Power and confidence roll off him as he moves closer. "Hey, Red," he calls out as he puts his hands up. He pushes water droplets off his face, and slicks back some stray hairs that have fallen from the ponytail he sports.

She can barely whisper the nickname, "King," as a form of acknowledgement.

Andi moves to kick the ball towards him, but suddenly Arin has his arm around the back of her neck, squeezing her shoulder to him, keeping her in place. "*Arey bhaiya,* look who I found!"

Rayaan falters momentarily but continues his advance. "Water's warm. Why don't you two join our game?"

He bends to retrieve the ball, and Andi watches the muscles ripple across his back. Her earlier assessment had been wrong. He still has a swimmer's body, only bulkier. The strong deltoids in his shoulders and slimmer waist attest to his hours in a pool.

"Loser buys dinner?" Arin taunts.

Rayaan reaches out to shake his brother's hand, nodding silently.

Arin gives Andi another little squeeze, dragging his fingertips across the top of her shoulder as he steps away. He slowly unbuttons his shirt, keeping his eyes locked on her. Although she's talking to Rayaan about the beauty of the home and view, her attention is on Arin. As each button pops open, his tan chest is revealed, covered in small curls, darker and thicker than the last time she'd seen them.

She wishes to fan herself, or to take a running leap into the water. She's getting too hot, and being so close to both men at the same time is not helping. Andi has no control over the way her body responds as a woman, different from her shy interactions and flirtations as a young girl.

The spell is broken when Rayaan throws the ball, hitting Arin square in the chest, forcefully at close range.

"Show off later," Andi's brother, Logan, yells from the pool, hands up to catch the ball.

Volleyball in hand, Arin charges towards the water, throwing it mid-jump, creating a large splash on the poolside.

"Sure you don't want to join us?" Rayaan asks quietly.

Laying out her towel, Andi replies. "I've got a book I've been dying to read."

"Always with your nose in a book, *jaan*," he chuckles and shakes his head. "Some things never change." The men in the pool shout at him to get back to the game. He retreats a few steps. "Don't forget sunscreen. You don't want to burn."

He makes a run for the pool, jumping higher than his brother, and folds his knees to his chest to create an even larger splash. Andi rolls her eyes, as the men laugh, and she removes her sunglasses to wipe away the spray.

"You won't melt, Princess," her dad calls out, grabbing the ball from Logan and putting the game in motion.

As the sun moves across the sky, Andi shifts and changes locations of her chair, to soak up the best light. She's intrigued by her book and can't wait to reach the twist. Whenever a romance is going too well in a book, there's always got to be a twist. The other women have joined her, and her nephew splashes lazily in a small baby pool placed on the ground between them. He laughs and giggles, covered by the attached sunshade.

Her swimsuit cover up is off her shoulders, but still covering her belly. Andi reapplies sunscreen, shutting her eyes to the dreamy vision of one of the 'boys' coming to do it for her. Surrounded by everyone, those are not the thoughts she should be having. She flips over on the lounge, laying her book on the ground, and continues to read well into the afternoon.

Water droplets on the back of her legs cause her to blink slowly. When had she drifted off to sleep? She jumps with a start when she realizes Rayaan is shaking his wet hair all over her. "Wake up, sleepyhead. You're looking a little pink."

She rolls over on the chaise and slowly sits up, wiping her hand across her mouth. She yawns lazily.

"I really wish I had my camera, Red." Rayaan laughs,

caressing his thumb across her cheek.

"Why? Cause I'm so beautiful?" She jokes.

She watches him swallow slowly. Something strange passes over his face, but it's gone before she can identify it. He says, "Well, that too, but mostly because you have lines all over your face from the lounge chair."

Her hands fly up to her cheeks and she can feel the little indentions in her skin. "Oh, that's just great."

"Looking good, Red." Rayaan's eyes are on her cleavage, her coverup having come loose, exposing herself.

Blushing, she looks down. "More chair marks. Lovely. Eyes up, King."

He chuckles, holding out his hand. "Go get cleaned up. Arin lost. We're all going to dinner."

Taking her hand, Rayaan pulls her up gently. Her foot tangles in the chair, and Andi topples into him. He grabs around her waist to catch her, supporting her. Her hands are pushed against his bare chest, solid yet soft, and she involuntarily gasps.

In a comforting hold, he bends slightly to look in her eyes. "You okay? You've been in the sun all afternoon."

He's too close and she can barely breathe. Her fingers flex and she notices his own intake of breath. "Good," she says quietly. "I think I stood up too fast."

He loosens his grasp, stepping back. "Drink some water

90

before dinner. We can't have you passing out."

She shakes her head, bending to gather her towel. "No, we can't have that."

"Do you need that?" Rayaan looks around. "I think your dad took all the towels inside."

Andi hands him the brightly colored cloth. In her peripheral vision, she can see him toweling off while she gathers her book and phone. She jumps back when cold water splashes her feet as he squeezes water out from the hem of his swim trunks.

"Watch it," she laughs, kicking water from the puddle back at him.

"You watch it before I dump your ass in the pool." Rayaan grabs her wrist and starts to pull her toward the water.

The sliding door opens and Prisha yells out, "If you toss her in that water, it will be the last thing you do, *beta.*"

"Ah, Ma, you're no fun!" Rayaan laughs as his mother joins them. She hands him a shirt and he pulls it over his head. The shoulders instantly become damp from his wet hair, hanging loose around his face.

Andi itches to run her fingers through the curls. She muses over how she is going to survive this weekend, in such close proximity to her childhood crushes.

"Arin made reservations for dinner at the club. Dinner is at 6:30. Get a move on- Rayaan, dress slacks. Not jeans."

He nudges Andi with his shoulder. "Sometimes she acts like I'm still eighteen."

"You dress like it," says his mother, moving around to collect glasses and plates left out by the pool.

Andi isn't sure of the dress code and doesn't know what's in the back of the car. She wasn't planning to stay and left most of her things at the hotel. "Auntie Prisha, what are you wearing?"

Prisha describes the spring-like sundress she plans to wear. Semi-casual. Andi hopes there is something in the clothes Janessa loaned her from the fashion closet at the magazine office.

Rayaan looks at her, confused. "Are you coming in?"

"No. I have to go check my car for clothes."

They go their separate ways, Prisha walking in the house with her son.

Chapter Eight

"Dammit," Arin mutters. His room overlooks the pool, and he's not happy with the scene unfolding down below. He'd always suspected Andi had a slight crush on his older brother, and the last two days don't seem to be proving him wrong. He knows he fucked up. He was young, in his early twenties when he broke her heart. Arin wishes he'd done things differently. He doesn't know if he can win her heart back. But he'd like to try.

And he needs to make sure her magazine article shows him in a favorable light.

With a scowl, he takes his shower bag, and walks down the hall to shower in the guest bath.

Grabbing his watch from the dresser, Arin walks over to the full-length mirror and flips his wrist over to put it on. His pink shirt sleeves flop open at the wrists and he cuffs them carefully, pushing them to rest just below his elbow. "Chick bait," he says quietly, and laughs about his commonly used stance in his videos. He stands tall, smoothing out the front of his pants, and checks out his appearance.

"Not bad," he says, reaching up to brush a short curl

behind his ear. He needs a haircut, like Andi said, but he didn't want to get one before the interview and risk looking foolish.

Turning away from the mirror, Arin reaches for his cologne on the dresser. He pauses when he hears cursing from across the hall. His brow furrows, curious. He quickly sprays the fragrance across his chest and exits the room.

In three short steps, he crosses the hall to Andi's room. Arin raps his knuckle against the door. "Everything okay?"

"Fuck me," he hears her whisper. He bites his lip to keep from laughing. Andi had always been the neighborhood good girl. When everyone else developed a tongue for curse words, she held strong. She'd always said even though she passed her time with the boys, she didn't want to sound like one. He'd had a good laugh the first Thanksgiving in college when she came home and cursed a blue streak about a speeding ticket she'd received. Through the door, he can hear her stumbling against something in her room and muttering some more.

The door flies open, and he can't hold in his laugh.

Standing there, in hair curlers and her make up half-finished, Andi glares at him. "Shut up and help me zip this."

She turns around, the smell of her perfume swirling around her, intoxicating him.

"Oh honey, it's a little tight," he sighs, stepping in the room and closing the door. He can't believe this stroke of luck!

"It's all I have. My things are still at the hotel. It's designer swag from the office." The spring dress hugs her curves, and she sucks in as Arin tugs up slowly on the zipper. "I just won't breathe, eat, or walk."

"You smell the same." He struggles not to inhale too deeply, the smell of her apple shampoo tickling his nose. He drags his fingertips up her spine, watching as goosebumps break across her skin. Arin can't help but notice the dress is so tight, she'd passed on wearing a bra. Gripping the dress at the top, he stretches the two sides together. "Suck in your breath," he commands quietly.

She breathes in again, holding it, and he gets the zipper closed. He smooths his hands down her sides, stretching out the fabric.

"Do you still like the back of your neck kissed?" He murmurs. "It was your favorite."

"Arin-" Her warning escapes her lips but sounds more of a plea.

Pressing his mouth to her skin, he peppers light kisses across her shoulder blades. Her skin is smooth and warm from the afternoon sun. When she doesn't protest, he scrapes her shoulder with his teeth, opening his mouth a little wider to dart out his tongue for a quick taste of her.

"We shouldn't. Everyone is-"

He spins her in his arms, covering her mouth with his, effectively stopping her weak protest. Arin deepens the kiss, pulling her to him and holding her close. Andi tentatively lifts her hands and tugs on his shirt collar, her fingertips brushing his skin.

She pulls back with a pop, brushing her hand over her bottom lip, her eyes hazy.

"Arin, I don't think-"

"Good then don't. Let's enjoy it." He looks her over, and with no signs of complaining, he kisses her again. She caves in, her tongue teasing his. Small gasps for air are released between them. He grips tightly to her rounded hip, drawing her closer. Her fingers tease the collar of his shirt and she faintly moans, weak at his advance. He moves his mouth from side to side, attempting to taste all of her, to light her on fire.

Somewhere down the hall, a door slams. Andi slowly leans back, returning to her senses. Andi pats his chest, slightly off-balance, sighing. "You always were a damn good kisser. You knew how to make my head spin."

She wipes her thumb across her lip. Arin is unable to overlook the fluttering of her pulse behind her ear. His cock stirs to attention and he wants her mouth on his again, her curvy body at his side.

"Good, because I'd like to kiss you again-"

Her phone buzzes on the dresser.

She chuckles, stepping away from him. "I don't know about that," she walks around the side of the bed, "but it was nice to relive old memories." The pretty redhead holds up her phone. "Alarm. We have ten more minutes."

"We could do a lot in ten minutes." Shit, he didn't mean for that to sound so arrogant.

"Oh, I'm sure you think you could, but-" She stops herself, and a blush flashes across her cheeks. With the unspoken thought, she crosses to the makeup vanity in the room.

He's curious about what she wanted to say, but doesn't ask. Although connected for that brief heated moment, there's still a lot of reparations to make before Andi owes him any kind of explanation for her thoughts or behavior. Arin can't keep his eyes off her reflection as she pulls the curlers from her hair. Her voluptuous breasts nearly spill over the top. He aches to snuggle between them as he had when they were dating. He licks his lip before offering advice. "I bet Ma has a shawl, or scarf, you can wear over your shoulders."

"Good idea," she replies, smiling up at him in the mirror.

Texting his mother quickly, he enjoys the process of watching Andi complete her beauty routine. She shakes out the curls, throwing half over her shoulder, leaving the remaining curls to hang down her back. She grabs a bright pink tube, twisting it, and pulls out a mascara wand. She opens her gray, stormy eyes wide and dabs at her lashes. From another tube, she puts two pink dots on her cheeks and blends them with her fingers. A glow highlights her face. Unconsciously, he mimics her pucker as she runs a mauve color over her lips.

"God, I love watching women get ready. It's so intimate."

Andi tosses the lipstick into a small straw clutch lying next to her. She shakes her head and stands, looking around the room. "Do you see my sandals? They don't match, but they're all I have."

Arin scoops up the shoes from the side of the bed, in one hand, and holds his other out to her. "Come on. You know how Logan is when we're not on schedule."

She pauses. "Like you care about being on his schedule!" Andi looks at his hand for a moment before taking it. "I swear, when we were kids, you liked making us all late to school, just to get him angry."

Her hand feels good in his. Like it's right where it belongs.

The pair laugh over old memories as they walk down the stairs, reminiscing about the carpool the mothers arranged.

When the closed stairwell opens up into the living room, Arin's eye instantly catches his brother's in the crowd, waiting to go to dinner. Helpless to stamp down the puckish impulse, he winks and raises their hands so everyone can see.

"Women, always running late," he jokes.

She drops his hand and gives him a slight push. "Whatever. I'm on time."

Her shoulders are flushed, matching her cheeks, but he didn't miss the deadly glare.

Arin will have to be on his best behavior to win her over. But the irritation on his brother's face dictates he'll play nice later. Provoking Rayaan is just an added bonus to his plan. Adjusting his sleeve, he holds his head high, impervious to the slight tension he's created.

As the families walk to the door to put on their shoes, the fathers continue discussing the driving arrangements, and Andi steps to the side to confer with Prisha over the shawl options she has to go with the dress.

Before Arin can take another jab at his brother, Rayaan announces he will drive separately. "I have to run back into town to the office. Forgot some papers that must be signed."

Prisha smiles and nods. She tilts her head to Sarah and Andi. "My son. The fancy lawyer," she says with pride.

Neal Collins pushes the large group out the door. "We're going to be late. Just get in a car. Let's go!"

Chapter Nine

Dinner with so many people was a fiasco. The baby wouldn't stop crying, so Logan took him outside so his wife could eat in peace. Prisha argued it was too much for Arin to pay for everything and slid some cash under his plate. Neal had so many questions for Andi about politics and life in DC, she could hardly speak to anyone else. And Rayaan sat sullen most of the evening, only perking up for a few moments when his brownie and ice cream were delivered to the table for dessert.

Andi was sad he left before the rest of the family finished their meals. He kissed his mother on the head, quietly telling her if work ran long, he'd stay in town and return to the house in the morning.

The drive back to the rental house is quieter. She rests her head against the window, the cool glass comforting after the stifling heat of the crowded restaurant.

Andi knows Arin wasn't happy she'd decided to ride home with her brother, but she needed space. She'd been carrying out the diaper bag and the travel seat, so it only made sense for her to ride with her siblings. Little Jackson was out like a light before they'd even turned down the winding lake road.

Smoothing out the small bag in her lap, she appreciates

Logan made a quick stop at one of the souvenir junk shops so she could buy a t-shirt and shorts to sleep in. She set an alarm to wake up early in the morning so she could drive into the city to get her things.

Listening to the couple in the front seats murmur about dinner is relaxing. She catches phrases here and there from conversations they had been a part of at the table that she had not heard. She smiles when Logan reaches over the console to grab his wife's hand.

"You two are really cute. It's sweet," she says sleepily.

Lauren looks over her shoulder. "You'll find the right guy too. Don't worry."

Andi nods, looking out the window, watching flashes of lights from homes as they whiz past. She's not worried. She just wants to make sure he's the right one, not just the one that feels easy.

Turning into the drive, Logan hisses out some curse words. "If they wake him up, he is their responsibility for the rest of the night. I'm done; reached my limit of parenting today."

"You played volleyball in the pool all afternoon," Lauren reminds him sarcastically.

The parents are standing in the circle drive, talking. Arin rests on the stone steps, his legs splayed out in front of him. Andi swallows hard, but looks away.

Her father moves close to the car as it pulls in. Logan stops, and her dad opens the door for her. Lauren and Logan frantically mime, indicating the sleeping baby.

"You okay?" Stephen questions softly, reaching his hand out to take the diaper bag. "You were awfully quiet at dinner."

Through the front window, she watches Arin lean forward, resting his elbows on his knees.

Her dad. Always so perceptive. She grabs his shoulder, and steps down from the vehicle. She can't wait to get out of the tight dress. "Why don't you join us for movies tonight?"

He begins to rebuke the invitation, but Arin moving towards them changes his mind. "That new movie on Netflix is supposed to be good? The media room has an account we can log into."

"Sounds like a plan." She rises on her tiptoes, kissing his cheek. "Thanks, Dad," she whispers.

He pats her back before bending to retrieve the boxes of leftover food that had been at her feet.

Before Arin can reach her, she loops her arm in her mother's, and asks for assistance with her dress.

Padding into the media room in her bare feet, she can't believe the whir of activity in her absence of twenty minutes.

After her mother had helped her unzip her dress, she'd answered a few quick emails for work, and changed into the clothes she'd bought at the touristy shop. Nothing matched and the t-shirt was so large it hung off her shoulder. Watching Prisha organize movie snacks, she attempts to tug it up, to hide the strap of her sports bra, but it instantly falls again.

"What is this, Auntie? We barely finished dinner!" On a side table in the room, chocolates, pretzels, popcorn, and an assortment of beverages are laid out. She pops a small, colorful chocolate into her mouth.

"Growing boys," Prisha waves her hand. "Just because they're adults now, doesn't mean they've changed."

As proof of her statement, Arin and Logan practically tumble through the door, obviously having raced from upstairs. Logan jumps in triumph, waving the baby monitor in the air like a trophy.

"Oh, who's gonna wake the baby now?" Andi laughs, stepping aside as they rush the table.

Her dad silently enters the room, taking one of the leather padded chairs designed to seat two.

"Mom's on baby duty," Logan explains, taking a beer from the table. "Lauren was exhausted and went to bed. And they're on the other side of the house, so we don't have to worry."

Arin slides up next to Andi, a large bowl of popcorn in his hands. "Where do you want to sit?"

"Dad's saving my spot," she says, reaching for two beers and the bag of pretzels.

She doesn't miss the look of disappointment on his face.

Grabbing a blanket off one of the other chairs filling the room, placed on leveled platforms, she walks over to her dad. Handing him the beer bottles, she plops in the chair, tugging her legs up under her and wrapping the blanket over her knees. She pokes her toes against her dad's leg.

He laughs, opening her beer and handing it back.

She shifts over, so she's not touching him. "I see Prisha brought the drinks, none of that cheap crap you buy." She raises her bottle and Neal and the boys chime in, a rousing "Hear, Hear!"

"Cheap beer, old cars, and camping vacations paid for your college, my dear." He takes a slow drink, savoring the flavor.

She lifts her head, seeing him as an adult, maybe for the first time, and not just her father. "Thank you. I don't know if I've ever really said that to you. Thank you for the sacrifices you and Mom made when we were younger so we could have a good life." He leans over and kisses her temple. She shakes her finger at him. "But you work for the university system. Don't give me crap about my education being expensive."

"But you were a deer killer," Logan reminds her, sitting in the seat in front of her. "How many times did you hit a deer and need to have your car fixed?"

She pouts. "It's not my fault I didn't have great vision."

Arin hands her a napkin. "Yes, that's what's different! Where are your glasses?"

She laughs, running a finger under her eye. "Lasik. As a foreign correspondent, I didn't want to worry about someplace with unsanitary water and taking care of contacts."

"You. Miss Squeamish- I- Can't- Dissect- the- Frog- in- Biology, got lasik?" Arin teases, getting comfortable in the chair next to her.

"I know, let's not talk about it," she shudders. "It was traumatizing."

She still has nightmares about it.

Neal enters the room and dims the lights. "All here?"

Not waiting for an answer, he turns on the entertainment system, and the all familiar red N fills the screen. With a few clicks of the remote, the movie starts and the chatter ends.

Andi can't keep her focus on the movie. She thinks Ryan Reynolds is trying to save the world... Again.

For the first half of the show, Arin occasionally threw popcorn kernels at her, trying to get them stuck in her hair, like he did when they were kids. Now, his attention span has waned, despite the explosions and sexy woman on the screen. Andi can see him scrolling on his phone, occasionally typing out something. Her phone vibrates in her pocket, but she ignores it. If it's work, it can wait. If it's Arin, she doesn't want to know what he might be thinking.

She huffs out, annoyed. Why hasn't he grown up? For all his accomplishments, it's no wonder he's still single. She feels like dating him would be a full-time job, taking care of him, and entertaining him.

But another kiss or two might be nice. She's only in town for a few more days. Where's the harm in a little fun?

Is that so wrong?

Arin wants the family togetherness of watching the movie, but his vacation day has created a backlog of messages for him to answer and deal with. As a social media influencer, there's more to the job than just posting videos. He'd pre-set three to post during the day, but one of them didn't work. In the dark room, he tries to use his phone to figure out the problem, but really needs to be working on his tablet or laptop.

His mother, sitting behind him, has already told him three times to put his phone away. Twice, he waved her off, but the third time, he snapped slightly, telling her he was working, and drawing attention to himself. He apologized to everyone, and turned the brightness down on his phone, making it harder for him to see the screen.

Not invested in the movie, he tries to squeeze in some work. He replies to a request for an interview, telling them he's unavailable until summer. The contract he has with Andi's magazine better be good, because he's having to turn down too many offers.

Typing up a list of ideas for upcoming videos, he's surprised to look up and find the movie has ended. His parents are cleaning the snacks, and Logan is picking up trash. He looks to his left, and Andi is sound asleep in her chair. Cuddled under the fuzzy blanket, she has popcorn stuck in her hair.

He smiles, rising and stretching. Dropping his phone in the chair, he kneels in front of her. She's so peaceful when she sleeps- less opinionated. He pats his chest at his silent joke. Reaching out, he tenderly picks the kernels from her hair, trying not to disturb her.

Stephen taps his shoulder. "Let's wake her and help get her to her room."

Arin shakes his head no. "She's so clumsy, she'll trip on the steps." He reaches for the pillow Logan had thrown at him. "Is there another blanket? I'll sleep here, until she wakes up."

Stephen stares silently for a moment, before giving in. He points his finger. "You don't know what it was like after you walked away." Arin hangs his head in shame. "She's going back to Chicago in a few days. Nothing stupid. And if you hurt her again, they'll find your body at the bottom of that lake."

Despite the older man's smirk, and chuckle, Arin doesn't doubt it for a second. Arin had always appreciated Stephen's honesty, and thought of him as a second father. There were many times when he was younger, he'd be in a scrape he didn't think he could talk to his parents about. Stephen had always been good to him, and offered whatever advice he could.

"Hear you loud and clear." He salutes the older man.

Pulling the blanket over his daughter's exposed shoulder, Stephen sends another glare towards Arin before leaving.

"What he said," relays Logan, pointing two fingers at his eyes, and then back at his friend.

Arin puts up his hands in a question, and waves to his parents as they say their goodnight wishes. His father adjusts the dimmer switch, turning the lights up to a slightly higher setting.

Great, even his own father doesn't trust him to be alone with Andi.

Laying on the floor next to her, he continues to type away at some emails, before drifting off to sleep himself.

Chapter Ten

Andi wakes, disoriented. Sitting up, she swings her legs around, but they land on something beneath her.

"Oof," Arin breathes out.

Andi yelps. "What the hell?" She reaches for her phone, fumbling with the flashlight.

"It's me, it's me," Arin says in the darkness. "You almost stepped on my dick."

"Ah, that's what was soft and squishy!"

"Fuck off," he mumbles.

She leans over and pushes his hair out of his face. "Is that any way to talk to a lady?"

"Why the hell are you awake?" he growls, throwing his arm over his eyes.

"Jeez, I'd forgotten how grumpy you are when you wake up." Andi scoots to the end of the loveseat and puts her feet on solid ground. "You know, this should be a topic for one of your videos."

"Please stop talking," he pleads.

Wrapping the blanket around her shoulders, she tells him. "No worries. I'm going up to use the restroom, and then going to bed."

His hand wraps around her ankle. "Don't go."

Andi hisses. "Arin! I have to go to the bathroom." She kicks her leg free from his hand.

Andi sits upright in her bed, searching for her phone. She blinks rapidly, trying to remember. She and Arin had talked for a while in the hall after coming upstairs. She scratches her eyebrow, remembering how he had her pinned against the wall, kissing her neck. Her stomach had been full of butterflies, and she'd felt good, in a way she hadn't in a while. But the voice in the back of her head told her this wasn't what she wanted. All the little run-ins, the flirting, hinted at Arin trying to win her back out of some sense of duty, to right the wrongs of the past. Holding on to that clarity for self-preservation, she hadn't let him in her room, and had sent him back to his, alone.

That's a step in the right direction, isn't it?

As she shakes her head, she returns to the present. "Dammit! I didn't set the alarm."

Momentarily contemplating driving into town in the clothes she slept in, Andi decides against it. The Regency is too high class for her to stroll through in booty shorts and a tie-dye shirt. Climbing out of bed, she digs through her beach bag to see what she can put on to walk into the fancy hotel. Oh! And stop at a coffee shop for a caffeine fix!, she thinks to herself.

Finding a tank top and some leggings, she decides to wear those, with her swimsuit cover up as a jacket. She shakes out her hair, a few remaining kernels of popcorn falling out. Knowing her shoes are by the front door, she reaches for her phone and purse.

Taking the back stairway, she passes through the laundry room into the kitchen. Someone is awake, and already has the coffee pot started. It smells wonderful! There's a large assortment of muffins, bagels, and donuts on the table.

Standing over the table, deciding to take a snack to go, she spots her bright yellow suitcase by the doorway. She rubs her eyes, thinking she's imagining it. Rayaan walks through the patio door with a large bouquet of fresh flowers.

"Did you do all this?"

"Good morning to you, too," he smiles, reaching for the vase on the counter.

"That's my suitcase. How did it get here?"

He casually places the flowers in the glass container, and they look perfect, as if arranged by a professional. She's caught off guard by it.

"I figured you needed your things, so I got them when I was at the office last night." He avoids eye contact with her.

She turns fully to face him, hands on her hips. "What do you mean, you got it? How the hell did you get permission to go into my room?"

He runs his tongue across his teeth and reaches up to scratch his thumb over a spot in his beard. "Well, it's kinda easy." He dips his head sheepishly. "I own the place."

"The Regency. The ritziest, priciest hotel in the tri-county area, and you own it?" She stares at him incredulously.

Stepping closer, he places his finger under her jaw, and closes her mouth. "You really don't use Google for your research, do you?" Pulling his hand away, he cocks his head. "In all these years, you never thought to Google me, us?"

Andi raises her hands in defeat. "Ha, ha. Very funny." She smiles. "Research is my job." She doesn't care to admit how often she's checked up on the Collins brothers. "But, if I want to keep up with you boys, I can just ask my mother. She delivers more news than TMZ."

Rayaan chuckles, leaning over the chair, folding his hands together. Andi's working hard to ignore the visual he creates in a green tank top, forearms on display and his shoulders, a golden tan. The tattoo on his shoulder peeks from behind the cotton cloth.

"So you never found anything?"

"Maybe something from social pages back before your divorce, but nothing related to your work." Andi knows she would definitely remember reading about such a large business acquisition.

"Some investigative reporter you are…" Rayaan shakes his head in shame, toying with her. "C&A Industries. Ever heard of them?"

She thinks quickly of the financial pages. "Yeah, owns half the hotel and resort industry up the East Coast, some things here in the West, a few newspapers, some radio syndicates…" Her jaw drops again. "That's you?"

"Not just me. C&A- Collins and Associates. A collection of my closest pals from law school. We all have our areas of expertise-"

"Do you own my magazine?" She swallows hard.

He looks her straight in the eye. "No. No, I don't." He stands up tall. "This, seeing you again, is purely coincidental. When the magazine reached out, I said they had to send their best journalist. They sent you."

Andi blushes at the praise the company afforded her. Her blush deepens when she remembers the state her room at the hotel was left in. "Oh, God. Rayaan! My room was a mess. I was only coming for the day, and-"

"Don't worry," he holds up his hands. "I didn't go in. I thought it would be an invasion of your privacy. I had a member of the cleaning crew gather any clothes, makeup or medicine." He explains. "The room is still yours. If there's anything not here, it's back at the room." He nods to the display of food on the table. "You still like blueberry donuts, right? The hotel bakery had them fresh this morning."

She nods, feeling more settled knowing he hadn't been in her room. Curiously, she wonders if he asked them specifically to have blueberry donuts this morning. "Plates?"

He points to the cabinet next to the sink. "Nice hot pink panties, though." With a smirk, Rayaan walks to the counter, reaching for two coffee mugs as she walks to the cabinets for plates.

Mid step, she turns. "What? I thought you said-" Seeing the mirth on his face, she knows she's been had. "You fucker."

She can't help but laugh with him at his trick. She walked right into that one. His eyes crinkle when he laughs, and his dimples deepen.

"Sorry," he shrugs. "Couldn't help myself. Hot pink, huh?" He tilts his head to look at her ass.

Placing the plates on the table, she turns her back to the wall, away from him. She mumbles, "You're horrible."

He chuckles again. "Do you drink coffee?" Rayaan asks, pouring a tall mug for himself. She can see it's battered and covered with travel stickers. "You used to hate it."

How can he remember so many little details?

Probably the same way she remembers he takes his black.

"Yeah, two sugars. Is there any vanilla creamer?" Answering her own question, Andi reaches inside the stainless-steel refrigerator and pulls out a jug of creamer. "Mmm… this breakfast sure beats the one I was planning to get."

"Oh, really," he asks, full of curiosity. "What were you planning on?" He fixes her drink according to her order.

"A coffee," she takes the cup he offers her, and carries it to the table. Using a fork, she stabs a donut and adds it to her plate before sitting down. "And a boring egg white bite, probably with spinach."

Setting a large bowl of fresh fruit on the table, Rayaan eyes her carefully. "Who are you? That doesn't sound like the Andi I knew."

She can feel the flush rising up her cheeks. Scooping out some fruit onto her plate, she dips her head. "I know, right? Adulting sucks. All that 'eat healthy, live longer' bullshit." She pokes at a blueberry with her fork, popping it in her mouth. "At some point, I have to finish this interview."

"How's it coming? If you don't mind me asking." He places two muffins on his plate, before grabbing a piece of cantaloupe from the edge of hers.

A baby cry pierces the air, loud enough to wake anyone still sleeping. Sounds of movement from upstairs filters down into the kitchen.

She rubs her hands on her thighs. "I'll be honest. I'm not sure I can write what needs to be written. This is a fluff piece." She breaks the donut in half. "You should know, even before I knew it was about Arin, I asked to be taken off the story. I'm trying to do more serious journalism."

"I can see how this doesn't fit in your usual beat." Rayaan's eyes show his interest in her work. "Your personal interest stories on the people of Sudan were fascinating. How you could show life still trying to carry on, as normal as possible, during a time of such unrest, was beautiful."

Andi beams with pride. "Oh, I was so fresh! Just out of college, and I get sent overseas like that," she shakes her head. "It was an unreal experience."

He contemplates her over the top of his mug. She can feel him sizing her up. "Not many people battle heartache by going into a literal warzone, Red."

"I was young-"

"And very stupid. What if something had happened to you?" Rayaan asks, resting his hand over hers.

Logan enters the room, carrying Jackson like a football. He sees the two at the table and raises an eyebrow. "Fall asleep with one; wake up with the other. I can't keep track with you, Sis."

Rayaan swallows hard and pulls his hand away.

Andi burns in shame and wonders what she can throw at her brother that would cause damage.

Tossing her hair over her shoulder, she brushes off his

117

comment. "Oh, please. I fell asleep watching the movie, it's no big deal." She picks at her donut, slowly losing her appetite.

"Try telling that to Arin," Logan snickers, bouncing the baby carelessly. His ease into fatherhood appears seamless. "All he's done the last two days is ask about you."

Rayaan clears his throat. Taking his plate, he walks to the trash, throwing away a half-eaten muffin. He exits the room, without saying anything.

Andi jumps from her seat. "Logan, you ass!" She hisses. "That was rude!" She thumps him on the chest, careful not to hit the baby.

"What? It's not like you were making the moves on- Oh, my God. Were you making the moves on Rayaan?"

She pulls an empty mug towards her, and pours him a cup of coffee, remembering he takes it black with one sugar.

Maybe?

But she's not going to admit that to her overprotective brother.

"No! I just-" she sighs. "I want to get through this weekend unscathed, okay? They get weirdly competitive, and I just wanna relax, finish my interview, take some photos of my cute nephew," she taps Jackson's nose as Logan swings him towards her, "and go home. End of story."

"He's really attractive," Logan concedes. "Nothing like

when we were growing up. Less nerdy. Fit, but not like he goes to the gym all the time."

They both turn to the sound of splashing water. All Andi can see are Rayaan's feet in the air before they submerge under water.

"Good. Fine, then you go have a crush on him."

Logan laughs, passing Jackson off to his wife as she walks in the room.

"Crush on who?" Lauren asks sleepily. She leans her head side to side and Andi winces when it pops.

"Rayaan." Andi pours her a cup as well.

"Oh yeah, totally hot." She giggles at her husband's pout. "But I work in his office, and workplace relationships never work out."

"Wait, we met at work," Logan reminds her.

"Yeah," Lauren reaches for a bagel. "And I'm still trying to decide if this is going to work out."

Andi laughs at their banter, watching as Rayaan slaps his hand on the side of the pool before flipping around to do another lap.

She shakes her head, confused before something strikes her memory. "You work for Rayaan?"

Lauren tears off a piece of the bread, barely larger than a crumb, and feeds it to Jackson before sitting him in the highchair. Logan tosses a few pieces of cereal on the tray and takes a seat. "One of the corporate offices. Really with one of his partners, he's only in our office about once a month." Plopping the bagel in the toaster, she reaches for the honey cinnamon cream cheese spread. "He offered me the position after last year's neighborhood Christmas party. It was such a raise in my salary, I couldn't turn it down."

Logan scratches his forehead. "That's why I get to stay home with Jackson three days a week, and work from home. I'm a kept man."

Lauren sits down next to him, placing her plate in front of her. She pats his arm. "You're so good with him. And it's such a relief not to put him in daycare yet."

Andi is filled with warmth, watching the two of them. "You guys are amazing. So comfortable together, and complementing each other."

Logan blushes at his sister's praise. "When you know, you know." He reaches over, pulling his wife to him, and kisses her temple.

More noise fills the kitchen as the other family members slowly make their appearance.

"Oh, daisies!" Prisha exclaims, admiring the flowers on the counter. "My favorite." She smiles at Andi. "Did you do this?"

"Rayaan. He was up before everyone, or just came in from town, I guess." She steals another blueberry from the fruit bowl.

In answer to Prisha's unspoken question, there is another splash from the pool.

Neal reaches over her for the bowl. "He was pulling in the drive when I went out for my run. Said he slept at the office. He's an early bird. Not like that other one." He points up to the ceiling.

"Oh, let him sleep, *priya*. We're all on vacation, and he's not running off to make videos. That's good."

Andi's ears perk up. "How does that work? Arin said he has to post several times a day."

Andi smiles as her mom enters the room, giving her shoulder a squeeze, but her focus is on Prisha.

Prisha scoops up some fruit, adding it to a bowl of cottage cheese. "He tells me he has several stored up, for days like this." She picks out a sour looking grape. "Have you seen his set up? It looks a little crazy, but he really has perfected it."

Thinking about the content of some of the videos, Andi is curious. "How do you feel about his new career path? His content?"

Taking the tea cup her husband hands her, Prisha smiles at everyone seated at the table. She announces proudly, "Do you know he has over three hundred thousand followers now?" She blows across the top of the cup. "I found it strange at first. When he first came to me with some sample videos, he was thinking of making the theme about growing up in a multicultural household. Oh, those made me laugh!" She giggles, hiding behind her hand. "They were so honest and colorful, honestly, but I didn't want him to insult any of our family in India." She takes a small sip of her drink. "Arin made a wise choice, playing into the belief people already had about him, as a lady's man."

Neal chuckles, "Takes after his old man."

Everyone around the table has a story about Arin, and his early days, mishaps he had as a young man, often trying to juggle too many girlfriends. Andi enjoys the stories and laughter, even getting up to grab pen and paper to jot down a few notes, as anecdotes for her feature.

"I even thought he found the one. We were shocked when he announced he was moving to-"

"Dad! Enough-" Arin growls, entering the room. He turns to Andi. "If you have questions, you ask me."

She drops her pen, stunned by his defensiveness. "Like you were asking Logan questions about me?" She pushes her chair back and stands up. "I wasn't asking out of curiosity. I was doing my job- gathering information about you, for the article. If you don't like it, we can be done. I don't have to do this. Shit, I had forgotten what a pissant you can be in the morning."

Sarah steps behind her. "Now, let's not start the day on

122

the wrong foot. Arin, your coffee is on the counter. No one was talking poorly about you, honey. We were simply reminiscing, and I'm sure Andi wouldn't use anything too personal in her story..."

He takes a deep breath, looking at everyone seated at the table. "Sorry, Aunt Sarah, Ma. You're right." Arin deflates. Stepping closer to Andi, he says quietly. "Please accept my apology for coming in like an ass. Not everyone knows why I left," he gives his father the side-eye, "and that's something we should talk about, but not out in the open."

Andi pushes in her chair and picks up her notepad. "For that? It's too late for an apology or an explanation now, Arin." She looks around the table. "Everyone in this room watched me throw myself at you for years, and when I finally had you, like I was some 'second place' trophy, like you knew I'd wait, you walked out." She swallows hard, keeping her voice steady, saying what she'd needed to say for years. Grateful she didn't let him in her room the night before, she continues. "You can't come crawling back, just because your life didn't work out the way you wanted." All eyes are on her, but hers are on Arin's, noticing the small tik in his jaw, and the tears swelling in his eyes. She shrugs. "You know what I've missed most, these last ten years? My best friend."

Her mother nods, whispering, "Both of them."

"Yeah, yeah," Andi says, voice choking. "When you left, I

lost Rayaan too."

"Give her a hug, asshole," Logan says quietly.

Arin's shoulders lift in an unspoken question. Andi steps forward, accepting his hug.

Holding her, he whispers quietly in her ear, apologies and a promise to make it better.

But her eyes are on Rayaan, watching the embrace through the window, and him running off, around the side of the house.

Chapter Eleven

"I don't know if he's coming."

"Did you pack enough sodas in the cooler?"

"Sarah, I forgot my sunscreen up at the house. Do you have some?"

The boat dock is full of noise and familiar chatter as Neal and Stephen return with the boat they rented for the afternoon.

Andi sits in an Adirondack chair by the water, observing the commotion.

The solitary pose tugs at his heartstrings.

"Come on, Red, we don't wanna get left behind." Rayaan taps the back of the chair with the bag he carries.

Andi seems shocked to see him. "Oh, you're going? Your mom wasn't sure." She stands up, gathering her bag and a stack of towels from the other chair.

"We haven't had a family boat ride in forever. Would I miss this?"

"I just thought-"

"You thought wrong. Come on."

Rayaan will be the first to admit, he hasn't been acting like himself. He hates watching Arin back at his old games, and he doesn't want to see Andi hurt. Although he's fearful his behavior is hurting her too.

Walking down the dock, the wind catches Andi's dress, swirling it around her as she walks. Realizing he was short with her, he offers. "I was on the phone with Elias. He had his first soccer practice today. Gemma took him and some friends for pizza. He was telling me all about his spelling test yesterday."

Andi nods in understanding, and the group on the dock raise up a cheer at their arrival.

"Got pretzels, *bhai*?" Arin asks, while helping the women into the boat.

"Didn't forget," Rayaan replies coarsely, as Andi hands over her things before taking Arin's hand to climb into the boat.

Andi turns and holds out her hands to take Rayaan's bag, gifting him with a wide smile.

He stays on the dock, untying the boat before hopping on at the last minute. Looking for a seat, he's disappointed that Arin and Andi are sitting together. His brother's feet are propped up on one of the coolers and he kicks them out of his way to pass by to get to an open seat across from them. Rayaan flops down on the bench seat, while they laugh at something, their heads bent together to look at something on Arin's phone. He adjusts his sunglasses, his stomach tightening in irritation when his brother leans back, placing his arm up on the seat behind Andi.

The boat pulls aways from the dock as everyone continues to get settled and items are stored out of the way. It knocks on the waves from another passing boat.

"Arin, switch seats with Rayaan," Stephen calls out from the driver's seat. "Gotta balance the boat."

Stephen was always his favorite person. Growing up, Rayaan had been of the belief that he and Stephen both had a distaste for the way Arin played with Andi's emotions. Seated in his new spot, he doesn't hold in his chuckle when his brother flips him off, and Stephen gives him a thumbs up.

Andi's curly hair is caught on the wind and slaps him in the face. Apple blossoms and cinnamon. The smell he remembers from their youth.

"Sorry," she reaches behind her and braids it quickly. "Forgot my hat."

Inhaling deeply, he hands her a hair band from his wrist.

She giggles. "I guess Gemma got tired of sharing hair stuff with you?"

Passing her the bottle of sunscreen everyone is sharing, he contemplates his answer. She liberally puts some on her cheeks and nose. Choosing to keep things light, he simply says, "Something like that." He wonders if their voices carry on the sound of the wind, if others in the boat can hear them? If they will join in their conversation?

"Can I tell you something?" Andi leans forward and lotions the top of her feet, playfully squeezing some out onto Arin's feet as well.

"Shit, that's cold," he bitches. "Rub it in, Ands."

A stab of jealousy pierces his chest, hearing his brother call her that.

"I'm not touching your feet."

She laughs easily and Rayaan likes the sound of it, even if it's aimed at his brother.

"Sure, Red, what do you want to tell me?" Rayaan asks, pulling her attention back to him.

"She was never good enough for you, King." She sticks out her tongue at him when he shakes his head at the nickname he hates. "She didn't deserve to be Queen."

Funny. He remembers Gemma not being a big fan of Andi's either.

Distracted by a stray red curl blowing in the breeze, Rayaan reaches up and catches it. Tucking it behind her sunglasses, he briefly touches the tip of her ear. "Why didn't you ever tell me that?"

"Would you have listened to me, any more than all the times I listened when you told me to be careful?" Andi juts her chin in Arin's direction. She smiles, watching him make faces at her nephew, sitting in the back with Sarah and his mom. The poor kid looks miserable in the baby life jacket,

128

but he's being a good sport. She looks back at him. "And I did, I told you she was only after the life you promised, reaching up the social ladder."

Rayaan remembered that; the first Christmas he'd brought Gemma home to meet the family. Andi had warned him that his new girlfriend had been preoccupied with appearances and the cost of things in his family's home. She had been excited about the prospect of being a senator's wife.

"Do you remember when we all went skiing together? I was up late, working on that paper. You don't remember what you said to me, do you?"

The wind makes it hard to hear as the boat speeds down the lake.

"What?" he asks, raising his voice. He inwardly wonders what confession he may have forgotten.

He and Gemma had been dating about three years at that point. She and Arin had officially been dating for a few months. He remembers one of the dads had found a good deal on a late season house rental in the mountains.

Andi leans into him, turning her head to look over his shoulder, to speak closer to his ear. "You told me you thought you should just give up and marry her, since she'd had so much patience while you were in law school, but you didn't really know if you loved her."

The boat hits a large wake, crashing against the next wave,

and she falls against him. Her hand grips his thigh, supporting herself so she doesn't totally fall over. Andi's fingers flex, and he can swear he hears her gasp. Jackson laughs at being jostled, and she rights herself as soon as she can.

Rayaan doesn't remember the exact conversation. He vaguely remembers Gemma being on that family trip. They had been on the verge of breakup, both stressed about their adult lives and beginning new careers. Adjusting his sunglasses, he has a memory of waking up in the middle of the night to go downstairs for a glass of water. He'd found Andi downstairs hunched over her laptop, pounding away at the keys. She was stressed about getting a paper finished on time, but Arin had wanted to go to a movie, so they'd gone out instead. Because they always seemed to do what Arin wanted to do.

Rayaan had made her a pot of coffee and sat up with her well into the morning hours, helping her with the paper. When it was finished, they'd talked over a second pot of coffee, and watched the sun come up over the mountains.

It had been the best night of his life.

Hanging out with his brother's girlfriend.

She shifts on the boat seat again, turning sideways to face him, putting her leg up on the seat. It rests against his thigh. Andi tucks the billowy skirt under her, to keep it from blowing in the wind. "When Mom called, and said you were

130

engaged, I was shocked." Andi taps his shoulder with her fingertip. "Did you know everyone thought you guys were pregnant? That was the only reason they could come up with since it was all so rushed."

"It wasn't that rushed. We were together for almost three years-"

"And you didn't love her."

No. He didn't really love the woman he married.

"After being friends for so long, it really bothered me that you couldn't make it to the wedding."

Andi bites in her lips and then puckers them out, like she's waging some sort of mental conflict. Opening her mouth to speak, they pop so slightly, sounding like a kiss.

All he can think about is kissing her, feeling her soft, plump lips against his.

"I couldn't watch you throw it away- your hopes. I knew you didn't love her, and I didn't want to be in that place. Celebrating something that wasn't real."

He cocks his head, letting her confession sink in. "But you had surgery?"

Andi scoffs. "Dental surgery. It could have waited."

"It had nothing to do with Arin being there?"

Over the wind, Arin shouts, "What?"

"Hand over some water bottles," Andi replies loudly. She shrugs, and says quietly, "He doesn't have to know what we're talking about…" She takes the bottle Rayaan passes off to her. "That was a part of it, too. And I had my first job. I couldn't easily get more time off to travel home."

He ponders her words for a few minutes. "Why weren't we friends after that?"

"Uh, you were married? I was overseas." She turns her head, watching the water in front of them. "It was difficult, getting back on my feet, after he left. Being friends with you would mean still being connected to him." She tosses her braid over her shoulder before taking another drink of her water. "Besides, Gemma hated me."

"No, she didn't-"

"Men. Clueless." She shakes her head. "Yes, she did." Andi presses. "Not like I was any kind of competition against a goddess like her, but she warned me at Logan's wedding to stay the hell away from you."

Rayaan is shocked. "She what?"

Her brother Logan had asked Rayaan and Arin to be groomsmen in his wedding. Arin had made up an excuse, probably to avoid seeing Andi. But Rayaan had accepted the honor and stood up with his friend to claim Lauren as his bride. He'd been paired with Andi, as a bridesmaid, to walk down the aisle. She'd looked so beautiful in the sage colored dress Lauren had chosen for that warm, fall day. They'd danced under the trees. His wife had been irritable most of the day. He'd assumed it was because she'd been dealing with a cranky toddler while he was busy with wedding duties.

Andi shrugs, "Yeah. It was late. Your parents had already taken Elias for the night. She was a little drunk. For some odd reason, I guess she felt she needed to stake her claim."

"I had no idea." Rayaan places his hand on her knee. "I'm sorry she did that." He caresses his thumb over the fabric of her dress. He's surprised to realize his ex-wife had been more attentive to his true feelings.

"I can't say I was too heartbroken when Mom told me about the divorce. I'm sure it was awful for you, but I thought you deserved better."

He leans back, removing his hand from her knee and absently scratches his belly. He tugs on his shirt, fanning it against his chest. "Entertainment law and real estate wasn't exciting enough for her." Why was he even questioning if he should remove his shirt in the heat? Logan has his off; Arin has his unbuttoned. "When I decided not to go into politics, as I'd originally thought, she swore I'd broken a promise." It's a hot spring day, why is he even second guessing himself? Leaning forward, he grabs at the neck and pulls it off quickly. Dropping his arm down, his elbow hits her sunglasses, knocking them from her face.

"Oooh, sexy." Logans barked laughter carries over the water.

Bending to pick them up for her, Rayaan flips off her brother.

Even though she hides her eyes quickly with her sunglasses, he can sense them gazing over his body. He somehow feels even hotter now without his shirt on. He takes a long drink from a chilled water bottle and tries to keep his focus.

"Having lived in DC for so long, might I just say, she would have made the perfect politician's wife. Stiff, fake, and insincere. More worried about her appearance to others."

Rayaan nods his head. "Maybe that's why we didn't work out. I want someone a little more laid-back, down to earth. Not spending every penny I earn."

How can he be hotter sitting next to Andi with his shirt off and the breeze against his skin? His arm rests against hers as she shifts on the seat once more.

Rayaan says. "You look overheated." He brushes his thumb across the line of sweat beading on her upper lip.

Andi grimaces. "Eww. Yeah, I think I should move to the shade."

Like being struck by lightning, he realizes he doesn't want her to move. He likes having her close to him, chatting with her in the little bubble of privacy speeding down the lake provides, as wind and waves whip against them.

"You could take off your coverup?"

She bites the edge of her lip, and leans in. "When I packed for the week, I was going to be sitting poolside at a resort pool. Not hanging out with family."

Rayaan chuckles. "So you're telling me your swimsuit is suitable for strangers to see, but not people you know?"

Andi huffs. "Fine. You know what-" she begins to unbutton the top of her dress and stands.

He grabs her arm, wondering if anyone is paying attention to their conversation. "You don't have to do anything you don't want to, but... You look uncomfortable in this heat."

"It's not necessarily the swimsuit; it's the way I look in it."

From where he sits, as each button pops open, she looks pretty good. The bright yellow suit cups her breasts, the support holding them high. When another button pops open, the swimsuit reveals itself to be a high-waisted two piece, stretching over her round figure. A daring choice. From behind her, Rayaan can see his brother watching with anticipation too, but not quite getting the show he is.

"Andi, the boat is in motion," Stephen yells over the wind. "Sit down!"

Another button frees the dress to fall over her full hips, landing at her feet.

"Oh, who's sexy now?" Lauren shouts. "Look at you!"

Arin gives a wolf-whistle, moving his hands in an hourglass shape, while Logan teases her to cover up.

135

Andi begrudgingly accepts their praise. Exposed for just a moment, Rayaan has the full view of the voluptuous woman in his sights. A vintage swimsuit, boldly colored, with a strawberry stitched on the hip. An overwhelming urge to bite it surges through him. Boy-cut shorts hug her thick thighs, and his eyes follow down her legs, noticing for the first time the bright red polish on her toes matches the embellishment. He catches another flash of color as she twists to sit down. A bounce on a wave practically causes her to land in his lap. Sliding back to her own spot on the bench seat, Rayaan can see her blush begins at the curve of her lovely breasts, rising up her neck. He reaches down to pick up the dress for her, and the forgotten sunscreen from earlier that had fallen to the ground.

Arin whispers a foreign curse only he can understand. Their mother is too far in the back of the boat to hear. "I fuckin' hate you," Arin says under his breath. "Lucky bastard."

Arin's already figured out what is slowly sinking into Rayaan's head.

Simply by pure luck, he's sitting next to Andi. And she'll need help putting lotion on her shoulders and back.

And he's the lucky bastard who gets to do it.

Andi says something quietly, but he can't hear her over the boat engine.

"What'd you say, Red?" he asks, speaking into her ear.

She holds out her hand, cupping her fingers. "Give me some… Can you do my back?"

He can feel his length hardening, and his shorts become tighter. To avoid the obvious sexual innuendo, he hands her the bottle instead of squeezing any into her hand. He shakes his head at the X-rated vision in his mind.

They both turn in the seat and face the front of the boat. He can see a sailboat off in the distance on the large lake. He can't observe what she's doing, but Arin is making jokes and trying to get her attention.

Andi hands him the bottle over her shoulder. She holds out her arm, and begins applying it to her shoulder and down the arm, rubbing it in.

Holy hell, it's like a dream he had once. He sighs and licks his lip nervously. From across the aisle, Lauren is talking to her, and watching him with a knowing smirk.

He can see Andi missed most of her shoulder and starts there. Slowly applying the cream, he massages it into her skin. He can see she still leaves the cream visible, in a thick layer, but if he's being honest, he's enjoying watching his hands slide over her velvety skin too much to apply it in the same manner. Besides, she needs to be able to sit back against the seat without getting the cream everywhere.

Arin coughs, breaking him from his thoughts. He quickly

finishes applying the summer-scented lotion.

Hitting a series of waves, she tumbles against him, her mostly bare back to his chest. His heart races and he wonders if she can feel it pounding out of his chest. The boat goes over the wake and knocks sideways again.

"Hang on, everyone," Stephen yells. "That cruiser was too fast."

Andi grips the back of the seat, and Rayaan wraps his arms around her, bracing his legs on the ground, as the boat rocks side to side. It rises up in the front on a series of waves and crashes back down, the water coming over the bow and drenching Logan and Lauren. Water flows through the center walkway, getting everything in the path wet. Jackson cries from the back seat, nestled next to Sarah.

As Stephen crests the boat over the last wave, he announces it's time to head back.

"Too many crazies out drinking and enjoying the first really nice spring day."

"Good driving, man," Arin compliments.

"You look beautiful," Rayaan whispers against her ear. A smaller wave pops up and they bounce in their seats, his lip brushing her skin. It turns bright pink from a blush he can't see on her face. "*Meri jaan*, you don't ever have to hide from me."

Chapter Twelve

As the last bites of dinner are eaten, Neal clears his throat. "Ok, everyone. It's time for me to make good on a promise I made many years ago. Andi, do you know what I'm talking about?"

She tilts her head, looking at him quizzically. He's aged, more than her own father- or maybe she just doesn't see it in him. The salt and peppered hair around Neal's temples is attractive, and like Rayaan, he wears his hair longer since he semi-retired from the local TV station. "Uncle Neal, I have no clue."

"When you were younger, and Logan and Rayaan were old enough to go out on their own, you always whined and complained you wanted to go with them. You wanted to go to the bars too, you said-"

"Oh, God, are you talkin' about that bar you took me to when I turned twenty-one?"

"You didn't appreciate it-"

"It was awful-"

"I don't think I know this story," Rayaan interjects.

She shakes her head at the memory. "It was so bad. They got me all hyped up about going out for the evening. I was all dressed up-"

"- where was I?" Arin asks, leaning his elbows on the table.

"Off with some girl, probably," guesses Logan.

"-I was all dressed up, thinking how awesome this was going to be. I finally get to go out, have some fun, really enjoy the lake life, right?" She looks at Rayaan, smiling at the fond memory. "Live up to all the tales you and Logan always told when no one was around."

"What happened when we weren't around?" Sarah asks, placing a cake and a pot of coffee on the table.

"That's why it happened when you guys weren't around," says Logan, pointing at the parents.

"So much stuff happened when you all weren't looking," laughs Arin.

"Who is telling this story?" Andi says, raising her voice. "Anyway," she stretches out the word, "I'm all ready. Got my ID, money for the cover charge. Ready to dance the night away."

"I thought your father and I took you to a very fine establishment," Neal says defensively.

Andi puts her hand on Rayaan's arm. "That was my first mistake, going out drinking with our fathers. I don't even want to think about what that looked like to anyone watching us together." She shudders and everyone laughs at Logan's whispered, "Eww." "I'm thinking we're going to the nightclub on the waterfront, and instead, they pull up to the little dive bar where all the fishermen go."

"- Oh, no! They took you to Hook and Sinker?" Rayaan asks, throwing his head back in laughter.

"Yes! It's like 9pm, and there's only about five people in there. It smelled of stale beer, moldy pretzels, and goodness only knows what. But your dad was so proud of himself." She smiles across the table at Neal. "So I ordered something on the drink menu, I don't know what it was-"

"- Something fruity," her dad remembers.

"It definitely had coconut rum in it," she nods. "We sat at the bar, talking and drinking. I could barely choke it down, but I did."

"She didn't make it all the way home, poor thing." Neal turns up his nose at the memory. "I pulled over the car just in time-"

"Still can't drink anything with coconut in it-"

"- I felt so awful the next day when I realized she didn't really want the bar experience. She wanted the club; to go dancing," explains Neal. "I promised one day, I'd get her a VIP table, to make up for it."

The words he's speaking dawn on her. "You didn't?" Andi asks gleefully, bouncing in her seat.

"I did. Go get dressed, kids." He shoos them away from the table, waving his hands. "Reservation starts at 9. Cabana

141

by the pool, as close to the dance floor as possible. And the tab is paid up in advance-"

"- To a limit," adds Stephen. "Your server will let you know when it's time to stop or pay your own bill."

"And we're keeping Jackson for the night. No parenting duties until noon tomorrow."

The 'kids' all shout their thank yous as they exit the room.

The small club caters to the tourists, although many locals frequent the establishment. After leaving the car at the valet station, the group is escorted by an attendant to their cabana, overlooking the lake, off to the side of the pool and dance floor.

"Ooh, Uncle Neal pulled through!" Logan exclaims appreciatively as a complimentary bottle of wine is set on the table.

The waiter explains that the seating includes locked storage for personal items and provides them with a code to get in and out of the box.

"Remember to rope off the opening if you all leave at once, and your space is safe for the evening. Is there anything else I can get you to start your night?"

As he takes everyone's drink orders, Andi asks if it's always so busy during the off season.

"College kids on Spring Break usually draw a crowd. The last few weekends have been busy, but it will quiet down for a few weeks before Memorial Day."

Slipping the young server a tip, Arin tells him to leave the drinks on the table, they'd be on the dance floor. He grabs Andi's hand and pulls her along.

Taking her to the center of the floor, he spins her around…

Stepping up to the bathroom sink, Andi stares at her reflection. Arin always was a good dancer! Being in his arms again felt so natural. "But that's not what you want, is it?" She whispers to herself.

Her cheeks are flushed from excitement and dancing and having a good time. Her hair has frizzy curls around her face, some matted across her forehead from sweating. Her head pounds from the alcohol and the music. Andi can't remember the last time she felt so relaxed.

She runs water over her wrists, trying to cool herself off before heading back to the dance floor.

The other stall door opens. Seeing the woman in the mirror, Andi drops her head.

The woman walks forward and puts her purse on top of the hand dryer. As she washes, she turns her head from side to side, admiring herself, not looking nearly as frazzled as Andi does. After drying her hands, the woman moves back, smoothing down her outfit over her thin hips. The leather dress looks like it's practically painted on.

Andi flips her hair back, trying to avoid eye contact in the mirror with the well-known actress, Brooklyn Nash.

The movement catches the woman's attention, and she peers at Andi. "Don't I know you? Oh my gosh! You're that journalist? The one who grills politicians and serves them up for lunch… Oh, I know it…" She rubs her finger across her eyebrow, thinking. "Andrea Jennings, right?"

"Right," Andi shakes the actress's extended hand. "We've met before. I work for The Edge. I interviewed you about two months ago?"

Brooklyn squints. She reaches for her purse. "I loved watching you on the news, I'm actually a big fan. Why don't I remember talking to you?"

Andi taps her fingers over her mouth, debating what to say, but her slight alcoholic buzz gets the better of her. "You know what, fuck it." She whispers. More loudly, she states, "You don't remember, because you were too busy being a diva, complaining the lighting wasn't right, the food was horrible, and you asked your manager how much longer you'd have to sit and talk to someone who looked like a floral sofa. That dress was Vera Wang, you bitch."

Whew! The sass! Maybe she's had more to drink than she thought?

The woman gasps as Andi turns on her heels to leave the room.

In the small hallway outside the restrooms, Arin waits for her.

"I came to check on you. You've been gone awhile."

Brooklyn steps out of the restroom, grabbing Andi's arm. "How dare you talk to me like that!"

"No, how dare you." Andi points in the tall blonde's face. "I was doing my job and keeping it professional. Just because you're famous, or high, which I left out of the article by the way, gives you no reason to treat people like shit. I'm not on the payroll, and I can talk to you however I want right now-"

"Oh, my God. You're Brooklyn Nash. I love your movies," Arin says, stepping between the two women.

Looking at him, in his black suit and teal shirt, recognition falls across Brooklyn's face and her whole demeanor changes. "You're the cute internet guy! What's your name?"

"Oh, gawd," Andi rolls her eyes. "Arin, Brooklyn. Brooklyn, Arin." She pokes Arin in the shoulder. "I'm going back to the table."

His eyes are on Brooklyn, and he only nods as Andi walks away.

She makes her way through the crowd to the cabana.

"Where's Arin?" Lauren shouts over the music, handing her a shot of tequila.

With one hand, she grabs the salt shaker Rayaan is rolling between his fingers, and licks the back of her other hand. Dousing it with salt, she licks it again and shoots the drink back, avoiding his watchful eyes. She slams the glass on the table. "Talking to a woman just as self-centered as him." Andi knows her anger is irrational, but she can't help it. She reaches for a lime wedge from the plate in the center of the table and sucks it between her teeth. She rocks on her feet and grips the table ledge.

Rayaan grabs her hip. "Take it easy, Red."

"Shit." She spits the lime into her hand. "Why do I always forget I hate that?"

"Have another one," Lauren giggles, reaching out with another small glass. "It'll make you forget that you forgot."

Easing between Rayaan's knees and the edge of the table, she sits down on the lounge chair beside the table. Preparing another shot, she points to the dance floor.

"Brooklyn Nash, people. I introduced him to Brooklyn Nash." She leans back, tilting her head up to the sky as she downs the burning liquid. "Two beautiful people, finding love in a dance club, introduced by the fat friend-"

"-You're not fat," Rayaan negates quietly, handing her another lime.

146

"I'd say a hook up, not love, from the looks of it," says Logan, watching the pair grind against each other on the dance floor.

"Shut up," his wife whispers, hitting him in the arm. "You're not helping."

Andi sits up, leaning into Rayaan. She taps his bearded chin. "I'm slightly tipsy, but I know what I look like. You don't have to mollify me, Rayaan." She sits up, running a hand down her side, gripping her full hip. "I'm curvy and soft, where a woman should be soft. I'm not fat. That's how others see me, that's how she saw me." She laughs. "But I don't give a shit. I've met people like her. They're not real, I don't even think her boobs are real… I don't let people like that bother me." Logan hands her a bottle of water, but she waves it away. She grips Rayaan's arm, giving it a good squeeze. "I entirely deserve better treatment from a friend, ya know?"

Rayaan places his large hand over hers. The silver rings are cool against her skin.

He opens his mouth to say something, but she cuts him off. "You're a good friend. Always." She squeezes his arm again, before turning to look at Logan. "Hey, big bro, I think the party's over. Can we go?"

"No, Sis," Lauren whines. "I never get a night out like this. A paid tab, and free babysitting?" She raises her hands to her sister-in-law and friend, pleading. "Please? Just a bit longer. You know Arin's a jerk. Let him do what jerks do."

Andi bounces her head. "Ok, great. Like thirty minutes. In case you've forgotten, we're all too old for this shit." She slurs her words slightly. "And no more tequila. Done with that."

"I don't know," Logan teases. "A fight between you and Brooklyn Nash, over Arin, would be epic."

"Uh, no. Not worth it." Andi throws her words over her shoulder as Lauren drags her to the floor again.

Rayaan sits like a lonely wallflower under the canopy, nursing his drink. He's rebuffed nearly every woman who's approached him for the evening, only dancing with Lauren and Andi.

Rayaan watches with growing annoyance at the number of men lining up to dance with the full-figured redhead.

He can't help but think that her "curvy and soft" makes him hard. His mind is stuck on the feel of her in his arms, smelling like apples and summer, as the boat rocked over the rough waters earlier in the day.

Dropping the glass to the table, he needs to get home, to a cold shower, to clear his head. He rubs his finger over his bottom lip, his beard catching against his skin. Watching her, so carefree on the dance floor, stirs his imagination.

A cold shower won't do. He'll need to run it off.

Rayaan has a vivid memory from days gone by, dancing with her under a moonlit night like this. He doesn't remember all the details; the old campground had some sort of celebration and hired a DJ for the night. There had been food and games, and a promise of fireworks. She was still young, and awkward, not quite a woman. Young enough-maybe she'd finished her first year in college?- he shouldn't have been thinking about her the way he had...

In the summer heat, her hair had formed ringlet curls around her soft face. Sitting off in the dark, watching everyone else dance, her mouth curved perfectly around the soda straw pressed against her lips. The way Andi perched on the edge of her chair showed off her great legs in the sundress she'd chosen for the occasion. He could hear the chatter, small snippets of things people were saying about her, her dress, and the way she looked. People could be so cruel; they weren't really seeing *her*. To him, she was beautiful. Soft. Full of life.

Making up his mind, he'd crossed the dance floor. Andi's eyes sparkled from the party lights, but flashed a moment of sheer terror when he approached her, holding out his hand. Sliding the chair back for her, she tangled her foot in the leg of the chair, and nearly knocked them over.

He smiles at the memory. *Always the graceful lady,* he thinks.

On the dance floor, Andi had held her hands up, as though preparing for a waltz. Something about the vulnerability on her face caused him to wrap his arms around her, more like a swaying bear hug. Her head rested on his shoulder, and she'd tentatively crossed her hands over his back. Her heart raced and pounded against his chest. His own galloped, softening his anger at the voices he'd heard, but he'd hoped she was so caught up in her own emotions she wouldn't notice. Halfway through the song, she began quietly singing, the lyrics evident to him for the first time, though it was a ballad he'd heard on the radio millions of times. A sad tale of unrequited love, but the singer was forever hopeful. As the music ended, he pressed a tiny kiss to the top of her head. She gripped his shirt, not ready to let go, and the melody drifted to another slow piece. Almost like it was simply to freeze the moment a little longer. He'd suspected it before, but he knew in that moment he would love her forever, even if he could never have her.

She was his best friend's sister.

The one he and his brother had declared 'off limits.'

As the beat of the music changes, Rayaan is pulled from his memories, recognizing a thumping rhythm from their youth. Lauren and Andi high-five and although he can't hear them from where he sits, he can imagine their squeal of

150

delight. The loud music swells to a pounding pulse, echoing off the water. Another man, younger, takes Andi into his hold. She willingly turns into him, her arms above his head, swaying to the music. This man is more bold than the others, placing his hand on her ass and pulling her closer to him. Rayaan feels a rush of blood to his head as he leaps from his chair, an animal-like snarl escaping between his gritted teeth. With swiftness, he crosses the dance floor to the unsuspecting pair, and as the rhythm moves into the chorus, he spins Andi to him, separating her from the predator.

"My turn," he growls, eyeing the man.

The stranger takes the hint and moves away, finding another partner.

"Rayaan, you can't just do that shit." Andi doesn't miss a beat, continuing to dance and grind, now moving into him. "I'm not a kid anymore. Maybe I wanted his attention? I'm not the girl you knew-"

"Fine. Then let me get to know the woman," he says in a low purr against her ear as he brings his leg between hers and pulls her close.

Playing with fire, he chooses to give into the fantasy. Just for tonight.

Her eyes widen as he swings her around in time to the music, keeping them joined at the hips. He leans over her, causing her to arch backwards. Andi grips the shoulder of his jacket, holding on, and he can feel her warmth against him. Reaching down as they sway to the music, he caresses her leg, slowly drawing her dress up, exposing her thigh. Touching her skin ignites him, and he grows hard, spurred on by her seductive movements. In the flashing lights of the club, he can see her eyes darken and can sense she's holding her breath.

Leaning in, he can smell the liquor on her exhale. He moves so close, he can almost taste her. Rayaan brushes his nose against her cheek as he tilts his head to speak in her ear when the song nears its end.

"These are just boys, don't play with them." He can feel her breasts brush against his chest, filling him with a desire he can't bring himself to act on. "A woman like you needs a man."

The music fades and he separates from her, leaving her stunned on the dance floor.

Chapter Thirteen

Walking back through the hallways to make sure they'd locked the front door, Rayaan picks up Andi's sequined heels, laying haphazardly in the hall. She'd kicked them off, one flying up and hitting the wall, when they'd entered the house. In deference to his mother and her customs, he lines them up neatly against the wall with the others.

He continues through to the kitchen, placing a left-out container of cheese back in the fridge. He pushes in a chair and throws away a napkin left on the table. Flipping off the light by the back stairwell, movement on the porch draws his attention.

Andi.

He pulls out his ponytail, shaking his fingers through it before gathering it up again and wrapping the band around it tightly. He watches her through the window. She was quiet on the way home, mad at Arin for not leaving with them. He and the actress had been huddled up in a booth together when they left. Logan had some choice words, but Rayaan told him to let it slide.

At the expense of hurting Andi, if Arin was seen in public with Brooklyn Nash, that could be good for his brother's career.

Rayaan sighs out, hitting his fist against the window frame. Putting business first? What kind of monster had he become?

He slides the glass door open and steps out on the patio. The surface is cool beneath his feet in the night air. He removes his jacket and walks closer to her. Quietly, to not wake the baby, he crows like a bird, using her family's gesture to alert her to his presence in the dark.

Andi turns slightly, looking over her shoulder, and calls back with the mocking sound.

Stepping behind her, Rayaan places the coat over her shoulders. She looks forward again, keeping her eyes on the lake, watching the moonlight hit against the rippling water.

"Whatchya doin' out here alone, Red?"

She chuckles, brushing her cheek against her covered shoulder, inhaling the scent of his clothing. "Smells like you," she says quietly and shrugs. "Just needed to clear my mind, King," she tells him absently.

He should have taken that run.

Rayaan takes in the view in front of him. She's unpinned her hair, and long curls hang down her back. Barefoot, the porch railing is nearly as tall as she. The flared skirt hangs at her knees, a little shorter in the back than the front, as it falls over her rounded ass.

Knowing where his thoughts center, his voice is gravelly. "What are you thinking about?"

"Memories. What could have been… Finishing this article…" She huffs out. A sadness fills her voice. "Having to get back to my real life."

Reaching for her arm, he gently spins her around to face him. "Good memories I hope?"

She offers a weak smile. "Maybe it was good to come relive all this stuff, to have the families together again… Maybe it wasn't." She blinks slowly. "I missed you boys. My friends."

Rayaan swallows hard. His eyes scan her face, seeing every freckle, every laugh line. The scar on her chin from falling while trying to learn to rollerblade. Her face tells a story he wants to remember… His gaze stills at her mouth.

Stepping forward, closing the distance between them, he breathes her in as he speaks. Jumping in feet first, he asks, "What if I don't want to be friends anymore?"

Her pulse flutters and she inhales slowly, her eyes drawn to his lips as well. She blinks rapidly and looks up into his deep brown eyes. Breathily, she whispers, "You don't?"

He brushes his nose against hers. "Nope, I'm not a boy anymore, and I don't want to be friends."

Rayaan's lips gently land against Andi's, soft and velvety, the briefest touch. He reaches his hands up, cradling her face as he kisses her tentatively, controlling himself. He can feel his beard scraping against her upper lip as he presses against her mouth with more force. The sweetest kiss he's ever tasted, a hint of alcohol on her breath.

Andi reaches up, gripping her hands around his wrists as the jacket falls to the ground.

Releasing slowly, with a satisfied smile, he pulls back enough to see the look of confusion in her eyes. He can imagine a million thoughts racing through her mind, and longs to talk about each of them with her.

With acceptance, she leans forward, kissing him in return, capturing his bottom lip between her teeth. Loosening her grip, she lifts her arms to wrap around his neck. Tilting her head a little more to the left, she tangles her fingers in the curls he missed.

One of his hands slides down, pressing against her breastbone, feeling her pounding heart.

He pulls away slowly, resting his forehead against hers. "I think we should go inside."

In a daze, she nods. But before they can go anywhere, she rises up on her tiptoes, pressing her body fully against him, crashing her lips into his. In her grasp, he flicks his tongue out, dragging it across her lip as she pulls away from his mouth-

His heart turns somersaults at the realization she's kissing him in return.

Rayaan longs for more, but they are rudely interrupted.

"Get a room! I don't need to see that!" Logan whispers loudly from the balcony above, throwing an empty can down onto the patio.

Rayaan laughs, waving at his friend, while Andi hides against his shoulder.

When the door above closes, Rayaan kisses the top of her head. "It's not a bad suggestion-"

"You think because you give me a knee-melting kiss, I'm going to hop in bed with you?" She wraps her arm around his waist, her voice light and teasing.

He reaches down to retrieve his coat, and they walk toward the door, his arm slung over her shoulder protectively. "I don't think it's totally out of the question?"

In the shadows of the trees, she comes to a standstill. "Rayaan, this is a lot. I'm just," she sighs, "I'm just not sure."

He nods. "I understand, no pressure."

Rayaan stands in front of her, his gaze taking in every aspect of her womanly body. He touches her with his eyes, not his hands, and he hopes the look says everything he can't bring himself to say.

Andi seems to grow more confident under his assessment. She steps closer in the dark, caressing his beard. "I like the man you've become. I'd like to get to know him better, and still be friends."

Her arm snakes behind his neck and she pulls him down

for another kiss. Angling closer, she pushes her weight against him. Rayaan expertly holds her close, his hand stretching across her lower back. As she continues to kiss him, she balances herself to raise her foot and run it down his pant leg. Shivers run down his spine and he picks her up off the ground, turning her slightly before setting her back down. She exhales quietly, "Oh."

He advances a few steps, and she retreats, as he corners her against the wall.

Digging his fingers in her hair, he tilts her face up to his and kisses her again. This time he shows no restraint, allowing his mouth to cover hers, pushing his beard into her skin. She whimpers quietly, bringing her hands up to his chest. He stills, resting his nose against her cheek as she begins to fumble with the buttons on his shirt. His breath is warm against her skin and he can feel her stormy, gray eyes watching him.

Rayaan drops his hands to her shoulders, pushing aside the strap on her dress. He nuzzles into her neck as she begins to caress the smattering of chest hair she's exposed. Her skin is warm from a day in the sun and smells like sun lotion. She gasps when he takes a quick nip of her shoulder. Her hands continue to fight the buttons, all the way down his shirt as he breathes her in slowly, fearful of making a sound.

A light in the kitchen comes on, the sounds of dishes

clattering on the counter.

Putting his finger to her lip, he motions for her to stay quiet. He lifts her hand, pressing his lips to it gently, before tugging her around the side of the house.

They dart around the porch, arriving at the front door.

"Rayaan, I don't-" she bows her head sheepishly. "I don't want to go in, and leave this moment, but I can't make any promises."

His shirt flaps open in the night breeze, distracting her. Andi pinches her mouth nervously and looks at him questioningly. Not knowing the seductive appeal she truly has on him, she bites her lip. "Can I sleep in your bed? Cuddled next to you?"

Rayaan grows hard at the thought. He wants nothing more than to have her in his bed. And the last thing he wants to do is sleep.

He smiles, his dimples showing. "Of course. Let's get your stuff."

Unlocking the keypad on the front door, he mentally kicks himself.

Arin will just have to forgive him.

Chapter Fourteen

Andi stares out the window at the lake from Rayaan's room. From the highest point in the house, she can see further down the channel. She watches the red and green lights bobbing on the waves, indicating a few boats are out, probably fishing.

She says to the closed bathroom door, "I didn't even realize this place had a fourth story."

Her buzz has worn off, and the reality of the moment is setting in. Rayaan Collins groped her on a dance floor. Rayaan Collins kissed her. She pinches herself. She has to be dreaming.

The door opens and he steps out, wearing what he called his comfortable clothes. In a baggy V neck t-shirt, and athletic shorts, he looks more boyish, reminding her of who he used to be.

Andi's heart flips over itself, seeming to pick up an extra beat or two.

If this is dreaming, she doesn't want to wake up.

He's still drying his hands on a towel, twisting around his rings to dry them. "It seems more like a hide-away. Like it was constructed as an attic, but then renovated to be able to hide from any of the craziness on the other levels of the house."

Rayaan tosses the towel back on the counter behind him, and steps fully into the room. Smiling, he brushes his mustache over his lip. "Are you gonna stay in your party dress all night?"

Giggling, Andi does a little spin. "It has pockets!" She pulls lip gloss from one of them. "All that dancing and didn't lose it."

He chuckles, walking towards her in the dim light. "Doesn't look very comfortable." He walks around her, admiring the navy blue, one-shouldered dress. He runs his finger under the strap, hanging off her shoulder. "Need some help getting out of it?" he asks quietly.

Andi bites in her lips, blushing. "I think I can manage, King. It's got a side zipper."

"Dammit," he mutters, pushing her towards the open bathroom door.

Behind the closed door, she can't stop grinning. Rayaan Collins kissed her.

Rayaan Collins wants her.

Reaching up, she removes her earrings, while looking over his cologne, watch, and other personal items left on the counter. She tentatively reaches out to touch the frame on a pair of glasses. Andi places her things in the small make-up kit she grabbed from her room on their way upstairs.

Reaching for the sink faucet, she warms the water. She quickly steps out of her dress, grabbing it before it falls to the ground. Not wanting the borrowed dress to wrinkle, she hangs it on a hook on the back of the door.

Eying a hair tie on the counter, she shakes her head. "He comes better prepared than I do." Deftly, Andi twists her hair up into a tight bun, using the band to hold it in place. With the precision of a nightly routine, she removes her makeup with a small wipe she pulled from her bag and washes her face.

Stepping back, Andi looks at herself in the full-length mirror. Rising on her tiptoes, she does a small pirouette, taking in her dimpled thighs, with their colorful ink, and the stretch marks on the sides of her belly. Thank goodness she'd had the forethought to wear a pretty black panty set with a strapless bra. Dropping on her heels, she sighs. "This is as good as it gets," she says quietly, walking back to the sink and her pile of folded clothes.

She slides on her favorite plaid shorts; also grateful she'd shaved her legs before dinner. Tying the waist, she looks at the remaining tank top on the counter. Rayaan can't see her in that. It's too revealing.

She spins around, looking for her t-shirt, hoping she's dropped it on the floor.

"Fuuuck," she whines, stretching out the word.

Andi stares at her reflection in the mirror, wondering what to do, when there is a knock on the door.

"Everything alright?"

Grabbing a towel, she holds it over her chest, tucking it in under her arm. Walking to the door, she speaks through the wood. "Can I borrow a shirt? I thought I grabbed mine, but it's not here."

There's a pause, and she can only wonder at what he might be thinking.

"What are you wearing now?"

She chuckles. "A gray towel. And my pajama shorts."

His finger taps the door. "Show me."

She inhales deeply. Closing her eyes, she considers her options.

"Don't hide from me, Andi. I want all of you."

Nervously, she opens the door inward, peeking around the edge.

Rayaan smiles grandly, his dimples showing through his beard. "No good hiding, Red. I can see your reflection in the mirror." He looks behind her. "The band on your bra is cutting into your skin, your back is slightly pink from the sun, and freckles are popping up as we speak."

She pouts and steps around the door. He backs up, giving her space. He's watching her like one watches a skittish colt, not sure what will happen next.

163

She's not sure either.

Keeping tall, she stands under his gaze, as she had done on the patio. Rayaan reaches out, low, his fingertips grazing the tattoo on her leg. "Flowers?"

Looking down, she watches his finger drag across her skin, leaving goosebumps in its wake. "Magnolias, like the movie I always watched with Gramma Lou."

Rayaan drops to his knees for a better look at the artwork covering her outer left thigh. Her mouth goes dry at the visual of him kneeling before her. From above, she takes in her view of him. The sun kissed streaks of lighter colors mixed in with his dark hair. The bump on his shoulder from a motorcycle accident he had when he was younger and broke his collarbone. The flecks of gold in some of the ceramic beads he wears around his neck. His long, dark lashes rested against his cheek as he looks down.

Gently, he sketches over the outline of the largest flower. "It's a really good watercolor, all the different shades of pink."

He looks up at her, his brown eyes smoldering, but promising tenderness. With that look alone, she becomes an instant puddle, warmth flooding her.

His touch becomes more exploratory. He drags his hand up, pushing the fabric of her shorts higher to see more of the ink. With deep reverence, he says quietly, "Your grandmother loved flowers. Ah, and she was the best cook."

On instinct, her hand drops down, brushing the side of his beard and under his chin. Tilting his head back so she can look at him, she asks, "You remember my grandmother?"

Rayaan smiles, his eyes gleaming. "Andrea Louise Jennings, there's very little I've forgotten about you over the years."

Her thumb caresses his bearded cheek. "I guess I could say the same about you, Rayaan Andrew Collins. Same shared middle name as your father."

He shrugs. "Sounds like you know too much about my father."

Andi lifts her head up and laughs, dropping her hands tightly to her sides as the towel begins to fall. "About that shirt?"

Rayaan gently tugs on the hem of the towel, but not enough to pull it from her, and she respects that. With her next breath, she raises her arms away from her body, allowing the towel to fall.

In a low voice, she says, "This is all of me."

Trying not to fidget, she stands perfectly still while his gaze contemplates all of her, from head to toe.

He lets a low whistle escape between his lips. "God, you're beautiful, *meri jaan*."

Rayaan licks his lip, seemingly speechless. His hand

reaches behind her, cupping her ass and drawing her closer to him. Andi slowly puffs out air, feeling another flood of wetness, sure a wet spot is developing where he can see it.

So close, his lips brush against her thigh as he begins to knead her ass. Rayaan hums, a low growl to her ears. "Getting a tattoo is so intimate," he muses, outlining the design with the tip of his nose. "Do you think the artist noticed your scent, or is that just for me?"

"Fuck," she whispers, going weak at the knees as he begins to run his fingers along the edge of her panties. Inhaling deeply, she too can smell the evidence of her arousal in the air. "No, just for you," she admits. Cheekily, she adds, "King."

"Huh," he ponders, "never really liked that until just now." He smiles up at her, a cocky grin growing on his countenance. "This is all mine?"

Rayaan turns his hand under the hem of her shorts, pushing his thumb against the wet spot of her panties, causing her to jolt.

Butterflies taking up residence in her stomach, and knees weak, Andi places her hand on his strong shoulder. Digging her nails into his skin for better purchase, she rocks forward, pushing against his thumb. On a breathy exhale, she simply says, "Please."

Upon her signal, Rayaan wastes no time. Still groping at

her ass with one hand, he uses the other to push her underwear aside and begins a desired assault on her already throbbing button. Small circles of his touch send shivers down her spine. Andi moans from his handling, gripping his shoulder tightly.

"You have no idea how many times I've thought of this," Rayaan says, delivering a kiss to her thigh. "How many times I've thought of you, Andrea."

"Oh, God," she moans, throwing her head back and leaning against the dresser. She whimpers, tugging on his hair with her other hand. "I've thought about you too."

Continuing to press against her clit, Rayaan teases another finger through her wetness. Finding her entrance, he pushes inside with a long, leisurely stroke.

"Oh, fuuu-" she whispers, never finishing the sound as he begins to pull and push inside her.

Supporting her with his shoulder, her legs quake and he's barely touched her. His finger slides in and out, and the warmth in her belly spreads, creating more slick. Rayaan grips her hip, holding her down on his hand as he slips another finger in, fluttering against her velvety walls. His thumb circles around her tense bundle of nerves, and she doesn't know how much more she can take.

Rocking back on his heels, he tumbles to a seated position on the floor with his back against the bed. In the process,

Rayaan tugs down on the waist of her shorts and panties, pulling them down with him. Panting with desire, Andi steps out of them, eager for whatever comes next. He positions her over himself, standing above him, and guides her to his mouth. With no direction from him, she leans over, lifting her knee to the bed, placing her wet pussy to his beard. His tongue glides through the slick, accepting her and tilting his head back to reach further into her silky spot.

With one hand, he traces over her ass and down her thick thigh, touching all the dimples and imperfections in her skin. Her whimpers and moans fill the space, while his other hand dips in and out of her hole, working in sync with his tongue.

His nose brushes her clit as she grinds herself into his beard.

"That feels so good," she whines.

Having reached her ankle, Rayaan trails his hand back up her thigh. Her leg begins to quake, and she tells him she's close.

A few more dragging strokes of his tongue, and it doesn't take long for her to quiver and clench his hand. Her body bucks so hard that he braces her with his shoulder and other hand, holding her up.

With a low, keening whimper that pierces the quiet house, Andi comes, washing over his beard while her back arches into him for more contact.

Rayaan slows his strokes, lapping up her wetness, bringing her down from the peak before peppering her inner thigh with kisses and brushes of his beard against her delicate skin.

"So wonderful, Andrea," he announces solemnly.

In her sated euphoria, she falls forward onto the bed, and he lifts her other leg up, kissing the back of her thighs as she lays on her belly.

"Did I wear you out?" he chuckles, playfully slapping her ass.

"Not in the slightest."

Andi rolls over, up onto her knees. Putting her arms around his neck, she holds him close for a kiss. Not bothered by the taste of herself on his lips, she kisses him deeper as his hands roam across her back. She feels the tension release as he pops open her bra, her breasts falling, pushing against his chest. "I want to feel your skin on mine," she whispers, nibbling at his ear. Dropping her hand, she tugs at the hem of his shirt, fighting to lift it between them. Rayaan curves his back, pulling his upper body away from her, but not releasing her mouth or his roaming hands. He splits apart only for a moment as she yanks the shirt over his head.

Fulfilling her wish, skin to skin, he holds her closer. He places tiny kisses across her cheek, his nose brushing her skin. He whispers in her ear, "Wish granted, Red."

Andi giggles. She holds his arm tightly, squeezing his

corded muscles. "I have to be dreaming. I'm not that drunk, but this has to be a dream."

"Why?" Rayaan asks quietly. "Is it so far-fetched I would want you?" He runs his hand over her hair, tugging on the tie and letting her curls tumble over her shoulders. "I probably have loved you since you were sixteen, and I was teaching you to drive."

A small smile creeps onto her face and warm thoughts fill her. How does he even remember that? "Did you say you loved me?"

Ignoring her question, Rayaan continues with a teasing tone. "You were a horrible driver." He laughs at the memories. "Is that weird for me to say? I was too old for you; you were my best friend's sister."

Letting his words pass, Andi absorbs his sweet confession. Copying his motion, she watches his hair fall around his shoulders. "You're still old now," she says, teasing him, tugging on a curl.

He swats her bottom. "You're such a pain in the ass."

Rayaan releases his hold on her, stepping back to remove his shorts. Andi holds her breath, realizing he'd been going commando. In the soft glow of the lamp, she takes in his physique. All muscle, athletic and toned. The tattoo on his chest and shoulder makes his skin look darker. A slight dusting of hair across his chest, a small scar from his appendectomy, a larger scar on his thigh from a college soccer injury. She already knows him. Yet taking the next leap to know all of him strikes her as a huge risk.

Rayaan reaches up to push his hair back, and she nearly salivates, watching the veins roll under his skin. "Fuck," she whispers. Repeating his praise, she tells him, "You're beautiful." She smiles tenderly. "I always thought you were so handsome, but all this," she circles her hand in front of her, "like a damn Greek statue, carved by the Gods."

Blushing, he brushes the tip of his nose before dropping his hand to his hip. "Red, your eyes totally skipped over *all of me*." He emphasizes the words.

Turning as red as her hair, she covers her eyes. Her grin is so deep, she can feel her own dimples pushing in the sides of her mouth. "I've seen you before," she admits, falling back onto her knees.

She separates her fingers, taking a peek at what he has to offer. She exhales. "Quite impressive."

Rayaan crawls onto the bed next to her. "You have? When was this?"

He scoots closer, putting his leg between hers, lifting her ass up onto his thigh. She instantly feels another flood of wet hit her as his wiry leg hairs brush against her mound.

She thinks back. "I don't really remember. We were all camping, and you had a girlfriend with you? I don't think it was G- her." She can't bring herself to say his ex-wife's name in their moment of sexual awakening. "I had a friend with me. We were walking through the woods and came across where you were skinny-dipping. We stole your clothes."

Placing his hand on her hip, he pulls her to him, smearing her wetness on his leg. A small moan escapes her lips.

"That was you? We broke up not long after- She thought it was… someone else, and didn't want to feel bullied by anyone in my family."

Andi stamps down the name of the person that jumps into her head. She doesn't want to be thinking of him right now either.

"It's really not fair you saw me first, even if you were only playing a prank."

He slides her closer, speaking against her skin.

"You're seeing me now."

"You're beautiful. You always hid; I don't want you to hide anymore."

Rayaan kisses her again, his tongue teasing her bottom lip. Andi's hands slide down his waist, counting each muscle in her mind. Their kisses fight against each other as her hand traces blindly over the veins on his hips. He gasps when she takes his length into her hand, holding it tenderly. He releases her mouth, nuzzling into her hair and looking down to watch her.

Dropping her eyes, she strokes him in her hands. They seem small in comparison to him. Twisting gently, she watches him plump and rise, the tip taking a pinker shade. She'd read once a man's lips and the head of his cock are nearly the same shade. She blushes, having always been attracted to Rayaan's mouth. She raises her head to find his dark eyes watching her hands, but she can see his pouty pink, lush mouth hiding under his beard. His lips hang open, breathing in slowly as she caresses him. Continuing her ministrations, feeling him harden in her hands, she dips her head to catch his mouth with hers.

Andi's heart pounds in her ears, her chest heaving, all thought to time and place escaping her. Releasing her grip with one hand, she pushes him backwards. Gently tugging off his lip, she brushes her nose against his, as he's already done to her, breathing him in. As Rayaan lays back, she hovers over him. With a devilish gleam in her eyes, she lifts his heavy, thick cock, raising her hips to tease him between her folds. Rayaan hisses out a wordless sound, pushing down on her hip to slide into her. The stretch surprises her and she cries out as he grips her flesh.

"Fuck," he whispers, inclining his head to kiss her again. He caresses her side, her breasts pressed between them. Pulling back, he searches her eyes. "It's probably a little late to ask if you really want this?"

173

Sinking down on him, she grins. "I probably should have asked you that question. Guess I was caught up in the heat-"

"Totally fine with it," he growls, pulling her down harder onto his shaft, while wrapping her hair around his fist. With gentle pressure, he pulls her head back, exposing her neck and biting along her shoulder.

Andi shivers, her thoughts still whirring. "I might still be a little buzzed," she confesses. "But that doesn't mean I don't want this, or that I'm not aware of what's going on." She turns her head to kiss his cheek. "Probably wanted this, you, for longer than I care to admit."

Placing her hand on his tatted shoulder, she pushes herself up to a sitting position, impaled on his cock. A little unsure of herself, but knowing what she wants, she takes his hands from her hip and hair and puts them to her breasts, encouraging him to squeeze and caress them.

"Yes, ma'am," he chuckles, taking her direction.

Andi continues to rock against him methodically, closing her eyes to his observant gaze. Something about his acceptance makes her feel incredibly sexy, and she gives herself over to her desires. Andi rises up and down, alternating from rapid to slow, drawn out movements, feeling Rayaan swell inside her. She gasps when his hand slides between them, teasing her clit and feeling himself disappear inside her.

He groans, his voice raspy and begging. "The way you take all of me- so damn sexy."

Releasing his grip on her breast, his hand raises, gently holding around the front of her throat for a brief moment. With a tender squeeze, he lets go, sliding it around the back of her neck and pulling her down to his mouth. With a sensitive nip to her bottom lip, he whispers, "Are you ready?"

"Yes," she whines, so close the edge.

Rayaan gently tucks her hair back and holds her face in his large hand as she rides him. His dark eyes watch her closely, and she feels empowered by his gaze. With his other hand pinching her tight bundle of nerves, she teeters over the edge. Riding out waves of passion, she pants loudly in between whispers of "I'm coming, I'm coming."

Sinking onto him, she continues her ride, his legs tightening beneath her. Ready to feel him release into her, Andi is surprised when Rayaan rolls her over onto her back. He finishes by pulling out and tugging himself, long ropes of creamy white cum splattering her stomach and hip.

Spent, he falls next to her, kissing her shoulder. He reaches over his head for his discarded shirt and places it on her belly. He pats at the mess, apologizing. "That wasn't well thought out," he explains. "I didn't know if-"

Andi takes his hand, stilling it and resting it on her hip. "It's fine. I'm a big girl-" she pauses, "I mean, I'm an adult woman. I have an IUD."

She turns her head to face him, an awareness of what they've done sinking in.

This could all go so horribly wrong and ruin two families in the process.

The grin on Rayaan's face tells her that's the last thought on his mind right now.

The look feels her with warmth, quelling her doubts.

Rising up on his side, he brushes his nose against her cheek before kissing her affectionately. "That was amazing, Red."

"You're going to call me that, at a time like this?"

She chuckles and pokes him in the ribs.

"Red is hot, passionate." He caresses his finger down her nose. "I don't think I expected all that from you."

She giggles, flopping her arm above her head, stretching. "Thanks, I think."

"Don't move, I'll be right back."

Covered in the evidence of their lovemaking, and as limp as a noodle, she doesn't plan to move any time soon. He bounds from the bed, not bothering to cover himself up. Rayaan doesn't close the bathroom door all the way, and she's surprised to hear him use the toilet. She's never felt comfortable enough around a lover before to leave the bathroom door open. The water runs briefly, and he returns with a warm, wet washcloth to clean her up. Laying back down next to her, his touch as he cares for her is full of adoration.

"Rayaan Collins, you have really surprised me tonight, in so many ways," she says, resting her hand on his thigh.

"All good, I hope?"

Before she can answer, her stomach rumbles. Giggling, she pats her belly. "Shh... I don't have time for food."

"Ah, luv, are you hungry?" He runs his hand over his chin. "Now that you mention it, I am." Sitting up, he throws his legs over the side of the bed and tugs on his shorts. "Don't go anywhere."

Before she can tell him there's no place else she'd rather be, he jogs out the door.

Leaning over the side of the bed, she grabs her underwear and a jersey he had next to the bed. Wiggling into both, the last hour replays through her mind. "My dreams aren't that good," she says quietly.

Looking around the room, she sees where Rayaan has made himself at home for the short stay. He's set up a makeshift desk by the other window, his laptop open and a stack of papers next to it. His swimsuit is hanging over a drying rack, with a towel underneath to soak up any drips. His phone lights up as the hour turns over to the next, a photo of his son, Elias, as his lock screen.

She's thankful for the little glimpse into the man he's become. Rayaan obviously has a priority to his family and health, and he takes his responsibilities seriously.

She admires that in a man.

Andi can hear him coming up the stairs and is adjusting the pillows on the bed when he enters the room. His arms are laden down with snacks and treats. Rayaan gives her a crooked grin when he looks at her. His smile is warm and inviting, a bit of a boyish charm with the slight gap between his teeth.

"Didn't know what you wanted," he says, as he spreads out his arms, dumping items onto the bed before handing her a bowl of ice cream. "Strawberry. Still your favorite, right?"

Accepting the cold dish, she nods, "Yes but I don't-"

"Like strawberries," they say at the same time.

"You only like strawberry flavored things," Rayaan finishes, taking a drink from a bottle of water.

She angles her head. "You really haven't forgotten anything, have you?"

He hands her a pretzel and she uses it to scoop her ice cream. "I remember that," pointing at her, using the pretzel as a makeshift spoon.

"Salty and sweet." She hums as she devours the mixed treat.

Rayaan dips his hand into a bag of cookies. "I've probably

elevated you to the status of 'Perfect Woman' in my mind, after all these years."

He thinks of her as perfect? Her heart skips a beat.

"Oh, there's no way I can live up to all that then," Andi teases.

He nods. "We should quit while we're ahead."

She sighs, scooping up another bite. "Uh, at least let me fuck you again before giving up on me."

He laughs, before grabbing her wrist and twisting her hand to place the cold, melty ice cream in his mouth. His tongue scrapes over the tip of her finger as he savors the sweet, before slowly pulling her hand away.

"That wasn't fucking, Andrea."

Shit, that was sexy as hell. And using her full name too-

She scoots closer and uses her thumb to wipe up a dribble of ice cream from his beard. "No, no. You're right," she breathes out slowly. "That wasn't."

"And I want more of it," he confesses.

She swallows deliberately, not sure what to say. She bows her head, and focuses on her ice cream, eating the rest with a spoon.

They sit in a companionable silence for a few minutes, Rayaan's thoughtful eyes appraising her. The young girl he knew has grown into a beautiful woman. Her unruly curls have been tamed, she's comfortable in her full figure, and her bright eyes shine from knowledge she's learned in her travels. This is a woman he could take to the fancy galas he attends, impress the uptight socialites, and come home and sit down for pizza, in nothing but cozy sweats for a movie marathon.

Finishing the bowl, Andi sets it on the nightstand, taking one of the cookies he offers her. Nibbling it, she fidgets with the hem of his shirt she wears. For once, his habit of wearing clothing too big for him pays off. She looks good in his shirt.

She looked better without it, but-

Breaking the silence, he asks, "Penny for your thoughts, Red?"

Andi covers her mouth while she finishes chewing the cookie, "Gimme me a minute," she mumbles.

He leans over and picks a crumb from her shirt, dropping it into his finished water bottle. Sensing her nerves about something, he doesn't want to rush her. He waits patiently while she reaches for a pillow, plumping it in her lap and squeezing her arms around it.

She rocks forward, hugging the pillow to her. "I don't go around, fucking people."

"I didn't think you did-"

"Not that there's anything wrong with that," she rambles. "I'm just not that person." She swallows nervously and scratches the side of her mouth. "I guess you could say I was a late bloomer. I was working overseas when I... I didn't in college." She picks at the zipper on the pillowcase. She huffs out. "Your brother and I never-"

Rayaan fights the urge to laugh. This is what made her a bundle of nerves? Collecting himself quickly, he places his hand over hers, grabbing her fingers. "I know. I know. You didn't have to tell me." He tilts her head up with his other hand, gazing into her worried eyes. "But I'm glad you did. And even if you had, that was a long time ago, and wouldn't have changed a thing."

Andi stares in disbelief. "You know?"

Rayaan chuckles quietly, squeezing her hand. "I may have heard some complaints back in the day." He caresses his thumb across her cheek. "Truthfully, it made me laugh to think you'd leave him with blue balls every time you went to visit."

She giggles, wiping her free hand across her forehead. "I wasn't ready." She sighs. "I think there was a part of me that always thought he'd leave or ruin it somehow."

Nodding, Rayaan pries. "And the person you chose, for your first? He didn't ruin it?"

There goes her blush again, as pink as the sunburned spots on her back and shoulders. Releasing his hand, she sits back against the pile of pillows near the headboard. "He was a guide, hired to show the reporters around and teach us customs of the area. I was in Greece." She folds up her leg and absently scratches her knee. "Dimitrios was his name; he was a little older. There was something easy about him." She shrugs. "It wasn't anything either of us planned for. It just kinda happened and was fun while it lasted."

Rayaan feels a pang of jealousy as she talks about her former lover. "And what ended it?"

She waves her hand. "The job. I was sent somewhere else." She gives a crooked smile. "I wouldn't say I made a habit of bedding men in the countries I went to, but if it happened, it happened."

He's definitely feeling a stir of green envy. But she shared her secrets. It's only fair he does too. "Pilar. An exchange student from Spain, senior year," he blurts out. "I was so heart broken when she left." He settles in on the pillows next to her, taking her hand.

Andi rolls her head to the right and looks into his eyes. He would swear she could see into his soul. "I remember. She was sweet. She liked to braid my hair when she was at your house."

Rayaan scratches his chest. "You remember her?"

She clears her throat. "Between the two of you, there was always a steady stream of girls walking past your dad's library door."

Now he blushes. "You make it sound bad."

"No." She squeezes his hand. "You were both so handsome, pretty girls couldn't help but want to be around you."

She had thought he was handsome? Had she ever thought of him, the way he thought of her?

Reaching over, he traces his finger along her jawline. "Is that why you were always there too, *meri jaan?*"

In a quick move, she rolls over and straddles his lap. "I always liked you for the size of your library." Placing her hands on the headboard, she grinds down against him. "I had no idea the size of your-"

Crushing her mouth to his, Rayaan's kisses swallow her filthy words.

Chapter Fifteen

The morning sunlight bathes the room, spring birds chirping loudly outside the window. Feeling a presence next to him, hairs tickling his forehead, all the memories of the night before rush back through his mind. Rayaan blinks his eyes open slowly, not wanting to wake his sleeping beauty. *Meri jaan.*

The reality of their night together had been better than any dream he ever had.

So near, he can see her freckles up close, a fallen eyelash on her cheek. She smells like apple blossom shampoo and the faint hint of sex. His leg is thrown over her waist, but she breathes easily under his weight.

Andi begins to stir and Rayaan closes his eyes, feigning sleep. He can only imagine her response at waking together. He keeps still when she lovingly kisses the tip of his nose.

Her hand running over the back of his thigh is ticklish, and his eyes flutter open from her caress.

"Why are you tickling me?" he asks, his gaze on her gentle profile. His morning voice is slightly grumpy, raspy sounding to his ears. He can't remember the last time he woke up to someone in his bed and wonders if he always sounds this way in the mornings.

She turns her head to face him, resting her forehead against his. "Good morning! Are you ticklish?"

Her voice is sweet and cheerful, and he wants to wake up with it every day for the rest of his life.

His hand presses against hers, stopping the movement. "Not really, but you're rubbing the same spot. It's," he licks his lip. "It's tingly. Weird. Stop it," he chuckles quietly as she does it some more with her other hand.

"We slept together," she announces in awe.

Shifting his head onto her pillow, he whispers in his ear. "We did more than sleep, honey."

She giggles as he nibbles her ear. Pushing his leg off her, she rolls to the side. "What would you do now if you were home?"

"Ravage you again," he says, scooting down the bed and nuzzling between her breasts. He means it, too.

She yelps when he bites her nipple. Tugging his hair, she pulls him away from her chest. "We're not at home. The house is full of people."

He flops onto his back, pulling her over, on top of him. Rayaan glides his hands over her back, feeling the indentations of the wrinkled sheets on her skin. She folds her arms over his chest and rests her chin on the back of her hand. He lifts his hands and runs them through her hair, combing back the wild mane. His gaze takes in every inch of

185

her skin. Lifting her hair off her neck, his hands span across the back of her head from ear to ear as he lifts his head to kiss her.

Breathing deeply, he drops his head back to his pillow. "I guess we can't stay here forever, can we?"

Hearing the front door slam, she shakes her head. "'Fraid not." She twists her fingers in the tiny hairs on his chest. Literally tugging at his heartstrings. "King, I'm not ashamed of what we did." She slides her foot along the side of his leg. "But I don't want anyone to know yet. Not until we figure out what this is."

Feeling deflated, he squeezes her arm. He sighs out, "I know, you're right." He rolls her gently to her side, sitting up and looking down at her. "I want this to be more. I want us to figure it out."

"I do too," Andi says, caressing the hem of the bedsheet. "But they'll all have their opinions, and we need to decide on our own what we need."

Bending to kiss the top of her head, he sweeps the covers back. "Why don't you use my bathroom? Get ready for the day, and we'll take it from there?"

Patting his thigh before he exits the bed, she reluctantly agrees.

To avoid suspicion, Rayaan leaves Andi alone for her bath, despite her pleading.

Skipping his morning run, he quietly makes his way down to the kitchen. Turning the corner, he's surprised to find both sets of parents are already awake, from the sounds of things.

"Good morning, my handsome *beta*," says Prisha, welcoming him into the room.

He bends to give her a kiss, greeting the others. "What's that wonderful smell?"

"Baked French toast," Sarah replies, feeding Jackson another spoonful of some foul-smelling cereal. "It should be ready in about ten more minutes."

"Give the kid some of that," he grimaces, watching the baby spit his food back out. "He'd probably like it a lot better."

Stephen pats him on the back, squeezing his shoulder. Rayaan tries not to think about his daughter in any way. "Don't worry, son. I plan to share some of mine with him."

Neal asks about their evening at the bar, while turning the bacon on the stove.

"I'm sure there will be stories to tell," Rayaan admits, pouring himself a glass of orange juice. "It was a good time, Dad. I'm really glad you followed through on your promise to Andi."

Neal nods. "She's like the daughter I always wanted."

187

He can't make out the words his mother mumbled, but he's pretty sure she added 'in-law.'

He nearly chokes on his drink.

"Everyone made it home in one piece, I take it." Stephen's questions often come out as comments.

"I was a good boy, only had two slow drinks, and everyone," he falters, avoiding his mother's gaze. He huffs. "I think everyone made it home. We were down a man by the end of the night."

Prisha hits her oven mitt against the counter. "He can't go one family weekend without hunting?"

As if on cue, Arin enters the kitchen. "What, Ma? I'm here. I made it home before daylight."

She cuffs him on the chin. "Don't mess up, *beta*. You have another cha-"

"What's that?" Rayaan asks, pointing at Arin's shoulder and cutting off his mother's probing statement. One which he doesn't want to hear the end of.

Arin pulls the item down, holding up a large t-shirt. "Found it on the floor in the hallway. It's got DC landmarks on it. I think it's Andi's."

Thinking quickly, Rayaan says, "Yeah, she was doing laundry last night, must have dropped it."

Arin reaches for a piece of bacon from the plate Neal sets on the table. "I went to give it to her this morning, but she wasn't in her room. I figured she'd be sleeping off her alcohol haze. Stephen, did you know your daughter can really dance when she's had some liquor?"

Stephen coughs. He winks at his wife. "Must take after her mother. Maybe the parents should go dancing tonight?"

Sarah shakes her head and looks out the window to the patio. "If she's not in her room, where would she be?"

Rayaan grips the counter, feeling like he's coming unglued from this crazy family togetherness. "She came upstairs to use the bathtub in my room."

Licking his fingers from the bacon grease, Arin replies, "*Bhai*, that's ridiculous. She has her own bathroom."

Absently, Rayaan shrugs. "Yes, but it only has a shower. She wanted a tub, to shave her legs, she said."

"You sure know a lot about Andi's activities in the last few hours."

Rayaan tries to avoid Arin's quizzical gaze.

He sits down at the table, resting his glass next to a plate. "Well, I was here, unlike some people." He glares at his brother.

Unaffected, Arin grabs another piece of bacon, announcing, "She might need it today, so I'll go take it up to her."

With speed, Rayaan sends her a text message, hoping Andi sees it in time.

His mother's voice is full of disappointment. "Did he really leave you all at the club for some girl?"

Fidgeting with his silverware, he bobs his head once. "Not just any girl. Some actress."

"An actress?"

Andi smiles at the door. He's waiting on the other side, knocking. Couldn't stand to be away for even twenty minutes?

"Come in," she says warmly.

Not in a million years did she expect Arin to walk through the door.

She sinks down further under the bubbles. "What are you doing here?" She hisses.

"Who did you think was going to come through the door?" He says, closing it and crouching down.

"My mother," she stammers, thinking of a lie. "I'd texted her to bring my beach bag. I forgot it."

He grins. "Don't think she saw the message. She's in the kitchen, feeding Jackson."

On the ledge around the tub, her phone lights up and she can see the message on the screen. *Arin's on his way up! Sorry! If it comes up, you did laundry*

What the hell is he talking about?

Arin holds out a wadded up piece of clothing. "You must have dropped this while doing laundry last night. Thought you might need it."

She nervously smiles. "I was wondering what happened to it. You can just leave it on the sink."

Leaning forward, he puts it up on the counter before rocking backwards to sit on the floor. He lets his head rest back against the closed door.

Her phone vibrates with a new message. Andi shakes the water off her hands. "I'm sorry. I've been answering work messages. I need to check this."

Everything okay?

She types back quickly. *He's here. Send Mom to get my beach bag and tell her not to ask questions.*

Hoping the job is handled timely, she places her phone down.

Arin props up one leg and rests his arm out over it. He points to the water. "Still like it so hot?"

"What? The water?"

Why does she feel like her brain isn't working? How is it she's talking to one brother while she bathes, after having spent the best night of her life with the other? She can't seem to connect her thoughts.

"I remember the first time we had a bath together. I thought you were trying to cook me." He smiles, tilting his head to her. "Do you remember that? It was your little apartment, the one with the girl who was studying to be a nurse? She was gone for the weekend, and you had flower petals on the floor, leading to the bathroom."

She did remember. But she doesn't want to. She doesn't want to remember her old life with this man. Not when she's on the brink of starting a new one with his brother.

The doorknob turns but won't open.

"Andi, something's blocking the door. Are you okay?" Sarah's voice sounds worried.

Arin scoots over, reaching up to open the door. "Hey, Aunt Sarah."

"Arin Collins! What the hell are you doing in here? She's taking a bath!" Sarah steps into the room, blocking his line of vision to the tub. "Out. Get out. Before I tell on you to your mother!"

Arin chuckles. "I'm not seventeen anymore, Auntie Sarah. That doesn't scare me." Andi can only imagine the look her mother gives him. He holds up his hands in defeat. "I'm leaving, I'm leaving."

"Close the bedroom door," she commands. "We don't need any more guests!"

When the door closes with a satisfying thud, Sarah rounds on her daughter. "Screw not asking questions. What the hell is going on?"

She drops the bag in the center of the floor and sits on the small bench seat in the corner of the room.

Andi dips her head. "I have no idea. But I have a feeling today's going to be an interesting day."

"Oh, Andrea," her mother sighs. "You're not still crushing on him, are you?"

Of course, her mother would see right to the heart of it. Andi could probably blame her weight gain on her mother, using food as comfort growing up, whenever things went wrong. There were countless nights she'd come home from hanging out with the boys when her mother commiserated with her over ice cream and cookies.

She taps her toe on the faucet, water running down her leg. "Sorry, Mom. Plausible deniability; the less you know, the better. You won't have to lie to anyone if they ask questions, even Auntie Prisha. You can simply say 'I have no idea' and actually mean it." Caressing her calf, she checks for any stubble. Grabbing the razor, she goes back over a spot she missed.

"Andi," her mom sounds so disappointed, "I thought you decided a long time ago not to get involved with Arin again and-"

Andi decides not to correct her mother. "Yeah, Mom, it was those damn beautiful brown eyes. They got to me; you know?"

Sarah sighs, standing up. "Honey, this could be easy or hard. Be careful how you handle it the next two days. If it's meant to be, after you go back to work, you'll figure it out, and hopefully everyone can still be friends."

"I get it, Mom." She twists, reaching for a towel.

Walking over to her daughter, Sarah bends and kisses her on the head. "Your life always has been full of adventure and challenges. This is just another one. But if I know you, it'll all work out for the best." Crossing over to the door, she announces, "Don't take too much longer. Prisha made French toast."

If the water wasn't getting cold, she'd sink herself under the bubbles and stay a bit longer. Instead, she decides to face the day head on, exiting the tub. Drying off quickly, she's grateful she put a change of clothes in her beach bag and decides to cut out a step by putting her swimsuit on under her favorite floral sundress. Braiding her hair quickly, she walks out into the bedroom to look for all her discarded items. She sees them folded on a chair in the opposite corner of the room. She smiles at the idea of Rayaan making the bed and cleaning up, and grateful the room wasn't still a disaster when Arin came through to find her. At this point, she's thankful for any small favors.

Chapter Sixteen

Entering the kitchen, Andi sees an empty chair between the two boys- she can't seem to stop thinking of them that way. Getting some juice from the fridge, she realizes it's a thought so ingrained in her, even if she knows them well into old age, she'll always think of them as 'boys.' Pouring her glass, she rubs across her forehead, before taking a seat on a barstool at the island, next to Neal.

She ignores the look both brothers give her.

She tilts to the left and gives him a kiss on the cheek. "Thank you for a fun night out. I haven't been dancing like that since I was in DC."

"Such a pretty dress," Prisha murmurs, admiring her sundress. She hands her a plate of French toast and fruit. "No fun places in Chicago, *beti?*"

Spearing pineapple with her fork, she explains, "Haven't been there long enough to meet a group of friends yet." She bites into it, wiping the juice from her chin. "One of my college roommates is my boss, but she's always with her boyfriend, so-"

"And you, what about the guy you were seeing the last time you were home for the holidays?" Neal asks.

From her seat, she can see Rayaan's head rise quickly to

hear her answer.

She focuses on her food, cutting the tasty toast into bites. "He was a lobbyist. When his candidate lost his seat, he returned to Philadelphia. I didn't want to leave DC." She takes a small bite, savoring the sweetness, coughing from the powdered sugar. "We took the train back and forth for a while to visit each other, but it just didn't work with my job at the time. We fizzled out; I think it's been over a year ago we quit seeing each other."

Neal nods. "A beautiful woman like you, no one else on the horizon?"

"That's sweet, Uncle Neal." She takes another bite, chewing slowly, aware now that Arin is also listening intently. If she didn't know Neal any better, and his inquiring manner, she would swear they set him up to ask the questions they wanted answers to. "My specialty is political reporting. Between the campaign trail and the election, finding love was the last thing on my mind. And I don't know if you know this Uncle Neal, but I'm kind of set in my ways, and opinionated. Some men don't like that."

Neal scoffs. He looks around at the other men in the room, and asks, "What man doesn't want that?"

Stephen winks at his daughter. "A woman's place is in the kitchen-"

"Dear!" Sarah scolds, swatting his shoulder with a dish

196

towel.

"-Eating the meal I cooked for her."

"That is the only way to finish that sentence, Dad." Andi smiles at her parents. "I can't find something like that, Uncle Neal. Someone who is gonna stand behind me and support what I want to do, instead of pushing me out of the way to get where he wants." She wipes her mouth on her napkin, leaving her plate half-eaten. "We all," she waves to include the brothers, "grew up with some great models of what it meant to be in a supportive, equal relationship. If I can't have that, I don't want it."

She rises, carrying her plate to the sink.

"Andi's right. The four of you showed us what a good relationship should look like," Arin inserts. "And it's not easy to find."

"Because, *beta*, you have to build it. You think this comes easy?" Prisha moves to stand beside her husband, placing her hand on his shoulder as he wraps his arm around her waist. "This wasn't the type of love I grew up with. Where I grew up, women were taught to be quiet and submissive, following their husband's lead-"

"-which is why you left, to come to school in America-" Neal interjects, pulling his wife closer.

"-But it still wasn't easy for me to change that way of thinking." She kisses the tip of his nose when he turns to look at her. She looks back at the younger generation she is addressing. "I know my parents learned to love each other, but I didn't want an arranged marriage, like they had. I dreamed of finding the right man on my own, for us to raise children together seeing that we loved each other." She holds her hand out. "I wanted you boys to feel it. But it is something you have to work on, agree on together, or it falls apart."

"That's for sure," Rayaan agrees.

Prisha moves to pat him on the shoulder. "Well, your ex is a different story. She just wanted a social ladder to climb, not a true relationship. Why if you hadn't-"

Rayaan clears his throat, standing up. "Can we not spoil my day by talking about her? There's nothing between us now," he says, aiming his words directly at Andi. "I should have listened to everyone telling me it was a mistake, and the only reason I don't regret it is because I have Elias." He moves to the sink, taking Andi's plate from her. "But when I give myself again, I'll know she wants me for me."

Catching the look passed from Rayaan to her, Andi can see the realization dawn on her mother's face. Her mother's eyes are wide with surprise, somehow aware now her daughter has Rayaan, not Arin, in her sights. Andi cuts her a side glance, and her mother runs her fingers over her lips, like a zipper, and acts as if to throw a key over her shoulder.

Sarah runs her tongue over her teeth. "Your brother and sister-in-law aren't awake yet. We promised them baby duty-"

"But that was before we read about an estate sale up the road we'd like to go check out," Neal finishes her sentence.

"Mmm," Andi hums. "Likely story. Good thing the diaper bag is ready to go, and you have a car seat."

Stephen pats his daughter's shoulder as he walks past her with a handful of dirty plates. "We're passing over the responsibility of your nephew to you."

Her stomach drops. "Uh, Dad, babies and I don't really get along."

"He's actually old enough to be considered a toddler now," Arin chimes in, placing some of the leftovers in the fridge.

"They'll be up soon. It'll only be a short while," Sarah says.

Andi sighs, reaching in the cabinet for a new trash bag. "Fine. Only if Uncle Neal promises to bring back some books."

"Just for you, sweetheart." Neal kisses her temple before taking the full bag of trash out the patio door.

The other parents quickly disappear, leaving her and the boys with the baby, waving happily from his highchair.

Andi thinks of something, and chases after them. "Auntie Prisha, wait, I have a question!"

Prisha stops in the hallway, turning to smile. "What's that, luv?"

"Can you tell me what," she ponders, thinking of the right pronunciation. "Can you tell me what "*meri jaan*" means?"

Sliding on her shoes, Sarah is drawn into the conversation. "All this time as friends, and I've barely been able to pick up any Hindi words." She shakes her head. "That has a lovely sound," she says as she repeats the phrase.

Prisha's grin grows. "It is a lovely sound, used as a term of endearment, usually reserved for sweethearts and lovers. It means 'my life.'" Putting her purse over her shoulder, she reaches inside for lip gloss. "Where did you hear this, *beti?*"

Swallowing slowly, Andi places her hand against the wall, knees weak. Rayaan's been saying it to her all weekend. Thinking quickly, she replies, "I was watching a show online, and the character kept repeating it, but the English translations didn't seem to match up. Mom's right, it is lovely, and I was curious."

Reaching up, Prisha caresses her cheek. "I always loved teaching you about my culture. We will go to the store, and I will buy foods to cook tonight. We'll have a traditional dinner."

"That sounds so good," Andi says with a chuckle, patting her belly. To calm the nervous butterflies swarming in her stomach- "I need to get back to Jackson. You guys have fun," she says, as she ushers them out the door.

Her mind whirring, she practically stumbles down the hall to the kitchen. Arin is playing with Jackson, while Rayaan washes the dishes. She joins him at the sink, to dry, taking a plate from his hand without a word.

He bumps her hip. Looking over his shoulder to make sure Arin isn't paying attention, he squats down a bit to whisper in her ear. "I'm washing dishes. Are you ready, oh what was it you said?" He pauses, thinking. He presses his lips to her shoulder quickly. "To drag me off to the bedroom?"

She remembers their conversation from Friday, just three short days ago, when he'd asked about her favorite video Arin created. Shaking her head, she can feel the blush creeping up her neck. "Shh. He'll hear you."

"Well? Are you?" Rayaan hits his hand in the sudsy water, splashing her with bubbles.

Drying the plate, she closes her eyes, trying to control her breathing. "Not because you're washing dishes," she admits.

"What are you two whispering about over there?" Arin calls from across the room. "Let's get the day going!"

Rayaan caresses his fingers over hers as he passes her another plate to dry. "We were trying to decide what to do with Jackson."

Dishes washed, he shakes off the water and takes out

201

another towel to help her with the drying.

"Good thing you have a plan, because I have to bail for a bit. I don't have time to play babysitter."

"What? No! You can't leave us!" Andi spins on her feet to face him, practically dropping the glass she's holding. Rayaan watches her carefully for an explanation. "You don't understand. I'm scared to be alone with Jackson. Babies really don't like me. I need you there too."

Picking up Jackson from the seat, Arin bounces him on his hip. "Don't be ridiculous. Everyone loves you. Isn't that right, Rayaan?"

"Definitely," Rayaan grins, continuing to dry the bowls.

When Arin tries to pass the baby off to her, Andi grabs the stack of dishes and walks them over to the other cabinet.

"You're not kidding, are you?" Arin asks, placing a blob of soap bubbles on Jackson's leg, making him laugh.

She shrugs. "There were never any little kids around; I didn't grow up babysitting. I just kinda missed that mothering gene, I think." She stretches to put the dishes away.

Arin shrugs. "I really am sorry, but I need to make a few videos, or I'm going to get off schedule. I have some written and ready, that take place in other locations, like my car and the grocery store. I can film some of those this morning while it's quiet."

Rayaan nods. "It's okay, *bhai*, we got you. It's been a while since I've had a baby in my arms, but I think I can remember." Handing Andi the last plate, he says, "Go get the stroller ready, while I make sure everything in the bag is ready. Andi needs good walking shoes, and we'll meet you outside."

Continuing to put away bowls and glasses, Andi is aware of Rayaan in her space. The moment she hears Arin close the front door, he pushes her against the counter, running his hands down her sides, his nose in her hair. "I thought they were never going to leave." With his grip on her hips, he forcefully turns her to face him, instantly placing his lips to hers.

Breathing him in, she tugs on the chain around his neck. Her other hand reaches up and scratches the side of his beard. Enjoying the new sensation, she pulls back slightly. "The beard suits you."

He chuckles, rubbing it playfully against her cheek. "Thank you."

Hearing a car horn, Andi ruefully steps back. "I better go get my shoes. He's- Jackson's waiting for us."

She tries not to think about Arin as she runs up the back steps.

Meeting Rayaan out on the front driveway, she's surprised

by the impromptu filming set up Arin has created. Jackson is standing in the front seat of his car, hands on the steering wheel. Rayaan is kneeling lowly beside the open door, hands up to catch the toddler if he falls. Arin is filming and making commentary as though Jackson was in a high-speed chase.

She stays back, not wanting to interrupt the moment, watching Arin at work. He moves to the other side of the car, winking at her. He starts filming again, acting out the role of an officer pulling over a speeding driver, only his voice on camera while Jackson gives him a steely glare only a baby can.

Rayaan breaks the scene by laughing and Arin calls cut, dropping his phone to his side.

"That might be something, if Logan and Lauren would let me use it."

Rayaan nods, standing up. He reaches in to pick up the toddler, nearly having to pry Jackson's hands from the wheel. "Not gonna go peacefully, huh, Buddy? None of that. We're going on a walk with Auntie Andi."

Rayaan moves to hand Jackson to her, but she steps aside, putting two water bottles in the cup holder.

"You won't even hold your own nephew?" he asks, incredulous.

"We can save his tantrum for when we get back."

Rayaan feigns handing the baby off to her, and Jackson grabs at his beard, babbling angrily.

Andi shrugs. "See? I told you."

"Chat on the way." Arin pats her hip. "You're wasting my daylight."

Rayaan rolls his eyes as Arin gives her a quick kiss on the cheek. "See you when you get back."

She awkwardly pats his arm and steps away, ignoring the icy look Rayaan aims at his brother. She holds the stroller in place as Rayaan rests the baby inside. Buckled in, Rayaan takes the tiny ball cap she hands him, and places it on Jackson's head.

They wave goodbye to Arin and begin their walk.

After a few moments of peaceful silence, Rayaan asks, "So, you don't want children?"

She notices his tight grip on the handle of the stroller, and she reaches down to hand Jackson one of his teething rings.

"Maybe? I don't know." She looks straight ahead. "I've never been in the right place to have one, so I've never really thought about it." She tucks a stray hair behind her ear, trying to match Rayaan's pace. "What do you do with kids his age?"

He chuckles. "You do know your nephew is fourteen months old, right? He's been a little slow, but starting to walk?"

"Oh, hush! I brag about my amazing nephew all the time, showing off Lauren's pictures, and I babble with him on video calls, but no, I can't say we've really bonded." She begins to huff, not realizing the road was so steep. "Are we going to get to level ground soon? This is killing me."

Rayaan smiles. "Soon. It evens out at the next driveway." He nods ahead. "And I'm not picking on you. Not everyone is made for mothering. Gemma wasn't, but she's better at it now that Elias is older." Pushing up his sunglasses, he sighs. "Things could have been a lot different if I hadn't pushed her to have a baby." Unable to read his expression behind his shades, she watches him flex his fingers. "It's good you know that about yourself and won't make those around you suffer."

The sadness in his voice reaches her, twisting her gut. She reaches out, placing her hand on his arm. "Suffer? Was it that bad, Rayaan?"

Coming to level ground, their walk is smoother as they make their way to the old park hidden on the hillside. Rayaan slows his pace.

"That's probably not the right word. But you know Gemma. I don't have to explain her to you."

Andi nods. She can only imagine how cold their household might have been.

"So why split custody now?"

Turning onto the sidewalk hidden in the bushes, Rayaan pushes the stroller ahead. "We both travel a lot with our jobs. This provides us flexibility because we can plan around his schedule. Maybe things will change as he gets older. Her new boyfriend seems nice, and Elias likes him, so I guess that's the best I can hope for."

Around the crook in the path, Andi can see their old stomping grounds. She gasps. "Oh, my word! It hasn't changed a bit."

"This place has about 20 code violations waiting to happen," Rayaan amends.

The equipment is still old, but someone has painted it colorfully. Planters edge the trees, with blooming flowers. A few picnic benches have been added, and Andi can see where they have been chained to the ground. Jackson points and claps, watching a group of squirrels chase each other near the slide.

Parking the stroller and locking the wheels in place, Rayaan pulls Andi to him for a hug. "How do you feel about pre-teen boys? Elias could talk your ear off about dinosaurs."

Having given no thought to Rayaan's role as a single father, Andi says the first thing that comes to mind. "I think I'd like it very much. And he could teach me some soccer moves."

Squeezing her shoulder, he kisses the top of her head. "I was hoping you'd say that."

Walking around to the front of the stroller, he takes the squirming baby from his seat. "Come on, Bud. We need to show off for Auntie." Rayaan carries Jackson over to the playpad with a fairly evident new foamy surface. "She needs to see you walk." He stands Jackson next to the tiny bouncer, shaped like a horse and waits for him to balance. Then he moves back a few feet and crouches low. "Come on, Jackson. You can do it."

Jackson roves his tiny hands over the shiny animal, babbling away, telling his own story. Rayaan throws an abandoned acorn near him, and the little boy watches it roll away. Turning his attention to Rayaan, Jackson lets go of the horse, bouncing a bit to gain his balance. Rayaan whispers words of encouragement, clapping his hands together as the toddler begins to teeter his way forward. When he's within reach, and looks like he's about to take a tumble, Rayaan scoops him up under his armpits and stands quickly, swinging the baby high into the air.

Andi inhales quickly, worried, but Jackson's giggles echo off the trees. Rayaan swings him low and brings him up high again, this time letting go, the little boy momentarily flying before Rayaan catches him in a tight grip.

Face to face, Jackson babbles in delight, patting Rayaan's cheek.

"He trusts you," Andi says.

Tossing the kid over his shoulder, and letting the boy hang down his back, Rayaan turns to her with a smile. "When I'm in the Seattle area, every few months, I usually stay with

Lauren and Logan." Bending, he catches the boy in a cradle hold as he falls over his shoulder. "He loves when Uncle Rayaan gives free flying lessons."

Jackson makes a feeble sound, starting with the letter 'F' and Andi wonders if he's trying to repeat the word 'fly.'

"You try."

Rayaan swings Jackson towards Andi, and eyes wide, she quickly accepts the handoff. Turning in a fast circle, she swings Jackson around, but his reaction is not the same.

"He can sense your fear. Relax." Rayaan steps behind her, placing his hands on her elbows, and guiding another swing. "Dip, and lift."

Not a smooth movement, but better than the first attempt, Jackson shouts. Andi's pretty sure he's done with this game, if Auntie Andi is in charge, but she likes the feel of Rayaan's body against hers. Turning again, they complete a third attempt, and Jackson claps his hands.

"Told you you could do it," Rayaan whispers in her hair.

Pulling the toddler close, Andi kisses his cheek. "Was that fun, Jacks?"

Jackson pouts out his lower lip and reaches for Rayaan.

The brooding, handsome man softens in the baby's presence. He sweeps his thumb over Jackson's forehead. "It's okay, Buddy," he says softly. "Andi's got you."

The toddler leans back in her arms, looking her over as if

209

he's really seeing her for the first time.

And starts crying, real tears running down his cheeks.

About to cry herself, Andi requests quietly, "Please take him."

His wailing increases as Rayaan steps from behind her, keeping his body as close to hers as possible. Jackson is struggling in her arms, and she's afraid she'll drop him. But Rayaan doesn't take him. He places his hand on the toddler's back, calmly rubbing him, and wrapping his other arm around her waist. He begins to bounce them both. "Shh, shh," he coos. "It's alright. It's alright. I'm right here."

The butterflies in her stomach start fluttering again, and she's pretty sure the pang she feels is her ovaries exploding, telling her she'd have children with this man. And only this one.

She blinks away the thought.

Their caretaker moves more to the front, capturing Jackson between them, as his cries subside, and he hiccups. Andi giggles, feeling sedated as well. Her arms, around Jackson, are pressed tightly to Rayaan's chest as he holds them both. She can feel his heat radiating through his clothes as the sun starts to warm up for the day.

"Maybe we should head back?"

He kisses her temple tenderly. "Had all the 'aunting' you can handle for today?" He chuckles. Loosening his hold, he pats her hip.

"What do you say we go home and see if Mamma and Daddy are awake? Huh?"

Jackson kicks out his feet, and shouts, "Ma!"

Andi laughs, patting the baby's leg, now rested firmly in Rayaan's hold. "There's your answer," she says, as Rayaan places him back in his seat, buckling him in.

Returning to the house, Arin's equipment is gone from the driveway, but the parents haven't returned yet. However, a trailer with a large inflatable boat is parked in the drive.

"What's going on?" Andi asks, walking past it.

"Beats me," Rayaan replies as he parks the stroller next to the garage and lifts the sleeping baby.

Andi gathers all the baby gear- why do they need so much stuff just to go for a walk?- and follows him inside.

Depositing the baby in the playpen set up in the library, they carry the monitor with them as they seek out the sound of laughter and raucous voices.

Logan and Lauren are awake, and regaling Arin with some story. Lauren makes a grand gesture as they step out onto the porch, and the trio dissolve into laughter.

"And that's why I'm staying home," she finishes.

"Staying home from where?" Andi asks, reaching into the

cooler on the patio, taking a bottled juice for herself, and handing Rayaan water.

"I've rented you all a boat for the afternoon, to go floating, like all the stories Logan would tell from when you were younger." Lauren pats her shoulder, proud of herself. "I'm going to stay here with Jackson and answer a few work emails. Prisha texted, and I can help her cook when they get back. I love Indian food; it will be fun!"

Finishing a long gulp of his water, Rayaan brushes the back of his hand over his mouth. "This sounds like a recipe for disaster."

"Everything's gonna be wet by the time we get back," Logan adds.

Andi dips her head, avoiding the grin on Rayaan's face at her brother's comment. Imperceptibly, she shakes her head at him, willing him not to make an inappropriate joke.

"Miss Clumsy over here will tip us over," Arin predicts, pointing at Andi.

"Again," say all the boys in unison.

Scoffing, Andi puts her hands on her hips. "You guys always leave your shit out. It's not my fault I don't balance well."

"'I have this inner-ear imbalance,'" Logan mimics, repeating something she's said a million times.

"I do!"

Rayaan and Arin chuckle. Arin taps Rayaan on the chest. "Aren't you glad we don't have a sister?"

"You're a pain in the ass, too," Rayaan quips. "Thought you had so much work you had to do?"

Arin chuckles sheepishly. "I came inside to film, but they were in the way."

Shaking his head disdainfully at his brother, Rayaan claps his hands together. "When are we getting this show on the road? Let's make sandwiches and get ready!"

"You have really grown into this whole 'outdoorsman' thing, haven't you?" Andi asks.

He nods while Lauren tells them a cooler of food is packed. "Ordered everything. All you guys have to do is exit quietly so you don't wake Jackson," she waves the monitor in her hand, "and have fun!"

Kissing his wife, Logan jumps out of his seat and takes on a commanding position. "Twenty minutes. Sunscreen, snacks, towels. Arin and I can get the coolers loaded, Rayaan, you back up the truck to the trailer." He turns to his sister. "Don't tip us over."

"Thanks," she laughs as they all run off to accomplish their tasks.

She hangs behind with Lauren, thanking her for the outing, and helping her to clear up the patio table. In the kitchen, her sister-in-law traps her by the cabinet.

"Rayaan! Girl, good for you!" She claps her hands excitedly. "Oh, you guys are perfect!"

Andi blinks rapidly. "What are you talking about?"

Lauren steps closer, grabbing a bag of chips on the counter behind Andi. "Well, I sure hope all those sexy time noises last night were you guys, and not any of the parents."

Andi gasps, throwing her hand over her mouth.

"It was! It was you; I knew it."

Andi grabs her arm. "Shh. Shhh. They'll hear you!"

"Y'all didn't seem to worry about that last night." Lauren can't contain her grin. It spreads from ear to ear.

"Fuuuuck," Andi hisses out slowly, slumping against the counter. She scratches her forehead. "Do you think anyone else heard?"

Lauren shakes her head 'no.' "Logan sleeps like the dead. And with the placements of bathrooms and the laundry room, I think you were safe. They're all on the other side of the house, and Arin said he didn't get back until around 7am."

Andi scowls at the mention of his name.

Lauren grabs her arm. "Wait! Was this to get even with him for the leggy actress?"

"Ugh, don't remind me of her," Andi says, shaking the thought from her head. "No. No. This wasn't revenge. This was the inner-seventeen-year-old me, reading his books,

214

hanging on his every word, wanting to know for the first time what his lips felt like."

"Delicious," Lauren sighs out, dreamily.

Andi giggles at her sister-in-law and raises her eyebrow.

Lauren straightens up. She coughs. "I can only imagine they'd be delicious? They just look like the ripest strawberries, and-"

"You've thought about this before?" Andi teases.

Looking out the kitchen window, they both see him walking along the side of the house, carrying the cooler.

"Who sees him and doesn't think about that?"

"Shit, Lauren. What am I gonna do?"

"Him, apparently. Do him."

Lauren laughs again at the look of shock on Andi's face.

Andi squints. "You have a wild side we know nothing about, don't you?"

Lauren opens the fridge and takes out a bottle of water. "Why do you think I'm staying home today? I partied a little too much last night. Can't remember the last time I drank so much. Me and Jackson are gonna chill by the pool."

The women freeze when the front door opens and closes. Lauren laughs when Rayaan jogs into the kitchen.

"Are you ready?"

"No, I haven't even been upstairs yet. Lauren was handing me more snacks."

Lauren begins shoving things into another bag. "Sorry, I was the hold up."

"Go change. The cloud cover broke, and it's gonna be hot on the water. Bring extra sunscreen."

"Bossy," Lauren whispers as Andi turns to go up the backstairs.

"Wait," Rayaan calls after her, and she stops.

Looking over his shoulder, to make sure Lauren can't see them in the stairwell, he pulls Andi close. "Some girl talk?" He twists his finger around a loose curl, stretching it down and caressing over her shoulder. She shudders. "You can't breathe when I'm close like this, can you?"

She bites in her lip, blushing. She shakes her head 'no.'

"What about when I do this?"

Wrapping his strong arms around her, he steps closer. With her standing on the bottom stair, they are eye level. Rayaan brushes his beard against her cheek and gives her waist a squeeze. He runs his nose along hers, his mouth hovering above hers. Her eyes are down, drawn to his lips. With a quick flick of his tongue, he wettens them. "*Meri jaan*, breathe."

She breathes deeply before placing her lips to his, sighing as she melts against him. Her hand snakes under the edge of his t-shirt and she caresses over his back, before dipping her fingers below the elastic on his shorts. Rayaan strengthens the

216

kiss, quietly moaning as she curves her fingertips, pressing her nails into his skin.

Lauren drops something in the kitchen. "Sorry." They split apart, grinning shyly. He caresses back her hair, before cupping her cheek. "There's movement on the driveway. The boys are restless," she warns loudly.

Andi turns her head and kisses his palm. "Go. I'll be right out. I promise!"

She does her best to run up the stairs, knowing Rayaan is watching her from behind.

Chapter Seventeen

In the backseat of the truck, Rayaan rests his elbow on the doorframe, placing his thumb under his chin, and his index finger along his cheek. He leans his head against the window-making it easier to view Andi in the front passenger seat. Her hair is loose, billowing around her shoulders. She's wearing a crazy tie-dye shirt that keeps falling off her shoulder, loose fitting yoga pants and sensible shoes to wear in the river.

He can't wait to watch her take it all off for the float trip.

She was right about being curvy and soft. She had compared him to a Greek god, but she was reminiscent of a beautiful Renaissance painting. The way the morning sun created shadows in the valley between her full breasts was divine. The curve of her ample hip, her thick thigh thrown over his, pinning him down to the bed was downright sinful. Her lusty, boisterous laugh at the silly things he whispered. Everything about Andi was big and beautiful. And she hadn't been afraid to share it all with him.

Hitting a bump in the road, his head bounces off the window. Aware of the growing desire in his pants, he shifts in his seat. Sitting on the opposite end of the bench seat from him, Arin leans over to show him a song he's selected for the floating playlist he's putting together. He nods, noncommittally.

Not getting the attention he felt it deserved, Arin scoots forward, inserting himself in the open space between Logan, in the driver's seat, and Andi. Balling his other fist at his hip, Rayaan watches his brother totally invade her personal space, putting his hand possessively on her bare shoulder, and showing her some of the songs he's selected.

Andi's head tilts up and he can see she is watching him in the little mirror on her visor, but her eyes can't be seen behind her sunglasses. She shifts in her seat, creating space between her and Arin. But all that does is allow him to turn his face towards her to be closer.

Rayaan clears his throat. "We just leave the trailer, and the company picks it up, then comes to the meeting spot further down the river?" His voice sounds husky and irritable. Arin moves back into his seat and Rayaan can feel his whole body relax.

"That's what Lauren said. We float for four hours, until we get to the site, and there's time to swim and picnic." Logan signals his turn into the state park, to use the designated ramp and parking lot. "Someone will come and meet us, to get the boat. She said she'd probably send Dad and Neal to pick us up, because she'll be cooking with Mom and Prisha."

"The boat looks kinda heavy," Arin muses.

219

"It's supposed to float right off," Andi says, holding up the brochure. "We can get everything loaded on the ramp, and you guys can hold it in place, with the current. I can drive the truck out, and park it."

Rayaan grins, teasing, "Oh, little girl, you think you can do that?"

Andi was always horrible about backing up any vehicle with a trailer attached.

He watches her bite over her lips, looking straightforward before she speaks. "One of my boyfriends in DC, well, Arlington, had a boat. He insisted I learn how to do everything."

The phrase 'one of' sticks in his throat and he feels sick.

"That's right, bro. Jonathan made sure she knew it all." Logan backs the truck into place on the ramp and sets the parking brake. "I've seen it with my own eyes. I think she can tie a better knot than you."

Andi dips her head, blushing.

"Jonathan," Arin stretches out, "sounds like a dickhead politician name."

Rayaan mutters, "A knot tying contest could be fun."

She pulls her sunglasses down enough to peer over them, to glare at him through the little visor mirror. As she shakes her head at him, he can see the blush rising up her cheeks. Looking down to her luscious body, in the seat of the truck, her shoulders are red from the blush as well. He licks his lip, knowing now that blush goes lower.

"Because he is the son of a dickhead politician," Andi says, getting out of the truck as soon as Logan shifts it into park.

Standing in the open doorway, she digs through her bag, grabbing only the necessities for a float trip. Rayaan climbs out of the truck and begins loading the coolers into the inflatable raft.

He can hear Arin talking to her quietly, but he can't make out their words. Stretching out his work, he walks around in front of the truck on his next trip, walking past her open door, and sees Arin has his hand on her waist.

He doesn't have to worry about dropping the full cooler. His grip is too tight, as he grits his teeth before coughing.

"Personal space, Arin. Ever hear of it?" She says to his brother.

He can't help his cocky grin. She definitely can take care of herself.

Moments later, Arin appears at the back of the truck, grabbing the waterproof bag with towels, and the other with snacks.

Logan stands near the helm, readying the ropes. "Make sure the oars are onboard," he says to Rayaan.

Rayaan hops up onto the trailer and settles all the supplies so they can all comfortably sit. Andi appears around the back of the truck, now in a ball cap and only the t-shirt. In the sunlight, he can see she got some sun on her legs the day before. "Sunscreen, Red?"

"Got it," she holds her bag up high. "River map, emergency charger, cash. Medical kit."

He claps his hands together. "I think you've done this before." He reaches for the bag, taking it from her.

"Just don't hit anyone with an oar today, okay?"

Rayaan looks at her quizzically, trying to remember her reference. Then it registers with him. "Oh, shit. But he deserved it! And I didn't really mean to hit him-"

"You knocked him off the damn boat, King!"

"Are you talking about the time we were fighting over the last beer, and I hid it in my pants, and he clocked me with the oar?" Arin asks, coming around to hand Rayaan the life jackets.

"Why did my mother let me hang out with you hooligans?" Andi wonders aloud.

"Aw, Sis, your life would have been boring without us!" Logan pats her on the back. "We all good?"

Everyone jumps into action, knowing their role to play. Rayaan and Arin wait on the bank, while Logan walks along beside the trailer as Andi backs it into the water.

"Whoa, whoa," he yells, as it starts to float off. He hops inside and tosses a rope to Rayaan. "A little more," he advises, yelling at her through the open window.

"All clear," shouts Rayaan as the boat pulls free.

Using the rope as leverage, he and Arin direct the raft to the makeshift dock. The current is strong, with a good breeze. They'll get their money's worth today, and hopefully won't reach the destination too soon.

Andi drives the truck up the ramp and parks it next to a couple of fishing boats. Rayaan watches her hop out of the vehicle and bound over to them, without seemingly a care in the world.

"Holy shit," Logan calls from the boat. "Has Mom seen your tat?"

"Shh, and you aren't gonna tell her," Andi says. "Or I'll finally tell her who broke Great-Aunt Ina's vase."

"Glad we could have this extra time to bond, Sis," he says sourly.

Rayaan reaches his other hand out to her. "Get in here," he directs her. He holds it a second longer than necessary, giving it a little squeeze.

"Looking good, Andi," Arin says, whistling, working hard to keep the boat steady.

"Gimme the rope," Andi commands after stepping down into the raft.

Her tone is knowledgeable, so Rayaan follows through. She wraps it around the post in the center of the dock and holds it.

"Arin, give me yours too, and get on first, you're lighter."

Rayaan watches his brother follow her instructions, nearly tripping as he steps in. The lacing of the ropes hold it steady, making it easier to board.

"Rayaan, we'll balance better if you're up front, on the left, opposite of Sis," Logan directs. He takes the ropes from Andi, as she settles in the back. "Last chance. Everyone got everything?"

When no one complains, he pulls the ropes free, letting the raft loose on the water.

Unsettled, Rayaan waits for everyone to get seated, surprised Arin remembered to sit in the correct position, and not by Andi, to keep them balanced. He shifts a few bags, creating an island for everyone to prop their feet on. Andi quickly braids the ropes, making them easy to pull out when needed, without knotting up. He remembers she once explained to him it was similar to a crochet stitch her Gramma Lou had taught her.

"Toss me one of those," he says. "Teach me again."

She walks him through the steps of looping the ropes together, and pulling them just so, creating an intricate design with the nylon fibers. His isn't as tight as hers, and she pulls it loose laughing at him, making him start over. When he's got the hang of it, she loses interest and tosses the rope down by

224

her feet.

Andi takes off her ballcap, and readjusts her ponytail, looping it though the cap and creating a bun. "I'm an idiot," she mutters, looking up to catch his eyes on hers.

"Why are you an idiot?" he asks.

"Can't take off my t-shirt with my hat on."

"Everyone divert your eyes. No looking at my sister," Logan demands.

Rayaan laughs, brushing his bristly top lip over his bottom one, looking away to watch a family of ducks swimming along the shoreline. He wants nothing more than to turn and admire her, but she is Logan's sister, and he respects the brotherly instinct to protect her.

"I said turn around, Arin," Logan says sternly.

"Good lord, we're all adults," Andi mutters. There's another pause before she announces, "Ok, everyone can sit normally again."

Of course, his eyes are immediately drawn to her, and his intake of breath is sharp. A little more collected than his brother's expletive escaping between his lips.

"You look amazing, Ands," Arin says appreciatively.

Inwardly, Rayaan cheers the grim look Andi shoots at his brother for the use of her old nickname. He recalls it only came about when they were dating, and probably wasn't high on her list of favorite things since their breakup.

The floral ensemble suits her well. As the day before, it's another high-waisted two piece, this time with the top sweeping low over her cleavage, rising back up to a flouncy sleeve over each shoulder. Two tiny straps hold it all up, straining under the weight of her full breasts. The bright colors cause her skin to glow, and Rayaan aches to reach out to her.

Anger and jealousy knotting his stomach, he simply bobs his head in agreement with his brother.

"So much more confident than you used to be," Arin continues. "It's entirely becoming!"

Andi blushes at the compliment, folding her t-shirt and setting it in her lap.

"Yeah, dating assholes somehow makes you have more confidence," Logan snarks.

"Logan, stop-"

"Oh, I wasn't referring to anyone on this boat." His eyes are directly on Arin. "But if the shoe fits."

"Stop." Andi says determinedly. "I won't sit on a boat for four hours like this. None of us on this raft are saints. We all did stupid things when we were young. None of us have had perfect relationships- ah, nope-" Rayaan smiles when she stops her brother before he can even start. "Are you forgetting Melinda? She was horrible."

She digs through the pile of bags for hers and takes out

226

sunscreen. She applies a bit to her fingertips and rubs it all over her face. "But we all learned from them, and we keep trying until we get it right. We might have some scarred and bruised hearts, but I think we all turned out okay." She uses a different lotion on her legs, covering her tattoo thoroughly. "You found Lauren. We're all still searching."

"Fine. Apologies, Arin," Logan says, reaching out to shake his friend's hand.

"No offense taken. I was an ass," Arin shrugs. "But I had my reasons." He glares at Rayaan. "Not good ones, and I do wish I had done things differently." He shifts his attention to Andi. "I wish I'd behaved better. I'm sorry."

Rubbing in the lotion on the tops of her feet, she lifts the corner of her mouth into a half smile. "I know you do, Arin, and that's enough for me."

Chapter Eighteen

Waking from the couch, Andi doesn't even remember falling asleep when they got back from the float trip. Stephen had picked up the sun-beaten crew at the campsite, exhausted and hungry after their long afternoon on the water. Logan had begged for a burger, claiming he was ravished and parched from the heat. Taking the long way back to their starting point, Stephen made a pass through a drive-in for nourishment, telling them Prisha would have his hide if they weren't hungry at dinner. It always amazed her how the water could play tricks on one's mind. Although they had floated for hours, the truck was parked only forty minutes from the final destination of the float trip. She must have been asleep in her father's vehicle, because she didn't remember anyone getting out to get in Logan's rental truck either.

The house is still and quiet, but amazing smells are wafting from the kitchen.

In the kitchen, food trays are waiting on the counter, covered in foil, and waiting to be served. Something bubbles on the stove, but the room is empty.

The patio door is open, and she follows her nose outside. The smell of charcoal and grilling meat reminds her of long summer days of a time gone by. Stepping onto the patio,

Andi expects to see her dad manning the grill, but is surprised to find Rayaan with a spatula in his hand. He's chatting with Logan, sitting nearby, and bouncing Jackson on his knee. Both men turn to speak to Neal, listening intently to his words.

Stepping from under the shade tree, Andi is instantly aware of the bright sun. She squints and stumbles, still groggy from her nap, bumping into one of the chairs.

"Hey, Sleeping Beauty. We thought you were never going to wake up," Neal says, rising from his chair.

"That's our cue to go get ready," says Logan, standing up and lifting Jackson into his arms in one fluid movement.

Andi pouts and rubs her eyes. She feels like she's been asleep for hours. "Don't leave on my account," she whines.

"You're such a baby when you wake up," Logan says. "I'd forgotten that, Sis."

"No, I'm not," she instantly replies, putting her hand on her hip. She can feel the scowl on her face, but in the after-nap haze, there isn't anything she can do about it. "It smells good."

Rayaan nods, tilting his head in agreement.

"Yeah, it does. And Auntie Prisha said to let you sleep, but to get things moving when you woke up," Logan says. "I'll go get the ice and drinks ready for dinner."

"And I'll go let my beautiful wife know it's almost time,"

Neal says, disappearing into the house.

"I'm grumpy. I made everyone leave," she says, slowly blinking.

Rayaan lifts his arm and motions her to him.

"What if someone sees us?"

The movement of his hand is repetitive and rhythmic and continues until she complies. He tucks her against his side, flipping the meat with the spatula in his other hand.

"You didn't run me off," he says. "And what do you think I'm going to do? Undress you right here while I'm cooking?"

She giggles, feeling more relaxed in his arms. The haze begins to lift.

"That's for dessert, later," Rayaan teases.

God, she hopes it's a promise.

Andi places her arm around his back, resting her hand on his opposite hip. She likes the feeling of being beside him. "Why is this view of you standing at the grill so sexy?"

He chuckles softly, moving more of the food around on the heated rack. "Probably relates back to some primal instinct, the recollection of the caveman preparing a meal over a fire to provide for his woman."

She looks up into his dark brown eyes. "His '*meri jaan*?'"

He smiles shyly, his eyes washing over the soft planes of her face. She can feel him memorizing her.

"*Meri jaan*," he repeats quietly, like a solemn vow. He

squeezes her closer to his side. "You know about that?"

"I asked your mom," Andi admits, returning the squeeze to his hip.

"It's the truth." Rayaan tenderly kisses the top of her head. "Go on. Everyone's been waiting. Mom says she laid out a gift for you on your bed."

With her other hand, she gently caresses down his chest. "A few minutes. That's all I need."

She slowly pulls away, feeling her grumpiness return with each step away from him.

Feeling gorgeous in the sleeveless gold choli and lehenga skirt, coral pink with gold accents, Andi patters down the hallway in her bare feet. Auntie Prisha's gift was perfect, like it was designed just for her. She swirls the pink net dupatta around her and can't control her giggles. Lauren had sent her photos of herself in a similar outfit, in seafoam green, to match her eyes. She's bouncing with excitement and can't wait to see what the other women are wearing.

Halfway down the back steps, Andi halts. She hadn't even given thought to the men in traditional Indian dress for the dinner Prisha had planned. But the sight of Arin in a fitted gray sherwani at the bottom of the landing is quite yummy if she's honest with herself.

231

"You look really good," she says quietly.

He turns to smile and reaches his hand out to her.

Now aware of every move, she feels the dusty floorboards under her feet, and her curls bouncing down her back. The last few steps are an eternity as she ponders his appearance here.

"I was hoping I'd catch you before we were all together," he says, kissing the back of her hand as he guides her down the last step.

Standing on firm ground, he looks down at her. Not like when she and Rayaan were in this same spot earlier in the day, standing on the step, eye to eye with him.

"You're stunning," Arin compliments, his voice low and deep. He brushes his fingertip across her exposed belly, watching the movement of his own hand. He gently tugs the dupatta. "Ma's color choice was excellent. It brings out the golden strands of your hair."

Uncontrollably, she blushes. She doesn't want to react to his words or his touch, but she can't help it. He is attractive and knows how to use it to his advantage.

Swallowing hard, she reaches up to adjust his collar. "You clean up nice too," she offers, the phrase meant to diminish her opinion and to brush him aside.

He chuckles, rubbing the scar on his forehead. "No paddles to the head today," he says with a smile. He tilts his chin up. "Do you think you could make some time for me tonight?"

Andi nervously scratches at her neck. She sighs, deciding honesty is the best policy. Or at least a half-truth for the time being. "Arin, I don't think that's a good idea. How is it going to change things?" She swallows slowly, bringing her eyes to his. "I've forgiven you, and whatever noble reason you think you had for leaving me. But this won't move forward. I don't want that." She smiles from the side of her mouth, cocking her head to the side to look at him. "I don't think you really want me either." His raised eyebrow is noted as she continues, "If we met tonight, we wouldn't leave here as friends-"

"I want-"

She doesn't let him continue. Andi holds her hand up to his mouth but doesn't touch his lips. "-You would be disappointed, I'm afraid, and I would be angry. And I want you back in my life, as my friend. I've missed that the most, all these years."

Arin deflates and leans back against the wall, his eyes every bit as watery as hers. "I've missed that too," he says, kicking out his foot and hitting his shoe against the bottom step. "Do you know how many times I picked up the phone, to reach out to you, but was afraid you'd reject me?"

She softly chuckles. "I would have. I did," she breathes

out. "You saw me Thursday, at the hotel, remember?"

"Gah," he runs his hand through his hair. "How is it that feels like ages ago?"

She nods.

He stands up. "Hey, we never finished our interview, and we're all leaving in a day or two."

"Yes, we did. You just didn't know it." Andi moves towards the kitchen. "It's mostly written. Gotta find the perfect ending, and it's done."

He follows her. "But you haven't asked any questions-"

"A good journalist doesn't have to." She holds her arm up. "Now, can I get a handsome man to escort me to dinner?"

Laughter and music float into the room from the open patio door as he guides her out.

The trees are lit with white faerie lights. The table is covered in a beautiful silk scarf with threads of gold and silver running through the bright colors. A large floral arrangement sets in the center, casting shadows over the dinner plates and covered dishes.

Seeing her with Arin, Rayaan steps forward, anger and bitterness written on his face. Andi moves her head to the side, cutting him off, and she witnesses the flame fizzle out, although he still creates a fist at his side. Her father strides to her in a crisp tan colored sherwani and takes her hand from Arin.

"Pink is definitely your color, my dear," Stephen says, kissing her temple, and guiding her to the table.

Indian music plays over the sound system, and Andi is sure she recognizes the song from one of her favorite Bollywood films. She smiles at Lauren, seated across from her.

"Girl, why have we not been dressing like this all our lives? We look amazing!" Lauren says, laughing.

"We do!" Andi agrees. She looks down the long table, seeking out their benefactor. Prisha presides over the table head as matron and host. Her purple shalwar kameez brightens her golden skin, playing up to her youthful personality. Making eye contact, Andi blows her a kiss. "Thank you, Auntie Prisha."

"It was my honor, *beti*." Looking around those gathered, the pride on Prisha's face is evident. She claps her hands together, her golden bangle bracelets creating a chime effect. "You all look so lovely."

Everyone murmurs their agreement.

Admiring the table setting, Andi looks to her left, noting Rayaan has silently moved to her side. His navy blue sherwani is so dark, she can barely make out the black embroidery covering the front. His silver chain dangles down his chest and his rings clatter against his water glass when he reaches for it. So damn handsome, he takes her breath away.

Arin pulls out the chair on the other side of her, but before he can sit, Sarah stops him.

She can't remember the last time her mother looked so beautiful. The blue and silver shalwar kameez Prisha chose for her looks so comfortable and compliments her aging salt and pepper hair.

"Arin, dear, can you trade me seats? With my bad eyes, I can't sit facing the setting sun- oh, I saw your scowl, boy. Don't you worry. You'll have plenty of time to spend with Andi later." She smiles warmly and Andi realizes for the first time she gets most of her sassiness from her mother. "And think of it this way," Sarah touches Andi's shoulder as she sits down in the seat he wanted. "Now we can both admire you with the beautiful evening sky behind you," she says while Arin walks around to the other side of the table.

"Just like a magazine advertisement," Andi laughs. She laughs harder when he flips her off discreetly, running his middle finger down the side of his face.

Rayaan's thigh brushes against her when he moves his chair closer to the table. She can feel her cheeks turning pink as her body secretly hums, just being close to him. As everyone is listening to Prisha's description of the foods as the coverings are removed, his attention is on her. Putting his weight on his right side, he tilts towards Andi, and growls quietly, "You look like cotton candy. So sweet, you could simply melt in my mouth."

Andi bites her lip, and drops her hand to the table, causing her place setting to rattle. Is it getting warmer?

Lauren looks across the table and winks at her.

"Behave, King," Andi admonishes quietly.

Having ignored Prisha's explanations, Andi takes a little of everything as the bowls are being passed around. She recognizes the chickpeas and paneer cheese in the colorful salad, and her mouth waters over the buttery curry sauce to pour over the grilled chicken. She serves up a large helping of the rice, to soak up the sauce, and takes two chapatis from the basket before handing it off to her mother.

Lauren is regaling everyone with her tales of her personalized chef lessons from Prisha. "It was so easy. Like this chapati," she holds up a tortilla looking piece of bread. "It's so similar to the tortillas my Mexican grandmother taught me how to make. Really, Auntie. You need to teach some classes on how to do this."

Logan doesn't look too sure of his wife's enthusiasm. He grabs his fork and creates a taco like creation with his chapati, rice and meat.

Arin chides him, elbowing him in the side. "Like this, *bhai*. With your fingers."

He scoops some of the rice and chicken into his mouth, and hums in satisfaction. "Ma, you really do need to cook

Indian food more often."

Andi places her left hand in her lap, remembering her etiquette training from trips to the Middle East. The company she reported for at the time insisted all staffers attend conferences on ethnic diversity and how to compose oneself in another country in a way to not offend anyone. She remembers vividly her instructor threatening to tie her hand behind her back to keep from using it.

"I'm not two," Logan mumbles.

Andi's pretty sure from the jump off his seat, Lauren pinched his thigh.

Using her fingers, Andi enjoys her first savory bite, utilizing a torn piece of chapati as a scoop. "When I was in Dubai, everyone repeatedly told me, 'it tastes better in your hands,'" she tells Logan, holding up her hand to show it's not messy.

Lifting the wrap he created, he says, "I am eating with my hands."

Rayaan laughs. "You're missing out," he takes a bite from his fingers as well. "Your sister's right. The oils in our hands react with the foods, creating a different flavor."

Logan shakes his head. "Dude, we played in the river all day. I came home and changed a baby diaper. It's a culture thing, I get it. I respect it, but it's not for me."

"You think I didn't wash my hands before I ate?" His

laugh is more of a barking sound, patting his chest with his left hand, the one he's not using for eating. Andi can feel the heat rising off him, vibrating with irritation. The hairs on her arms stand up, sensing danger. His tone is serious. "Did you complain we didn't properly wash when we cooked hotdogs over the fire today, and ate with our hands? What about hamburgers, fries, or pizza? You eat those with your hands, and don't think twice. How is that any different from Indian culture?"

Logan's face drops, and he lowers his wrap to his plate. "You're right, man." He swivels in his seat to look at Prisha. "Sorry, Auntie. I meant no offense."

Waving her fingers at him, Prisha dips her head and silently accepts his apology. "It's just a different way of appreciating our food, its flavors, the nuances."

Stephen points his fork towards the serving bowls. "Isn't it considered offensive? I mean, I even felt a little uncomfortable putting this on." He gestures to his clothing for the evening.

"But you're not wearing it all the time, or eating like this, that's the difference," says Lauren.

"You're appreciating the culture," explains Andi. "Not trying to appropriate it."

Prisha rests her water glass back on the table and clears her throat. "The girls are right. You are accepting my culture, and being a part of it, but not claiming it was yours." Andi notices Jackson, in his highchair, has no problem eating with his fingers, and is really loving the rice and vegetables. His lip begins to quiver when he sees her watching him, so she quickly looks away. "You're not acting in a way to make fun of me. You're wearing the clothing of my country because I have given it to you, as a gift. You appreciate its beauty and design." She waves her hand to the display of traditional food. "By eating this meal with your hands, you are letting Lauren and I know you value our hard work and tasting the love we put into preparing this feast."

Whether she meant to guilt them or not, the others at the table still using a fork set them down and make modest attempts to eat with their fingers. With the rice and the curry sauce, it's not an easy task.

Talk changes to lighter subjects when Neal asks about the float trip. The four begin sharing their adventures, but Arin sums it up easily. "We aren't the dumbasses we once were-"

"-I was never a dumbass," Logan interrupts.

"And no one was hit with an oar, and Andi didn't tip us over," says Arin, raising his glass in a toast.

"We did lose a can koozie, a towel and a baseball cap," Rayaan says.

What a shame too, he'd looked so cute with his hat on and his aviator sunglasses.

"All in all, a good day," Andi agrees.

Lauren coughs. "What are you not telling, since the parents are all here? You're adults now. Fess up."

"Way to throw me under the bus, babe." Logan strokes his chin thoughtfully. "We drank all the beer and got to the campsite way too quickly."

"The current was really strong."

Andi watches as Rayaan washes in the finger bowl to the right of his plate and wipes his hands on his napkin, signaling he's finished eating. He rests both hands in his lap.

"What did you guys do then?"

"Thank goodness you packed hot dogs," she says, referencing the meal Rayaan alluded to earlier. Andi's pretty sure her voice jumped in shock on the last word, at Rayaan taking her hand under the table. As he squeezes it against her thigh, she exhales slowly. "We started a campfire and grilled those."

She's instantly warm and feels a rush of adrenaline. She squirms in her seat as his large hand holds hers, and he can still manage to caress her thigh with his thumb.

"Uh-huh. What else went in the fire?" Lauren asks, leading them out. "Come on. I know the stories."

"Shit," Arin hisses. "You're evil."

Sitting up straighter in his chair, Stephen asks, "What stories?"

"Babe, I'm in my mid-thirties and still scared of my father. Shut up," Logan says, reaching for more food.

All eyes are now focused on their end of the table.

Rayaan leans back in his chair. "That was all on you three, I wasn't usually around for those shenanigans."

"Oh, thanks," Andi sighs, shaking her head. More for his roaming hand than his sell-out. "Not me, they were the pyromaniacs." She gestures across the table.

"You were the one that always said it was for research," Arin remembers.

"But I didn't actually blow anything up in the campfires when we were kids," she insists. "I was too afraid of fire."

"Yeah, that's true," Rayaan agrees, moving her hand to his lap. "You never wanted to play with fire, just watch it." He slides their hands up his thigh.

On the other side of her, Sarah clears her throat. "Blowing stuff up?"

"You were playing with fire today," admits Arin, grinning wildly.

"Shh, I'm scared of my dad too."

Lauren can't hold it in anymore. "They used to blow shit up in the fire late at night, after everyone went to bed- to see how high things would fly."

"Like what kind of stuff?" Neal asks nervously.

Prisha questions, "Were you blowing up stuff today?"

Rayaan begins to press their joined fingers against his cock, holding her hand against him. She can feel him harden from his play.

She tries to keep her cool, but it's nearly impossible.

"Just a soda can," Andi admits. "We wanted to see if a modern can would blow out like they used to.'"

Sarah taps her daughter's arm. "Is that what that charcoaled old soda can is on the bookshelf in your room?"

"You still have it?" Rayaan asks.

"Yeah," she says quietly.

It was from one of the few nights Rayaan took part in their foolishness. He usually disappeared when they were done making smores and would start to goof off with talk of burning things in the fire. But one night, probably her senior year of high school, or her freshman year of college, he'd stayed with them. She vividly remembers it had been a cooler night, and he'd given her his sweatshirt. The other boys had said if she was cold, she should go get her own. As they were contemplating what to burn, she'd dropped a full soda into the flames. Rayaan shouted for everyone to get back, fearful of shrapnel if the can exploded, and he'd picked her up and swung her away, shielding her from the fire. She'd never forgotten the little flecks of gold that sparkled in his dark eyes, brought out by the amber flames behind him. Or the surprise that his lythe swimmer's body could pick her up.

Instead of exploding, the tin can had shot straight up, and sticky soda showered down on them. They heard it drop back to the ground and went in search of it in the dark. Arin had found it, the metal still hot. The can was singed. The bottom was rounded, as all the pressure was released from the top. They'd made fun of her for noting it was convex, when she had been sure it would be concave. The soda had pressurized the top of the can, escaping through three little openings, small tears in the metal.

Of all the things she'd packed away from her room over time, that metal can was still there.

Rayaan's sweatshirt was most likely in one of the boxes under the bed in her childhood room.

Even after washing away the sticky soda, it had smelled like him.

Andi smiles at him, seeing the same flecks of gold in his eyes brought on by the lights in the trees. She inhales deeply, surrounded by the same fragrance that had comforted her all those years past.

Cardamom. The missing scent. She smiles, thinking back to Friday afternoon, when she couldn't identify the third aroma that made up his essence. Saltwater, forest, and the spicy, sweet smell of cardamom. After being so close to him all weekend, it finally came to her.

"Those were good times," she giggles.

Stephen inquires, "Out of curiosity, did the new cans do the same?"

The night is pierced with the shrill ring of a phone. Arin slams his hand to his pocket. He coughs. "Sorry, I was expecting a work call." He rises from his chair and walks to the edge of the deck.

Andi shakes her head, defeated. "It wasn't a really good fire. It just rolled to the side, and soda started leaking out. It bubbled a little." She shrugged.

"Our little scientist," Rayaan chuckles.

Logan hits his hand against the table, making a declaration. "We'll have a better fire this summer. Just like the old days."

"Hold on," Neal ponders out loud. "Is that why I never had lighter fluid for the grill?"

"Oh, would you look at that!" Logan exclaims. "Jackson's asleep in the chair." He jumps up from his seat, patting Neal's shoulder. "I probably owe you about a hundred dollars' worth of lighter fluid, pal."

The movement stirs everyone, but Andi stays in her seat, her hand still pressed to Rayaan's crotch under the weight of his warm hand. He leans forward and takes a cold chapati, rolling it up and dipping it in the curry sauce. Taking a bite, he moans quietly.

Andi can appreciate his love for the delicious food, but she rolls her eyes at him. Pulling her hand free, she stands up to clear the table.

He jumps up as well and pushes her chair out of her way.

He offers her a bite, and she accepts it, chewing slowly as plates are cleared.

She avoids her mother's watching eyes.

Arin returns to the table. "Didn't mean to clear everyone out. Sorry."

Holding a stack of dirty dishes, Rayaan asks, "A work call?"

"Yeah, nothing to worry about." He breathes out. "I'm getting it taken care of."

Andi doesn't understand bro code, but she's sure that wasn't a work call.

Chapter Nineteen

With his feet propped up on the deck rail, Rayaan finishes off his drink. The liquor burns down his throat, feeling like tiny flames licking his insides. It reminds him of Andi dancing at the campfire earlier in the day. Setting the glass down beside him, he picks up his phone.

"Let's see if she still wants to play with fire?" he mutters aloud.

Typing quickly, he hits send before he can think better of it. *What are you wearing?*

Moments later, his phone vibrates with a return message. *Why don't you come up here and find out?*

He looks out to the water, an owl swooping overhead.

Rayaan rubs his finger over his lip, scratching the tip of it with his beard. She'd looked good enough to eat in her lehenga at dinner.

Slowly standing up, he pretends he doesn't hear his knee pop.

His phone vibrates again as he reaches for the glass, to take it inside.

I should clarify- I'm on vacation with family. Don't expect anything too exciting, just the oversized t-shirt from the tourist shop

In the kitchen, he guffaws quietly. Always so literal, she's funny and doesn't even know it.

Hearing the main door close, he walks to the front of the house. Through the window, he sees taillights disappearing as they go up the drive. Rayaan does a quick count of vehicles and realizes one has left.

Arin's car.

Straightening the shoes for his mother, he contemplates where his brother might have gone at such a late hour. His mind flits back to the leggy actress at the club the night before, but his brother is old enough to make his own choices now.

Grabbing the railing, he takes the stairs two by two. Walking down the hallway, he hears snoring from one of the rooms, and wonders how to get her attention without waking the others. Standing outside her door, he considers simply entering the room, but decides they aren't at that stage of any kind of a relationship yet.

Pulling his phone from his pocket, he types *KaKaw*.

He figures it must be close enough to the bird sound her family makes when they're communicating. Rayaan smiles when he hears her giggle. His grin grows even more when he hears a bump and 'oof' whispered quietly.

She's rubbing her knee when she opens the door, and grabs his shirt, pulling him into the lamp-lit room.

"You're accident prone," he chuckles, reaching down to

rub the offended area. "Do I need to bubble wrap everything in my house before you visit?"

Andi wraps her arms around his neck. "I don't know when this invitation is for, but why would that be necessary?"

She lifts on her tiptoes to kiss him, her lips warm and pliable, and he presses her close to him. He likes the way her soft curves mold against his hardened muscles. She fills in the gaps he has in his life. His heart beats faster as she deepens the kiss, using the back of her arm to pull him down to her height.

Slowly, she releases her hold, her eyes dreamy when she opens them. She takes his hand, and says, "We'll stay in bed the whole time I'm there, so it seems pointless."

He could take that challenge. Rayaan kicks off his house slippers, leaving them by the door. "Really? In bed the whole time?" he teases, following her to the bed in her guest room.

"Um, yeah. We can eat there too, it's not a problem." She plops down, bouncing on the mattress.

Crawling over her, and pushing her backwards, Rayaan purrs, "I can think of things I like to eat in bed."

Flat against the cozy floral blanket, Andi breathes out slowly. Searching his eyes, she winds her fingers through the silver chain hitting her chest. She bites her lip. "You sound so possessive."

Hovering over her, he shifts his weight to one hand, and

pushes back her hair with the other. "Do you always bite your lip like that?"

She giggles, raising her hips up to meet his. "Like what?"

Rayaan caresses over her forehead. "You have no clue how sexy you are, do you?"

She blushes as he lowers his weight on her. She says quietly, "I'm a lot of things, but I don't know if sexy is one of them."

His heart softens for the sweet girl, the beautiful woman that doesn't know how amazing she is. If he has to spend the rest of his life telling her, so be it. Rayaan kisses the soft spot between her shaped eyebrows and trails tiny kisses down her nose between each word he speaks. "Smart, funny, cute as hell, clumsy, and sexy."

Placing her hands on his hips, Andi pulls him down to rest between her legs, raising one to wrap around him. His lips fall to hers, sucking in her breath as he creates a seal over her mouth. She moans quietly, beginning to writhe beneath him. Tugging on his loose-fitting t-shirt, she finds his skin, and her hands are warm and soft as she caresses his lower back.

Breaking the kiss, he pecks her mouth again, his beard brushing against her cheek.

"You taste like sin on my lips," she says reverently.

He grins, and he can feel the happiness reaching his eyes, causing the delicate skin around them to crinkle. "Always a writer, finding the perfect words."

"Do it again," she says.

Her wish is his command, and they roll around on the bed for seemingly hours, kissing and fondling, testing each other out. Most of their clothing lies in a pile next to the bed. His lips feel bruised and he's sure he has tiny scratches on his back from her nails. Given the hickey in the crook of her neck, he's hoping she has something to wear the next day to hide it.

Andi playfully whines when he rolls away from her, climbing off the bed to go to the restroom.

When he returns to the room, he watches her quietly. She's on the bed, half asleep, clad only in her underwear, a pretty polka dotted set. Seeing her open suitcase on the floor, he wonders if she really does have pink panties.

Sensing his presence, she rolls over and smiles warmly. "Come back to bed."

He shakes his head. "No, you come here."

With a look of curiosity, she rises from the bed, and joins him at the door.

"That shower isn't big enough for both of us, King," she says, tapping his chest.

"Who said anything about a shower?"

Scented bubbles reach his nose, and he ushers her inside, to the surprise he has waiting for her. "Have a seat."

The small room has a barstool, which he's moved closer to the counter. On the floor below, he's filled the bin for wet swimwear with soapy water.

Andi crooks her head at him. "What are you up to?"

She settles herself on the wooden seat and leans her elbow on the counter.

"You've walked around this house barefoot all evening. You can't climb in bed like that."

Rayaan lowers himself to sit on the floor. His bare back hits the cool glass shower door and he jumps. "Shit that's cold!" he hisses, looking at the offending fixture. She giggles, watching him intently. He can almost imagine the wheels in her head turning and wonders what she's thinking.

Shaking his head, he lifts one of her feet from the floor and places it in the warm soapy water.

"Are you really going to wash my feet?" Andi asks.

Rayaan repeats the same with her other foot and swirls the bubbles around. Andi gently kicks out a foot, splashing water on his knees, getting his shorts damp.

"You got me wet!" he whispers, not wanting to wake the household.

She taps his knee with her toe before placing it back in the water. "Well now we're even," she says slyly.

Realization dawning on him, his jaw drops slowly. "Oh, really," he growls, brushing his hand over his beard. "You are trouble, Red."

She lifts her eyebrows and blows him a kiss.

Andi scoots forward on the seat and spreads her legs. The wet spot on her panties is proof of her words. Reaching for one of her feet, he begins massaging it in his hands, and pitches forward, pressing a kiss to her thick thigh. She runs her hand over his slick-backed hair and plays with the stray pieces from his man-bun. He flicks his tongue over her flesh, and she whimpers as his hands squeeze her feet with more pressure.

From his kneeling position, he looks up at her. "As a kid, I learned washing another's feet is a symbol of respect, of care. It's believed when you wash someone's feet, as your hands contact the other person, a circle of energy connects you together. It's supposed to fill you with good thoughts, and positive energy." He wraps his hand around her ankle, giving it a squeeze. His voice is low, full of emotion. "That's how I want to be connected to you, Andrea. With positive energy."

"Oh," she gasps, barely able to make words. "Yeah, okay."

Rayaan can smell her growing arousal and is heady from the scent. His mouth and beard roam her delicious thighs, biting and kissing, as he quickly massages and washes the other foot.

"Take me to bed," she demands.

Winking at her, he reaches for the towel on the counter behind her and begins to dry her feet. "Anything for *meri jaan*."

While he finishes tending to her wash up, she traces her fingers over the corded muscles in his shoulders. "What about your feet?"

"House slippers. Not dirty," Rayaan shrugs, pushing the water container aside. Standing quickly, to be sure, he wipes his feet on the discarded towel.

Andi rests both elbows back on the counter, pushing her chest out in front of her. "How am I gonna get to the bed without getting them dirty again?"

Rayaan chuckles at her sass, adding it to the list of qualities he adores about her.

He pulls her hair forward, over her shoulder, dragging his hand down through the curls and caressing the tops of her breasts. "I'll carry you."

"Really?" she asks, uncertainty filling her voice.

"Are you taunting me, woman? Implying I'm not up to the task?" He bites his tongue before he spews out his gym stats, instinctively knowing that would not be okay in this setting.

Bending slightly, he reaches under her on the bench and lifts under her rounded ass, tossing her over his shoulder as though she weighs nothing. She lets out a squeal and clasps

her hands over her mouth, not wanting to wake anyone.
Rayaan turns sideways, admiring their figures in the mirror.
He smacks her ass, then lovingly caresses his hand over it.
"This is a whole snack right here, and I intend to taste and
savor every bite."

He turns his head and bites her thigh, resting on his
shoulder.

She giggles, and he knows her blush is hidden in the blood
rushing to her head.

She smacks his ass in return, and he carries her to the bed,
unceremoniously dumping her on it. It skids slightly on the
hardwood floor, making him aware they'll need to be
conscientious of their movements. Her eyes open wide as he
lifts one corner of the bed, scooting a rug under it.

"That should work," he announces, not sure at all. He
can't hear other noises in the house, so he's pretty confident
they won't be discovered. Yet it adds another layer of
excitement to their secret tryst. Rayaan wonders how much
longer they'll be able to keep their affair hidden from their
families.

Andi rises onto her elbows. "Did you seriously just lift this
up, with me in it?" She asks incredulously.

He chuckles nervously, rubbing his hand behind his neck.
"Yeah, I did."

"Shit," she hisses out, crooking her finger and motioning

him towards her. "That is sexy as fuck!"

Pulling off his shorts quickly, he climbs up on the bed, positioning himself between her knees.

"You always go commando?" she asks, as he grabs her ankles and pulls her towards him, sliding her down the bed. "Ohhh," she says in awe, her mouth frozen into a silent 'o.'

His answer is lost when he reaches up and tugs down her polka-dot panties, diving between her legs. He kisses her tenderly, licking over a mark he left on her thigh moments ago. Heady with her scent, he keeps his focus, wanting to love every inch of her body.

Scraping her nails over the back of his neck, Andi tugs at his ponytail. "What did you say?"

Rayaan nips along her outer hip bone, caressing her stretchmarks lovingly, before lifting his head to look at her. "I was in a hurry to pack. Forgot them."

Andi's laughter fills the room, and he reaches up to put his large hand over her mouth. "Shh, you'll wake everyone."

"Oh my God, that's amazing," she finally spits out between her gasps for air. "I don't believe you!"

"You know what else is amazing?" Rayaan rolls to his side, rubbing his hand over her belly. He tilts his head to kiss her belly button before dragging his touch lower. He shifts slightly to be able to see her face. Her beautiful, sun-kissed, freckled face. "The look in your eyes when I touch you right here."

Already hot and wet from the bathroom, he reaches for her swollen clit, caressing around it, watching her head tilt back.

"Your eyes get dark and stormy, and I can see your pulse flutter." Beautiful. She begins to writhe beside him, opening her legs so he has more space for his large hand. He slides it back, pushing a finger inside, while continuing to stimulate her most sensitive spot. "And your breathing hitches, and you make tiny little sounds; happy sounds."

"Uh-huh," she says quietly, moaning the word, tapping her knee against his thigh.

"Are you happy, *meri jaan*?" he asks, penetrating deeper, her juices soaking his hand.

Pulling up on the chain around his neck, she brings his mouth to hers. Closer to the edge, her noises change, captured between their lips. She pulls off his bottom lip, whispering. "So happy." Andi rolls onto her side, throwing her leg over his hip. His cock presses against her thigh and Rayaan can't wait to sink into her. "Make me happier."

Lifting her head, she licks across his tattoo, dragging her teeth over his collarbone. Ignoring the ticklish light touch, Rayaan pulls away his hand, and pitches her over onto her back. Hovering above her, he lines himself up with her entrance. Dragging his weight through her slick, he leans forward, keeping his eyes on hers. His mouth hangs open, tasting her scent in the air. Remembering the previous night, he asks, "Where do you want me to come this time?"

Caressing her hand across his cheek, she replies, "In me. I want all of you, King."

With a low growl, Rayaan heeds her directive. He sinks into her with a deliberate slowness, feeling like his heart will explode. Andi's heat is almost too much to take. Finally stretched, he rows again and again, reveling in her hands all over his body. She instinctively knows he craves her touch, as she brushes down his nose, across his jaw, gripping his shoulders. As her senses heighten, she thrashes her head from side to side, stopping when he holds himself up with one hand, and uses the other to caress her cheek.

"I want your eyes on me. I want you to know it's me who makes you happy."

Andi nods, biting her lip. How can she be so cute and sexy as hell at the same time? Her curls are a mess, her shoulders are sunburned and marked by his mouth, and she takes every inch of him with each long stroke he delivers. She grabs his wrist, holding his hand to her cheek, tracing her fingers over the veins there. She turns her head to kiss his palm, shifting to bite gently near his thumb on the heel of his hand.

Knowing Andi can take it, he drops his weight onto her, moving his arms to cage them around her head. He plays with her curls as he stares into her eyes, continuing to pummel into her. Her mewling sounds heighten when he alters his rhythm, and she shifts her leg higher across his back. There's still so much to learn about her, but Rayaan's sure she's reaching her high.

He nuzzles his nose against her cheek, tenderly nipping the soft flesh. "Are you ready to come for me?" he asks, knowing her answer as she grabs his hip, pushing him down.

Wordlessly, he continues to saw into her until she falls over the edge, her walls gripping him and pulling from him his own release.

Chapter Twenty

Opening the door slowly, Rayaan peeks out the gap. Sunlight filters the hall and sounds are coming from another room down the hallway. He's sure he can make a run for the kitchen without being discovered. Keeping the handle controlled by his hand, he steps out and quietly closes the door. Turning quickly to make his exit, he sees Arin standing at the head of the stairs.

He holds in his profanities, and strolls down the hall, as if he hadn't just been caught sneaking out of Andi's room.

Arin walks towards his room, and brushes against him, his shoulder jabbing into Rayaan's bicep. "Nice night, *bhai?*"

Rayaan continues his stride, his blood starting to boil.

He makes it halfway down the stairs before his brother grabs his arm. "I asked you a question!"

Rayaan shrugs him off and jogs down the remaining stairs to the bottom before turning to look up. "I could ask you the same, sneaking out of here after midnight. Late night rehearsal with the actress? Clothes optional? Just slinking home?"

Arin dips his head sheepishly but makes no admissions. "Were you with Andi last night?"

Rayaan closes his eyes, silently praying the rest of the

house is still asleep. "That's really none of your business, is it?"

He steps out onto the patio quickly, taking what is sure to be an argument outside.

The speed with which Arin descends the remaining stairs is frightening, and the door nearly flies off the hinges when he steps out.

"The fuck it isn't!" he yells.

"*Bhai,*" Rayaan returns, his voice dripping with venom, "You lost your chance."

Taking a fighting stance. Arin yells, "That doesn't mean you step in and take over."

Rayaan moves out of the shadows of the trees and feels the morning sun on his shoulders. There's still a chill in the spring air, but it's not enough to calm his anger. "You don't deserve her, and you know it," he hisses.

"You piece of shit!"

Hearing yelling and more words of anger from the back patio, followed by a splash, Andi rushes down the stairs.

Seeing Arin spluttering in the pool, she opens the door quickly.

He yells, "Wait till she finds out you were the one who broke her heart, and it wasn't my fault."

"I didn't tell you to leave her, you dipshit. You did that on your own."

She steps from under the trees, seeing Rayaan lurking over Arin, his shoulders hunched and full of rage.

Confused, Andi confronts them. "Are you fighting over me?"

When Rayaan doesn't answer, she steps closer, and he relaxes a little. His eyes are full of sorrow when he turns to her. "What is he talking about?" she asks quietly.

Out of the pool, Arin shakes off the water. "It was him. He made me break up with you."

Dazed, Andi steps back. "What? Why would you-"

"-He wanted you. Said I wasn't good enough for you-"

"-You weren't; still aren't," Rayaan says, hands fisted at his sides.

Arin lurches toward him, hand raised, but Andi steps between them, holding him back.

"Is that true?" Andi asks, looking up into Rayaan's dark, brooding eyes.

Rayaan swallows and brushes his lip with his thumb. He nods. "Yeah. We'd argued for months about it, actually. I told him if he couldn't be good to you, he should break things off before it got too serious."

Andi steps back, feeling as if cold water had been splashed on her. "You what?"

As if her icy rage was palpable, Rayaan crosses his arms in front of himself nervously. "I told him if he was using you as his rebound, he shouldn't take advantage of you."

She can barely hear his words with her heart beating in her throat. Her stomach churns and she wants to throw up.

Rayaan continues, "I told him to let you down easy, not to run off to the other side of the country."

She looks at Arin. "And you just did it?"

Arin tilts his head up. "He was right. I was so lost. I was just going to hurt you and-"

"So, you both made this decision for me, and just walked away?" Her rage begins to build, the little hairs on her arms standing up.

Pushing back his wet hair, Arin says, "I told him if I couldn't have you, he shouldn't either. That we both needed to walk away, fair and square."

"Fair?" she screeches. "How was that fair to me?"

Rayaan steps forward, bravely standing in front of her. "It wasn't about you, Andi. It was about us as brothers, being able to keep our relationship as family."

He reaches his hand out to her, but she shakes it away.

"'Wasn't about me?' I was there- it affected me- how could it not have been about me too? I don't understand." She inhales deeply, trying to make sense of all the pain of the missed years. "You both just walked away? Left me?"

She whirls around. "You moved across the goddamn country instead of being honest with me." Andi points at Arin, accusingly. "Leaving me to drift aimlessly through endless unmeaningful relationships."

"And you?" She spins towards Rayaan, aiming her finger at him with fire in her eyes. "You married somebody you didn't love. And caused me to lose you both as my best friends; leaving me to think I'd done something wrong?"

Through her anger, Andi's eyes well with tears, years of pain written across her face. She gasps for air, waiting for one of them to speak.

Dipping his head, barely able to look at her pain, Rayaan mumbles, "We could have done things differently."

Andi throws her hands up in disgust. "I can't believe either of you. Knowing this is worse than what I've suffered all these years. I don't want to see either of you."

Turning on her heels, she leaves them to each other, bile rising in her throat.

Sliding open the kitchen door, she realizes they've had an audience. Prisha, Neal, and her mother busy themselves, trying not to look like they'd been eavesdropping.

"Auntie, did you know?" she asks slowly, licking her lip.

With guilt, Prisha nods her head. "But not at first."

"You did?" Neal asks in disbelief. Prisha shushes him as Andi moves on through the room.

Collecting her shoes at the bottom of the front steps, her mother follows, patting her back. "Oh, darling, I'm so sorry."

With tears in her eyes, Andi melts into her mother's arms.

"How could they do that to me? Just leave me?"

"I know, I know," her mother murmurs, rubbing her back.

Leaning back in her arms, Andi's tear-stained face looks at her mother with such renewed heartache. "Did you know?"

Sarah shakes her head. "Prisha always said the boys had a falling out… I suspected Rayaan was sweet on you- he was always so protective- but I never imagined it went this far."

Wiping away her tears, Andi hiccups. "Only I would be stupid enough to fall for two brothers."

"What's all the noise?" Logan asks from the upper landing.

Sarah waves him away, so he disappears.

"What are you going to do, darling?" Sarah asks, squeezing her daughter's arm.

Scratching her eyebrow, Andi sighs. "I don't know. Go back to my lonely life in Chicago, I guess."

The next day, while checking out of the hotel, Andi sees Rayaan sitting in one of the lobby chairs. He's spinning one of his rings around and around with his thumb, watching her intently. Her heart cracks again, but neither makes a move to

265

reach out to the other.

Walking out the door, she leaves the Collins brothers behind.

Chapter Twenty-One

Spinning in her office chair, Janessa reads aloud, "*Let me start this article by stating Arin Collins and I were high school enemies and college sweethearts. I didn't want to write this piece, not because of pain, or heartache, but because I hate the idea of social media influencers. But by going home again, reconnecting with Arin and old friends, I realized everyone influences something, everyone grows up; everyone deserves love. I mean it from the bottom of my heart when I say, even assholes like Arin Collins.*"

Andi rolls her eyes, "Are you finished now? I know what I wrote."

Janessa drops the magazine on her desk and thumps it. "Babe, that's some of your best writing. You really told it like it is, let the readers see the real Arin." She bounces her head. "The family angle was good."

Unfazed by her friend's praise, Andi leans back on the couch. "Just because I was pissed, I wasn't going to turn in shit writing. I'm not about to tank my career over him. The asshole."

Janessa snorts. "The asshole was out again with Brooklyn Nash last night. Some red carpet premiere. Did you see it?"

Huffing out, Andi picks at some lint on the pillow next to her. "Yay, I introduced them," she facetiously cheers.

"They've become quite the Hollywood 'It' couple."

"Yes, I know. I heard you got the magazine and my name mentioned in the recent TMZ story, about how I introduced them."

Janessa reaches for her coffee. "You say it like I threw you under the bus. You said I could leak that info."

"I know I did, and honestly, I am happy for him." She thumps her head back, hitting the wall. "I'm just sick of hearing about how the Internet's boyfriend found love."

"Why does she have to be tall and leggy?" Janessa muses.

Andi looks down at her thick thighs, then stares across the room at her leggy friend. "Look who's talking."

Janessa giggles. "Sorry." Her stony eyes pierce her friend. "It's not him you're upset about though, is it? His brother still didn't call?"

Andi stares up at the ceiling. To get Janessa, and her mother, off her back, she'd been saying Rayaan had not reached out to her.

They didn't need to know he'd called and left messages, and emailed, at least once a day, for the last four weeks. Or that her heart was broken in half…

Before she can answer, there's a knock on the office door. Martha peeks her head in and announces, "There's a delivery for Ms. Jennings."

Janessa waves her in, her eyes growing wide.

Andi sits up when Martha places the most beautiful arrangement of flowers in front of her. Spring flowers- all her favorites! Lilies, daffodils, tulips, hyacinths, and hydrangeas. The display gives off a heady aroma, and she inhales deeply.

"Beautiful," she whispers, breathing deeply again, and thanking Martha.

Janessa hits her hand on the desk, impatiently. "Well, aren't you going to open the card?"

Martha leaves the room, closing the door behind her.

Reaching for her laptop, Andi stands. "No. Only one person would send me those."

Janessa walks around the edge of her desk. "Fine, I'm curious." She gently caresses one of the tulip petals. "Can I read it?"

"Have at it." Andi shrugs. Her cold tone sounds foreign to her ears. "You can keep the flowers too."

Walking to the desk, she collects the notes for her next assignment.

Janessa reads the card aloud. *"MJ- I wanted to personally thank you for the coverage your magazine presented about Arin. The writing and storytelling was superb, as always. King"*

Andi stands frozen at the door.

"King, I get. His name sounds like 'reign,' but what's with the initials, MJ?" Janessa curiously asks.

Tears welling in her eyes, Andi whispers, "It's an

abbreviation for a phrase, in Hindi."

Leaving the room, she closes the door behind her. With no witnesses on a late Friday afternoon, she collapses against it, letting the tears freely flow.

Chapter Twenty-Two

Sitting on her bedroom floor, surrounded by piles of clean clothes, Andi knocks her head against the dresser.

She sighs heavily.

Nothing feels the same. Having Arin and Rayaan back in her life, even for just a quick weekend had brought her more joy in those fleeting hours than any experience of the last few months.

She missed them.

But she wasn't ready to forgive them yet.

Pulling her phone from the pocket of her favorite sweatpants, she begins to aimlessly scroll. Again.

Anything to keep her mind off 'the boys.'

"I don't wanna know what's going on in DC," she says aloud. Clicking out of that app, she decides to check if any good movies are playing later in the afternoon.

Distracted by a video about easy hair braids for the upcoming warmer weather, she's sucked into her phone screen for over an hour, without even realizing it.

Startled when the buzzer on her front door sounds, she pulls herself up. The laundry she had started to put away before her thoughts had begun eating at her would have to wait. A quick glance in the mirror tells her she's suitable for presentation to the morning intruder. The door buzzes again, and she slides on her slippers as she makes her way to the living room.

Looking through the peep hole, she's surprised to find Prisha Collins standing outside her door.

"Auntie!" Andi exclaims. Clicking the lock and opening the door, she asks, "What are you doing here?"

The regal woman steps inside, patting her on the shoulder and kissing her cheek. "I'm in town for a few days. My best friend from college needs help with her daughter's wedding." Andi returns the kisses. "And with you not answering anyone's phone calls, I felt a visit was in order."

Andi rubs her lips together, suddenly feeling called out, like a punished child.

"Auntie, I can explain-"

"-I just walked in, *beti*. Let's take a moment to breathe." Prisha takes off her shoes, leaving them by the door. "I know you weren't expecting me."

With a few short steps, she places her coat over the back of the couch. Her eyes survey the room.

Andi's eyes follow hers, and she sees the place through the woman's view. Cozy, with minimalist lines, old magazines and newspapers scattered over the coffee table and couch. The room shows little vibrancy of the occupant.

It demonstrates how little she's cared about anything since

returning from the lake trip.

She raises on her toes, fidgeting from the perceived examination. "I've only been here a few months; I haven't really had time to make it my own yet."

Prisha nods, making a noncommittal clicking sound in the back of her throat. She steps towards the fireplace mantel, drawn to the one spot of color and personality in the room. She lifts one of the colorful, chunky frames and examines the photo before putting it back.

"Would you like some tea?" Andi asks as Prisha picks up another photo.

Moving at the quiet flick of Prisha's hand, Andi walks into the open room kitchen. Knowing there's more to the reason for the unexpected visit, Andi smiles wanly. Sensing Prisha has come to deliver an important message, she reaches under the counter for the tea kettle. She spins around to the pantry, taking out some cookies she bought the day before at the market.

Without even looking up, she knows the photo Prisha is looking at. From the corner of her eye, as she fills the kettle with water, she watches her Auntie lift the two post-it notes on the frame. Without being prompted, Andi offers, "It's one of my favorite photos."

Prisha makes a humming sound.

"You looked so beautiful that night," Prisha says, turning

273

towards the kitchen.

Andi raises a questionable eyebrow. Her hair had frizzed slightly in the humid air, but the curls had framed her face. The green dress had taken the two mothers weeks to help her find, but it had been a perfect fit. She hadn't felt like a princess for her Senior Prom, but magically, for a few hours, she hadn't felt like an ugly duckling either.

The gas stove clicks to life before the flame bursts up to heat the bottom of the red kettle. Andi turns the handle, centering it on the burner.

"Me? I don't know about that. But the emerald green was stunning."

Prisha scoffs. "Why do you have it like this?" She flicks the corner of one of the papers.

Andi knows the image like she knows the back of her hand.

That night, Arin's teammates and their dates had descended on the Collins' lawn, gathering to take photos under the beautiful willow tree at the corner of the house. Her date had been late, but Andi had been included. The picture on their front porch, with both Collins boys squeezing her in a hug, had been placed into different frames over the years, following her from place to place, and always on display.

"The post-its?" Andi asks, taking the water off the stove.

She shrugs as Prisha sits at the small kitchen table, still clutching the frame. "Just cuz I'm mad at them now doesn't mean I always will be." Dropping tea bags into the two mugs on the counter, she says quietly, "It usually lifts me up when I've had a bad day."

Prisha smiles, her eyes filled with a sad warmth, and removes the purple post-it. She reveals Rayaan, his arm wrapped around Andi's waist, and places the paper on the table. "You know, he wasn't supposed to be home that weekend?"

Andi furrows her brow. "He wasn't? I thought he was the assigned photographer?"

Prisha takes the plate of cookies from Andi's outstretched arm and puts them on the table. "It was a week before his finals; he had so much to do. But he drove six hours; he came home for you."

Andi places the hot mugs on the table. "Why would he do that?"

Prisha purses her mouth, uncovering Arin when she lifts the remaining blue paper. His arm is loosely hanging around her shoulder, but his head is rested against hers. "Arin was worried about you."

Andi blows out a puff of air, adding milk to her tea. "Why would he be worried?"

Prisha sets the photo up on the table so they can both see

it. "Arin explained there had been a rumor your date might stand you up." She adds sugar to her mug. "Neil had told Rayaan to stay at school. That there would be nothing he could do, but he'd skipped class, and came home anyway."

"Neil took away the car? I remember something about that." Andi tries to recall the memory, but so much had passed since then.

"He said if Rayaan couldn't be responsible and not waste time or money, he wasn't worthy of the car." She lays her spoon down and looks Andi in the eyes. "Rayaan said it wasn't a waste of his time. That it was worth every second to see you in that billowy green dress."

Andi's brain can't process Prisha's words fast enough. "Auntie, I don't understand-"

"Do you remember the hole in the kitchen wall?"

Andi giggles. "When they were fighting over a plate of bacon? And it took Uncle Neil forever to patch it up, so instead you put a bookshelf in front of it?"

Prisha lays her hands flat on the table. "*Beti,* they weren't fighting over bacon."

Slowly, comprehension dawns on Andi. "Me? They fought over me?" She whispers in disbelief.

"It wasn't the first time, Andrea. But it all had been light, good-natured brotherly tussles… but this? This was different." She pauses to sip her tea. "The 'Bacon War,'" she says in air quotes, as the event had come to be known, "was two adult men, battling for the same woman. It was tearing them apart, and literally destroying my house."

Prisha stares at the photo on the table and sighs. "I did it, *beti*. I said neither could have you."

"What?" Andi's mouth drops open. "Why, Auntie?"

Dabbing at the tears in her eyes, Prisha explains. "Because you could bounce back, dear, and move on from your crushes, but they would never again have another brother. For the peace of the family, they had to let you go." She clears her throat. "And for a long time, you all had gone your separate ways, only running into each other at Christmas gatherings. But then, somehow you and Arin got together. And for a while, it seemed to work. Rayaan was with Gemma and showed no remaining interest in you."

"He didn't love her," Andi asserts quietly, running her fingertip around the edge of the mug. Her thoughts tumble, trying to process her Auntie's words and to keep the confession going.

Prisha bristles. "No. No he didn't, and she probably didn't love him either. He looked good on paper, and that's all that mattered to her."

"On the ski trip, I remember they were pretty strained."

Reaching across the table, Prisha pats the back of Andi's hand. "They weren't the only ones, dear. It was obvious you and Arin were both trying to be something for each other, but not being true to yourselves. You had different dreams and goals." She clears her throat. "But you were so hung up on finally getting your dream."

Andi's mouth opens in rebuttal, but she has nothing to say to her Auntie's honesty.

"You would have sacrificed all your career plans to have the life- the boy- you hoped for from the time you were fourteen. Think of all the travels and experiences you'd never have had?" Lifting her mug, Prisha blows over the top of the cup. "You'd have to ask Arin why he left, but it was the best thing he could have done for you."

Tears running down her cheeks, Andi gulps. "It took a long time to learn, but I know that. I know that now." Looking up at the ceiling, she sniffs, before noisily exhaling.

"I only know bits and pieces of what transpired after the ski trip, what the boys have shared with me." Prisha shakes her head. "But it split them apart, for the longest time. They weren't brothers anymore. They played the roles when they needed to, but it took a long time to patch things up." Her ring hits the side of the cup, the diamond screeching across the ceramic. "But, *beti*, that was not your fault; not your doing, and that was all on them."

Prisha abandons her tea, and rises, walking around the table to comfort Andi. Bending, she wraps her arms around

Andi, who instantly feels comforted. Whispering promises of better days, she pushes Andi's hair back from her face as they both release pent up tears.

When the tears turn to tiny hiccups and small titters of laughter, Andi chokes out, "Ugh, boys are stupid! Why did I let them do this to me?"

Prisha hands her a tissue. "Because they're handsome, and hearts want foolish things, my *beti.*"

Andi dabs at her runny nose. Lifting her head, she groans. "I thought I was done crying over those two!" She shakes her hair. "Enough." She sniffles again. "Enough. Dammit, they're both so pig-headed they won't resolve this until I step in." She stands up from the table, helping Prisha to rise as well. "But they can stew for another day or two. Let's get out of here for a while, huh?"

Prisha nods in agreement, setting the mugs in the sink. "I think first, you need to change out of those 'heart broken, depression' clothes you have on." She smiles warmly. "Let's go see what's in your closet!"

Chapter Twenty-Three

A few days after Prisha's visit, Andi decides to check out another restaurant Janessa had recommended to her as a new resident of Chicago. The meal was fabulous, and she contemplates dessert. Leaning back in her seat, she enjoys the night view of the city. The buildings slowly begin to light up as the sun sets, and streaks of orange, purple and pink touch the water of Lake Michigan. Her phone buzzes, and she picks it up, reading a text from her mother. She shakes it off, and quickly types back that she's out for the evening and will call later. That's the nice thing about having a two-hour time difference. She can call later, as her mother's settling in for the night, and they won't feel rushed to chat.

"Andrea? Andrea Jennings?"

She looks up at the use of her full name. Only people from her time in DC call her that. Andi's surprised to see Jonathan Stratford moving toward her. She hides her giggle, remembering on the drive to the float trip, Arin had said it sounded like a dickhead politician's name.

As he stretches out his arms, she quickly stands, wanting to avoid an awkward seated hug.

He holds her a little longer than necessary and she pats his arm, stepping back to break the embrace.

"That suit brings out the blue in your eyes," she says, remembering they were his best feature. His blonde hair is coiffed and in place, his nose a little too pointy, but his handsome crooked smile erases the flaws. Flaws she only noticed after his red flags had become more visible. "What are you doing in the city?"

"Well, I definitely wasn't expecting to run into my lost love, that's for sure!" Jonathan exclaims a little too loudly. "I thought you were working in St. Louis."

She shakes her head no. "My new magazine is based here," Andi explains.

"Mind if I join you?" he kindly asks, directing her to sit back in her chair.

She murmurs a polite yes, and he pushes her chair up to the table.

Jonathan points to her empty glass. "Another drink?"

Before she can even respond, he waves over a waiter and orders her a refill and a scotch and water for himself.

Her phone buzzes again. "Sorry, I was answering some work messages before you came over. Gimme just a minute."

Jonathan nods and admires his reflection in the window as she texts her mother quickly. *If I don't text you in an hour, you MUST call me. I'm OK, will explain later*

Andi turns the phone, face down, and pushes it up under her clutch. Accepting her refill, she turns down the waiter's offer of dessert, sending the message she doesn't want this visit to last any longer than necessary. "Chicago. Why are you here?" She repeats, a little more forcibly than she intended.

Ignoring her icy vibes, Jonathan leans his arms on the table, taking her into his confidence. "Dad's thinking about running for president. We're here to meet with some union members, and local politicians to test the waters."

Andi's journalistic senses kick in. "He's going against party. He's not in line with the correct beliefs anymore."

Jonathan chuckles hollowly. "I figured he wouldn't have your vote. He's going Independent; he doesn't agree with the other side either. It's how he figures he can make the most change."

"He's had his Senate seat for several terms-"

Jonathan puffs up proudly. "I'm going to run, to take over his seat."

Andi sighs. "Why am I beginning to think this isn't a chance meeting?"

Jonathan hangs his head sheepishly. "Ok, so I knew The Edge was based out of Chicago. But this is purely coincidental." He taps the table. "I was going to call you. No one understands the political game like you do. Your talents are wasted, interviewing actors and social media stars."

Andi raises her eyebrows. She can't disagree with that.

"I want you to manage my press."

She nearly chokes on her drink. Sputtering, she wipes her mouth. "We broke up, and don't see eye to eye. Why do you think I'd want that?"

"I thought you'd want back in the political world. With your knowledge and connections, it could be a real asset to my campaign."

Narrowing her eyes, she asks pointedly, "How did you know where I'd be?"

Leaning back in the chair, he holds out his hands. "This was a pure fluke. Coincidental, like I said. I had dinner with some suits earlier. Came into this room to check out the view; sit at the bar awhile." He takes a long sip from his glass. "What do you mean we don't see eye to eye?"

Like a freight train, memories speed through her mind. All the reasons why Jonathan was wrong for her. But somehow at the end of the lightning-fast montage in her mind, Rayaan appears.

Andi swallows hard. "Do you remember when we vacationed in the Caribbean, and you told me to change my swimsuit- you didn't think I should wear a two piece? That's example one. Two would be how you always talked me out of ordering cheesecake. And three is the fact you had me twisted up enough in your world that I let you get away with it. Every damn time." She cuts her hand across her throat. "I'm done. I'm not going back to that again. I will find someone who appreciates me."

Jonathan clenches his jaw, exasperation on his face. "I don't want to get back together with you, Andrea-"

"No, you just want to use me, to get what you want. Like last time, but it was too late for me to see it." She rises from the table, grabbing her phone and clutch, and signals the waiter. "If you want me to interview you for *The Edge*, I will. Your father too, but I'll be honest and fair." Looking at the total on her bill, she discreetly pulls out some cash and stuffs it in the folder. "That's enough for his drink too. Keep the change."

Grabbing her arm, Jonathan pulls her towards him. She looks down at him in his seated position and shakes off his hand. "I'm moving forward now, Jonathan. Working with you would be a step back." She scratches between her eyebrows. "Good luck to you and your father. I mean that sincerely. It will be a fun battle to watch, but I don't want to be a part of it." Andi looks out the window, the city dark now. "Enjoy the view."

She turns and walks away, leaving a potential disaster behind her.

Sliding into the backseat of a cab, Andi sighs with relief. She's always been bull-headed when it comes to her work, but a bit of a push-over in her personal life. She feels proud of herself for standing up against Jonathan. Accepting his offer would have been a regression, and the last place she needed to end up was in his bed.

"Time to move forward," she mutters.

The cab driver catches her eye in the rear-view mirror.

"Sorry, talking to myself," she mumbles.

Flipping over the flowered phone case, she types out a quick message to her mother. *I rescued myself. I'll be home in 20 minutes, and I'll call.*

Seconds later her mother replies with a smiling emoji.

Thinking over her dinner, and her interruption, she realizes she didn't have dessert. Pulling up the app for a bakery in her neighborhood that delivers cookies late, she places an order. She'll make it home just in time to meet the driver.

Andi leans her head against the window, watching the cityscapes whir by as the car weaves in and out of traffic. She envies the couples walking down the sidewalks, heading to dinners, movies, or home.

She knows exactly where to find that, but she's not ready to give up her stubborn stance yet.

Snuggled on the couch, her tabby cat Luna sniffs at the

small cookie crumb Andi has shared. She turns up her nose and hops down from the couch, running off to some unknown hiding place. "Alexa, music down," she commands, waiting for the noise level to drop.

Licking a smear of chocolate from her thumb, she taps open her phone and pulls up her mother's contact information. The phone barely rings before Sarah's soothing voice meets her ears.

"Why did you need me to rescue you? You haven't sent me a message like that in ages," Sarah starts.

Rolling her eyes, and picking apart a second cookie, Andi replays the run in with her ex-boyfriend.

"I never liked him," Sarah shares. "He didn't seem genuine. Sure, he had pretty smiles- all that dental work- but they never reached his eyes." Andi nods in agreement although her mother can't see her. "Find a man with laugh lines around his eyes," Sarah advises.

One particular face, with deep laugh lines etched in his tanned skin, fills her memory.

Andi waves her hand in front of her eyes, wiping it away like the mist of a ghost.

The women chat about their days, though the conversation is mostly repetition, as they've already talked several times during the week.

Andi scratches her head, sleepiness starting to creep in.

The cat jumps back onto the couch and begins pawing at the corner of her fluffy blanket. "Getting tired, Mom. I'm sure you didn't simply want to talk about the plant sale at the library this weekend," she chuckles. "What's up?"

There's a moment of silence.

Sarah sighs, and Andi braces herself for whatever may come.

"Have you talked to either of the boys since Prisha visited?"

Andi releases her breath.

"That's your big question that can't wait?"

"Prisha told me they're still not talking to each other, and I just wondered-"

Her mother continues to talk, but Andi doesn't take in her words. The extended weekend at the lake had been over a month ago. That was a long time for the brothers not to talk. But if Prisha's tale had been accurate, they had done it before. And they were just stubborn enough to do it again.

Andi's brow furrows.

A tiny voice in her head nags at her that she did the same thing.

"I know Prisha's at her wits end."

Andi gulps. "I don't know how I can help, Mom." She scratches the side of her nose, feeling uncomfortable. "I'm not ready to talk to them yet, either."

"I know. I know."

She can imagine her mother nodding.

After a moment of silence her mother asks, "I guess you didn't see Arin's video from yesterday?"

Andi reaches over to pet the cat, who snuggles into her hand. "I'm not paid to watch them anymore, so I don't have to."

"Huh, okay." Sarah is obviously bothered. "It was a good one. You should watch it."

Looking at the clock on the fireplace mantel, Andi says, "Sure, Mom. I'll get to it tomorrow. I need to go to sleep now. It's late here."

The women exchange wishes for good sleep and goodbyes before hanging up.

Scratching at the cat's ear, Andi says aloud, "Why does she do this to me?"

Feeling guilty, she swipes across the face of her phone, opening the social media app. She taps it closed before any posts appear.

"What could he say that's so damn important? Screw it."

Andi tosses the phone down, hitting the cat's tail. Luna sneers at her and yawns, putting her paw over her face.

Standing, the blanket moves with her, shifting the cat's position and she growls lowly.

"Grumpy pants," Andi says, reaching across to turn off

the lamp.

Taking the box of remaining cookies to the kitchen, she puts it in the pantry. Standing at the sink, she takes her nightly vitamins and tousles her ponytail in the reflection of the window.

The curiosity is starting to gnaw at her.

Moving to the bathroom, she washes her face and brushes her teeth.

Her phone flashes a message from her sister-in-law, saying '*HELLO? Call me,*' but she ignores it.

The app is right there, under the flashing message.

She sighs, glaring at herself in the mirror. "Fuck me," she whispers.

Leaning against the bathroom counter, she clicks open the app. A quick scroll takes her right to Arin's page, and she runs through a few reblogs to reach yesterday's date. Her finger hovers a moment before clicking 'play.' She turns up the volume.

The setting is different from other videos. It looks like Arin is sitting in a dark, deserted bar, although movement to the side of the screen could be a bartender. Her phone delays the sound, so she doesn't hear the first line. It's a skit featuring the friend persona. The two characters have been drinking, a collection of empty bottles on the bar.

"I don't know where I went wrong," whines the friend,

reaching up to push his ball cap back, making his eyes more visible.

The camera cuts to Arin, wearing a baseball jersey. His 'bro' character. "You forgot she was an independent woman, who could think for herself. She and I have been friends for a long time, and I forgot that too." He pauses, tapping his hand against the bar. "She expects the truth and works hard to get it." Arin takes another drink from the beer. "She doesn't always need to be protected."

The friend reappears, the baseball jersey hidden under a denim jacket. "How do I get her back? Tell her I'm sorry? She won't even answer my calls." He picks at the label of his bottle. "I'm miserable without her," he says quietly.

The camera swings around again, to Arin holding a bouquet of flowers that appeared from nowhere. "It's time for a grand gesture and tell her how you really feel." He pats his friend's arm, off camera, and Andi wonders at the camera work. "I've seen you two together. You're like…" His eyes look away and he swallows hard. His voice chokes. "Like magic. If two people are meant for one another, it's you two."

Not another word is said, but with some camera trick, the last shot of the short clip looks like the two men, both played by Arin, are hugging it out, clapping each other's back. The name Jennings- her name- is clearly visible on the back of the jersey in bold red print, with a giant number two.

Stumbling to bed, Andi watches the video three more times. Exhausted as hell, sleep eludes her, her mind racing with thoughts and memories.

Unable to find respite, she kicks her legs up, making a mess of the duvet and sheets. In the dark, she reaches for her phone. Pulling up the contact information, she quickly types out '*Why the number two?*

Not expecting an answer at the unholy hour, she flops over, punching her pillow before resting her head. Finally settled, she takes a deep breath, willing sleepiness to take over.

The phone buzzes, vibrating against her outstretched hand.

Rubbing her tired, dry eyes, she tries to read the words, bright green, lighting up the room.

He deserves a second chance

The phone buzzes again.

You awake? I'm gonna call

Before Andi can type a response, the phone rings in her hand. Swiping the lock, Arin's soft, raspy voice reaches her ears. "He deserves a second chance."

No 'hello.' No greeting of any kind.

Rolling onto her back, Andi asks petulantly, "Why?"

Staring up at the ceiling, she waits for his reply.

"Easy." She can almost picture him, with a casual shrug,

sitting on the tiny blue loveseat featured in his videos. "He realized your worth long before I did…" He sighs and she waits for more. "He's the better man."

Andi scoffs. "I guess I'm still confused. I thought at the lake you were aiming for a second chance?"

Arin chuckles softly. A warm, familiar sound. Damn all the butterflies it causes in her stomach. "I knew I wasn't getting that, pretty much from the start. When you decide to be icy, it's felt deep."

Andi noisily breathes out. She's not sure if that's meant as a dig or a compliment.

Arin continues. "But I could use you to get under Rayaan's skin. No matter how much we grow up, that's still my favorite hobby. I'm the loveable asshole, remember?" He references her words from the article she had written about him. He exhales. "I don't deserve you, Andi, but he does."

Her heart pounds, but she has to know- Ignoring the soft pleading in his voice, on his brother's behalf, Andi inquires, "Why did you leave? Tell me everything."

"Everything?" Arin guffaws. "That's a lot of shit under the bridge, Ands."

"No." The sound that escapes is a cross between a growl and an irritated giggle. "You don't get to call me by that nickname and think you can escape this. I want to know!" She can hear the rise in her voice, the irritation boiling in her veins.

"Shit," he hisses slowly. "I don't know. I can't remember all of it. We were young, and too serious, and it was all based around this idea we had about each other since we were kids. You were the cute, nerdy girl next door. I was the 'not quite bad boy' with a floppy curl on my forehead that got all the girls' attention. After a swim meet, I'd flirt with everyone at Dante's Pizzeria, and stay up all night reading history books."

Andi giggles at the truth to his view of himself.

"And I always had a soft spot for you, because you knew that about me. I didn't have to be anyone else around you. You were 'my Ands.'" He exhales and she hears his foot thump against something over the phone connection. "But you were also 'Red,' and *bhai* and I shared that friendship with you, and the camping trips and all the family stuff-"

"And those are all great memories, and I'm glad I had that with you both." Andi scratches across her forehead, almost to touch the instant replay of thoughts running through her mind.

"I can't rehash all the history, Andi." His words sound bitter, as though the same memories bring him sadness. "But I wasn't the only person to love you in that little white house with the amazing library, and tree swing in the backyard." He clears his throat. "Rayaan adored you but held back because he was older than us. You never saw it because you only had eyes for me."

The images in her mind change. Rayaan leaning in the doorway to the library, talking about a book. Rayaan pushing her in the swing. Rayaan sitting with her when she had her tonsils out. Teaching her to drive. Helping her with an assignment at a ski lodge. Dancing with her at her brother's wedding. Then the imaginary montage moves faster… Rayaan emerging from a pool. Helping her into the boat. Dancing at the club. Holding her close. Stepping towards her for their first kiss. Diving between her legs for a quick taste-

She gasps, her pulse racing. She grabs the neckline of her t-shirt and fans it against herself.

Trying her best to keep the emotion from her voice, she turns into the investigative journalist she is, and prepares for the hard-hitting question.

"Did you ever love me, or was I just a pawn in a game, a way to get back at your brother for some perceived wrong?"

"Ouch, damn you know how to get to the bottom of it, don't you?" Arin audibly gulps, the sound reverberating over the phone. His tongue clicks against his teeth. "Yes, yes, of course I loved you. That summer I came home, my heart was broken. And you were there to pick me up, like always-"

"- I'm not a consolation prize-"

"I know that, Andi." Arin presses on. "This is hard for me, dammit. Go easy. It's why I couldn't talk to you for

294

months after I left, because I knew how much you were hurting, and then I was ashamed, and I let us drift apart."

Andi sits up, reaching for the light on the bedside table. Scared to hear his confessions in the dark. Her heart pounds against her chest. She presses forward. "At the lake, that morning you were fighting, you said it wasn't your fault, that Rayaan made you break up with me. What the hell was that?"

Arin groans. "Shit, I need a drink for this. How do people sit so confidently when you interview them?" She hears his feet shuffling across the floor. For a split second she thinks of the uneaten cookies in her pantry, but decides she prefers the safety of her bedroom to hear this long-awaited confession. Hearing the metal click of a bottle cap bounce across a counter, she can almost feel the coldness going down her own throat. "I'll tell you my side of the story, and then you can corroborate with Ray, if you want."

Running her tongue across her teeth, Andi contemplates talking to him again. She's not ready for that. "Just talk. And I'm fully aware we should have had this conversation ages ago, but I was better at running from things then, rather than confronting them, when it came to my personal life."

Still, she pulls a pillow into her lap, and picks at the hem.

He blows out. "Have it your way." He puffs air from deep in his lungs. "I guess it was a few weeks after that ski trip- remember we were all there?" He ignores her murmur of acknowledgement and continues. "I came downstairs to check on you. You two looked a little too cozy, huddled over notes and your computer, and I got jealous- I'm not gonna lie. We were so close to graduation, I started thinking we should get married-"

"Fuck, what?" Andi asks. Was that a stab of loss or horror she felt in her chest?

Arin must have heard whatever the feeling was in her voice as astonishment, and replies, "Right? We both wanted different things, it probably never would have worked out, and we'd have hurt each other in the process. Anyway, he and I were having dinner one night, and there was probably a beer or two too many between us." He's quiet and she lets him stew in his thoughts. "We both said things we didn't mean, although I'm pretty sure I was honest about Gemma. That girl was trouble. He started in about how I wasn't right for you, and that's when I dug my heels in. I was gonna propose and prove him wrong. Great reason to get married, right?" He scoffs.

Andi nods, gripping the phone. "You never liked when he played 'big brother knows best.'"

"See? You get it. He never did... Until he did. The day you had that job interview, he came over while I was getting dinner laid out, roses on the table. Without even asking, he knew what I was gonna do, and begged me not to do it, not to propose and break your heart. By the way, Ma doesn't know this, that I was hours away from making you her daughter, and letting her own dreams come true, so I'd kinda like to keep it that way." Arin chuckles. "She'd kill me for messing up."

"Oh my God, Arin, this is like a fucking soap opera." Andi sighs. "Like something you'd watch play out on TV for weeks. But it's real, and you're telling me what my life was almost like." She licks her lip, trying to accept all his tumbling words.

"What's behind Door Number Two?" he jokes, repeating a line from a game show they watched after school as teens. "You win jealousy, jaded love, and an unused engagement ring!"

"Shit, that's not funny, Arin!" Andi scolds. "This is my life you're talking about."

Arin chuckles. "I had to learn to laugh about it, otherwise the therapy bills were adding up. Do you know how many times I've had to stop myself from writing skits about this?"

"Don't you dare!" She threatens. She slaps her hand down on the bed, causing the cat to flinch. "And then what the fuck happened- because I had a great interview, and was already to come celebrate with you, and-"

Shaking her head, she stops short of confessing she had planned to lose her virginity to him that night. She huffs out.

"What? What could he say that stopped you?"

"Dammit, I wish we were doing this in person," he says quietly.

Andi squirms uncomfortably. "I don't know if that would make it any easier. Just finish, okay?" She looks over her shoulder. The giant red numbers on the clock indicate the time. "I have work in a few hours. I have a feeling it's going to be a long day."

She knows a phone call with Rayaan is long overdue, but it will definitely have to wait.

Breathing out loudly through his nose, Arin picks up where he left off. "Rayaan confronted me, got me to confess my motives weren't altruistic, and told me I'd be making a big fucking mistake- not because of you, but because of me. That I wasn't right for you. We had a fight, and said more shit, but he convinced me I wasn't the one for you. But I made him promise, promise not to tell you why, promise not to make a move on you." He audibly swallows, and she can hear him scratch the stubble on his chin. "Reminded him how Ma always said we had to depend on each other as brothers, and never let anything come between us. Even if that meant neither of us could have you." His teeth hit the bottle as he takes a long swig of his drink. "I left town for a few days, didn't talk to anyone. I guess you called Ma when I didn't show up, and she called him. He told me you cried on the phone, and it broke my heart." He chuckles dryly. "It pissed me off when he married that bitch- because it was the same thing he'd said to me. 'A big fucking mistake.' And I was the only one who knew he married her to try to erase you from his mind." Arin huffs again. "He tried to make it work. But that woman was awful." A crashing sound carries through the phone. "Four lives were ruined by that one decision- five, if you count Elias."

"Oh, Arin," Andi sighs. Empathy rolls off her at the thought of all the pain they suffered. "Maybe it would have been different if we'd all been a little wiser, talked it out."

"When you got kinda famous, do you know how much it hurt to see you on TV or in magazines with some guy?" His laughter barks out. "It sucked. Really bad. How did you put up with that all those years? Watching me with different girls?"

A sense of peace washes over her. It wasn't anything she'd done wrong. Arin hadn't fallen out of love with her, necessarily. He simply loved his brother more. They should have had hard conversations, but who has the foresight in their early twenties to do that? She scratches the back of her head and yawns. Her voice softens. "I thought it was pretty obvious. I'd basically do about anything for the Collins' boys." She giggles.

He yawns in return. "I feel like this discussion isn't over, whether we continue it tomorrow or in a few days, after we've had a chance to replay it all. But you should call him... At the lake, I was the jealous fucker, and I ruined it. Instead, I should have been happy for you both. I'm sorry."

Andi smiles. "I've waited so long to hear those two little words from you, and to know you mean them." She exhales. "I don't know if I'm ready to call him yet." She reaches for the blanket at her feet, pulling it up and lying back, sleepiness finally taking hold. Her heart is lighter. Leaning over, she turns off the lamp. "Let me think on it a few days, like you said. I need to get some sleep now, and we'll talk more soon. But thank you. Thank you for telling me, and still being my friend. That's really important to me, Arin."

"Me too, Ands, me too."

And this time, his use of the nickname doesn't hurt so much.

Chapter Twenty-Four

Unable to sleep, Rayaan scrolls through his phone. He bunches the pillow up under his head and flips his loose hair over the top. Nothing holds his attention as he jumps between apps. Clicking on a political page he follows, a headline captures his attention, making him sit up straight in bed.

"Senate hopeful Jonathan Stratford and political pundit Andrea Jennings- back together and hitting the campaign trail!"

The vague story features paparazzi style photos of the pair sharing a table and hugs in a fancy restaurant in Chicago. In one of the photos, Stratford looks up to Andi, with a dazzling smile, his hand around her wrist in a possessive manner. Before he can finish reading about the retirement of the elder Stratford, Rayaan reaches for the book lying beside him on the bed and throws it across the room. In his fit of anger, a potted flower falls from the shelf and crashes to the floor.

"Fuckin' hell," he mutters, dropping the phone to the bed.

He tucks his legs to his chest and wraps his arms around them. Bowing his head to his chest, he breathes deeply. In and out. Trying to clear his mind. Trying to remember what she'd said about Stratford the day of the float trip.

Moments pass, and his breathing rate returns to normal,

his pulse slowed. The moment of jealousy passing, petering out before allowing it to escalate. Lifting his head, he purses his lips, his beard scratching his nose. He takes the phone and climbs out of bed.

In his bare feet, he pads over to the balcony entrance and steps out onto the overlook. The spring air is warm, almost summer-like. Below, traffic is still moving, despite the late hour.

He quickly types out a message. *Still awake? Call me*

Impatient, he paces the balcony feeling the natural dirt and grime under his feet. The rain shower yesterday carried in debris he hasn't had time to clean up.

The phone rings, and he answers quickly.

"Are we still set to make an offer on that project? The financials look good?"

Rayaan nods his head, listening to the caller. "Uh-huh, hmm…" He hums.

Leaning against the railing, his silver ring clangs against the metal. "Sounds good. Make the acquisition first thing in the morning and send me the paperwork."

Without a goodbye, he hangs up the phone, his grin reaching from ear to ear as he watches over the city.

Chapter Twenty-Five

Blinking awake, Andi is aware the buzzing sound of her phone is not her alarm.

"No one who loves me calls this early," she says, her voice full of sleep and gravel.

"What the hell, woman! Why didn't you tell me you two were back together?" Janessa screams through the phone.

Andi lazily licks her lips, her mouth dry and full of cotton. She blinks slowly. "Stop yelling. With who?" How would Janessa know she'd talked to Arin till the early hours of the morning? "I'm not with anyone."

She flops her arm down on the empty, cold side of the bed.

Definitely not with anyone.

She sighs.

"The senator's son? It's all over the media blogs this morning."

Andi presses her hand to her forehead. "What now?"

"Andrea Jennings, wake the fuck up," Janessa yells. "You're late for work, and you are the media darling this morning- it's everywhere. I'm fielding calls from New York already; people wanting to interview you."

She rubs the sleep from her eyes. "Why would anyone

303

want to interview me?"

Janessa screams, a sound of exasperation filtering through the phone. "You. And Jonathan Stratford, having dinner together last night. The photos look cozy and romantic. Why didn't you tell me?"

Andi swallows hard. Last night comes to her in a flash, and bile rises in the back of her throat. She sits up, whispering obscenities. "That fucker," she says loud enough for Janessa to hear. "It was all staged. To use my political clout, to get his name in the game." Swinging her legs to the floor, she finally pieces together what her friend is saying. "I wonder how he knew where I was… What's the time stamp on the first posting?"

"Hang on, let me look." She can hear Janessa's nails clicking across a keyboard. "Let's see… Looks like around 11:30, last night."

Andi sighs. "I'd already gone to bed." Well, not really- she had been wide awake, learning about what her life could have been, but Janessa doesn't need to know. "That shit would have known I go to bed early." She stands up and moves towards her bathroom suite. "If I get my hands on him, I'll kill him." She looks at her reflection, poking at the redness of her skin. "I'll be at the office in about an hour. If anyone else calls, tell them the story isn't true, and I don't back anyone in that political race."

"Ok, sweetie. What a relief- I never liked that guy. I really want you to be with Ray-"

"Goodbye, Janessa," Andi says before hanging up.

Reaching for her make-up compact, she wills herself to keep her redhead temper in check. Streaking highlights and contours across her cheeks and forehead, Andi's glad it's too early for her mother to have seen any of the gossip blogs yet.

Dabbing at her nose with her makeup brush, she wonders if anyone else of importance has seen the fake news yet?

Too tired to drive, she stretches out in the back of the Uber driving her to work. Thoughts are coming rapidly, and she's not ready for it. She should have called in sick. Trying to sort information from Janessa and the late-night call with Arin might just be too much on a day with so little sleep.

Remembering the unanswered text from Lauren, she types back a reply, thinking the busy mom might already be awake in her time zone.

Mere seconds later, the phone rings. She doesn't even try to hide her exhaustion. "Sorry, I got in late last night, and didn't get to call."

"Jonathan!" Lauren screeches into the phone. "Eew! Why? Remember that one whole drunken night, singing about never, ever getting back together? Sis, you told me to always

305

stop you from doing stupid shit? This is me. Stopping you."

"Good morning, Lauren." Andi replies, quietly. "Glad you checked all the gossip pages before you went to bed last night." She chuckles. "It was nothing. He somehow created a publicity stunt. I'd give up strawberry ice cream before getting back with him."

"Oh, ice cream? Ok," Lauren giggles. "I know you're serious then. You wouldn't give that up."

"Nope," Andi agrees. She taps the driver on the shoulder. "Stop at the corner. I'll get a coffee and walk the rest of the way."

The driver nods, and signals to pull to the side.

"Aren't you at work?"

"Nope," Andi repeats. "I overslept. I," she hums. "I was up late last night, talking to Arin, after watching his latest video."

"Wow. Oh," Lauren gasps. "How did that go?"

Climbing out of the car, Andi breathes deeply. "Better than I expected... Listen, I gotta call you back; I'm late."

"Ok, one thing- Have you talked to Rayaan? People at work are kinda worried about him."

"Yeah, really?" Andi bites her lip. "I know. I need to talk to him. Maybe I'll check on him later. I need to put out these senator race rumors first."

Twenty minutes later, coffee in hand, Andi rides up to the sixteenth floor in the elevator. In the brassy surface on the wall, she surveys her look, patting the chignon at the back of her hair. Ready for a fight, her style is put together and stern, navy slacks with a cropped military style jacket and a crisp white t-shirt. Thankfully she doesn't look as frazzled as she feels. When the elevator reaches the floor, housing the headquarters for the magazine, it seemed like an eternity before the doors open.

There's a flurry of activity, and Janessa is standing in the middle of it. The foyer silences as Andi steps off the elevator, and many of the lower staffers scurry away.

"Shit, did it get worse?" Andi asks, walking to her friend, who was approaching her.

Janessa waves her hand, brushing things aside. She lifts her head. "There's just a lot, today," she says, guiding Andi to her office. "A new development we need to talk about."

"Oh, God. Just rip the band-aid off. What? What is it?" Andi asks, anxiety creeping over her.

Janessa pauses at the door, her hand resting on the knob, holding it open, but not stepping inside. With her other hand, she pats her friend's arm. "It's not bad, not bad at all. Just probably not what you want with all this gossip blowing around."

"Fine, what is it?" Andi asks in exasperation.

Smiling, Janessa announces, "The web group DailyNewsBeat plans to expand their media services, and they want you to be their on-air political commentator." She can barely contain her excitement. "The new company owner wants to meet with you."

Swinging the door open, she ushers her friend into the room.

Andi stalls at the door. "Oh, I don't know, Janessa. I was thinking I should get back into the field, reporting on domestic issues overseas." She steps backwards into the room, still facing her friend. "I don't wanna be just a face on TV."

"The face is nice, but I want you for your brain."

Rayaan Collins' rich voice fills the room, and Andi spins around. Her jaw drops, and she looks at Janessa, still standing at the door. "I didn't know you meant a meeting now!"

With a knowing smile, Janessa says, "I'll leave you two to work things out." She closes the door with a loud click.

"Whatdya say, Red? Wanna come work for me?" Rayaan's hands are in his pockets, but she can see them twitching.

Her heart pounds in her chest and she's sure he can hear it. Wanting nothing more than to run into his arms, Andi takes two steps closer, and then stops. Her damn mouth speaks before she can stop it. "Didn't you hear? I'm an 'independent woman' who 'doesn't need protecting.'"

His smile turns up at the side of his mouth. "Didn't you hear," he stretches out the word 'you,' "I'm 'miserable' and we're 'magic' together?"

A smile begins to form on her face. "I think I heard that somewhere." She takes another step towards Rayaan. His presence makes her boss's office look smaller. She tilts her head. "Did you really buy the news outlet?"

He pulls one hand from his pocket and scratches his beard. He tips his head down but lifts his chin in acknowledgement. "Do you really want to talk business now?"

She licks her lip, her eyes twinkling. Playful. Full of joy, just being in the same room with him. "Isn't that why you're here? To ask me to work for you?"

Taking a step forward, he shakes his head. "Not for me. With me. There's a difference." Rayaan's admiring eyes take her in, hesitation reflected in his. "There's no one else in your life?" he asks, his voice wary and possessive at the same time.

Shit. He's seen the gossip blogs.

She starts with the truth first. "Not unless you count my renewed friendship with the internet star, Arin Collins? I think you know him?" She smiles, biting her lips over her teeth.

"I did hear about that this morning. I think that means we

have lots of things to discuss later, as well. Including the proper apologies." He rubs his finger under his chin. "I meant, are there any new developments?"

Andi shakes her head. "If you're referring to anything else, you should be aware I was an unknowing participant in a publicity stunt last evening."

"Good," he nods. "We can take care of that later. Sue on grounds of a libelous nature, something like that." Advancing another stride closer to her, he holds out his hand. "Buying a news outlet is my grand gesture."

Andi takes his hand and feels fulfilled, like the piece of her missing the last few weeks has found its spot. "I heard about that too," she muses. "Isn't this the part now where you tell me how you really feel about me?" She asks quietly, referring to his brother's video.

He chuckles, pulling her closer. "I think you already know."

She tsk,tsks and shakes her head. "No. I think words are really important, you know. Need to make sure we're both understanding each other." She grins. "Especially after years of failed communication."

Rayaan bows his head and caresses his nose down the side of her cheek. Andi giggles from the graze of his beard. "It's always been you," he whispers.

With a swift motion, he moves back, dropping to his knee

and pulling out the hand from his other pocket. "I've loved you for a lifetime and want to spend the next lifetime telling you how I feel."

Andi's heart jumps in her chest. Is this really happening?

Opening his palm, Rayaan offers her a beautiful ring, aged and weathered.

"Will you marry me?"

Andi gasps, staring at his palm and back up to his face. His beautiful, tanned face, with laugh lines...

"That's your grandmother's ring," she whispers.

Raising his eyebrow, he asks, "How do you know?"

"Your mother showed it to me once, when I was helping her decide what jewelry to wear to a party," she breathes out. "It's beautiful. I've never forgotten it."

With the hand holding hers, he caresses his thumb over the back of her trembling hand.

"It's yours, along with my heart, if you want them," he tells her solemnly.

"And we're simply- we're going to skip dating?" She can't stop the words tumbling from her mouth, ruining a romantic moment. "What if you have habits I hate, like leaving your socks next to the clothes hamper, or cheese wrappers on the counter, and we aren't compatible, and we-"

"So practical," he mumbles under his breath. Rayaan squeezes her fingers in his grasp. "We'll figure it all out.

You're my *jaan* and I'm your King. I've loved you since you were sixteen, and learning to drive, and we would talk for hours about our favorite books. What else do you need to know?"

With her free hand, she reaches under his beard and tilts his chin up and his head back to look into his eyes. "I was just a kid. How did you know?"

He turns his head and gently kisses her palm. "I've always been able to see you, your heart. I want you with me. In the newsroom, in my bed, washing dishes together, on the campaign trail."

Dizzying, she forms her mouth into the shape of an 'o.' "Wow. That's a lot of future dreams- campaign trail?"

He chuckles, and tugs her forward, pulling her down to rest on his bent knee. "Red, are you saying 'yes' or not? My beard is gonna grow white, waiting for you to answer."

"Do you want more children?" She looks unsure.

Clutching the ring in his fist, he wraps his arm around her waist. "I only want what you want." His deep brown eyes offer her all the reassurance she needs. "Whatever makes you happy."

"You make me happy." Andi bites in her smile. "Have you talked to Elias about me?"

Slowly bobbing his head, Rayaan admits, "I asked him what he thought about making you a permanent piece of our lives. He wanted to know if he'd still have to call you 'Auntie?'"

Andi giggles, pushing back the strand of hair that covers his eye. "I'm sure we could come up with a more suitable title." Sighing happily, she throws her arms around his neck, whispering in his ear. "A thousand times yes. I'll marry you." She tugs at his earlobe with her teeth. "Will you put the ring on my hand?"

Her gaze drops to their hands, and her eyes fill with tears as he slides the ring in place, fitting perfectly.

"You make me the luckiest man, Andi." Rayaan reaches up to caress the side of her face, wiping away the tears of joy. "I've missed you We've lost so much time when we could have been together... I wanna wake up next to you every morning, *meri jaan*."

Tightening his grip, he brings Andi's face to his, claiming her mouth. She can taste the lingering flavor of his morning coffee mixed with her salty tears, and she smiles against him. Sinking into his warmth, she parts her mouth and teases his with the tip of her tongue. Bringing her arms over Rayaan's broad shoulders, she nearly topples them to the floor as each French kiss chases after the other. She holds him tight while he quietly moans his adoration.

As he slowly pulls them apart, Andi flips her hand in the air, catching the light to admire the silver sparkle and

313

diamond.

Still in awe of the monumental decision they've made, she whispers, "Andrea Jennings Collins."

Rayaan squeezes her hip. "No 'Jennings.' You'll be all mine. For always."

With light laughter, she taps his chest. "You, King, have a bit of a possessive streak."

"Damn right I do." He lifts her hand and kisses the ring on her finger. "I take care of what's mine."

The words are out before she can reel them in. "How do you still have the ring? Shouldn't it have been for-"

Rayaan playfully covers her mouth with his large hand, clamping off the end of her sentence. "Ma never offered it to me before." He slides his hand back and pinches her cheeks. "She gave it to me after the divorce. Said I would know when to give it to the 'right one.'"

Andi's eyes grow wide. "She's a bit of a mystery, isn't she? How would she know?" Rising from his leg, she straightens out her pants. "Does she know you're here now?

Pulling himself off the floor, he rises to full height, shaking his head, and looks down at her. "Only two people on my sales team."

She straightens the lapel of his coat, still amazed at the glistening addition to her finger. "Did you really plan to propose, or just offer me the job?"

He chuckles, reaching for a strand of her hair and twisting it around his finger. "Why all the questions?"

She tilts her head. "I'm a new reporter for DailyNewsBeat. Questions are my job."

Rayaan gives the strand of hair a tug before dropping it. He takes her newly ringed hand and presses it to his heart. "I was so afraid the ring was going to get lost in airport security." His eyes gaze at her face, taking in every imperfection. "I was going to offer you the job first, and propose at a celebratory dinner tonight. But when I saw you, you took my breath away. I felt like a nervous kid again, wanting to be near you, but not knowing if I could touch you. Not knowing if you'd forgiven me yet."

She sighs, "I don't know if I've forgiven you yet, but everything we went through got us here. This is where we're supposed to be-"

"Guys, I have a meeting in thirty minutes," Janessa's voice announces over the speaker. "Can I get back in my office?"

Rayaan throws his head back in laughter. Andi looks around, having forgotten they were actually in her friend's office.

"Oh, my God, yes! We're so sorry! We've been going over important details." Andi smiles at her ring.

"All good, I hope?" Janessa asks.

The machine clicks off and Andi replies, "Very good. Just

what I needed."

Epilogue

Eight Months Later

Rayaan steps out of the closet, adjusting his cufflinks. "You about ready?"

He takes a deep breath as he waits for her. Tonight's a big night for them. Maybe that's why he's been oddly emotional all day, even nervous. But the past few months have proven to him what he's always known: there's nothing he can't do if he has his woman by his side.

Andi opens the bathroom door. Leaning against the doorframe, she bends to adjust one of the straps of her heels.

A low whistle escapes from his lips. "Looking good, Red." He practically prowls, moving towards her. The emerald green party dress compliments her bold red hair. It reminds him of the dress she wore when she walked back into his life last spring. It hugs her curves and dips low enough in front for an appreciative view of her ample cleavage.

With a faint blush, she stands and smooths down the silky fabric. Pointing over her shoulder, she says, "I can't reach the zipper."

He squints his eyes and grins. "Likely story." He motions for her to step closer.

Andi follows his lead, turning away from him. He grabs her hip and pulls her closer. He reaches up, and gently gathers her beautiful red curls, throwing them over her shoulder. He inhales deeply. "Apples," he sighs contentedly.

"Are you smelling my hair?" Andi giggles.

"Still can't get enough," he says, beginning to tug at the zipper. "Making up for all those missed times I wanted to smell your hair but couldn't."

"Have I told you lately that I love you?"

Pulling up on the zipper, Rayaan leans down and whispers against her ear, "What if I help you out of this dress instead of into it? We can stay up here and-"

"Everyone is downstairs!" Andi twists her upper body to look over her shoulder at him. "Your parents' anniversary party starts in less than an hour!"

Moving closer, he presses himself against her and delivers a soft kiss to the pale, bare skin on her shoulder. "The caterers have it under control."

She slowly breathes out. "We're hosting."

"Our siblings are downstairs; they can handle it."

She sags against him, pushing her ass against his cock. He should have worn looser slacks. He's hard and ready for her, and the evidence surely shows. "Now you're just teasing me," he growls.

"The zipper, King, the zipper."

318

She taps her foot impatiently.

"Where is your youthful sense of spontaneity and adventure-"

"Are you calling me old, because that will get you nowhere-"

"Shit. It's stuck." Rayaan jerks the metal clasp again, but it won't budge. "I wish I was joking with you, but I'm not. Let me get a closer look; I'll fix it."

He backs up against the bed, sitting down when it bumps against the back of his knees. Drawing her to him, he chuckles at her whispered series of expletives. "That is a creative use of words there, Mrs. Collins." He leans closer for a better look at the problem.

"Fuck. There's a word."

"Right now, you are not helping, *meri jaan*," Rayaan says, through his clenched jaw. "The fabric is stuck in the little metal teeth."

He can't forget his state of arousal. It's heightened by her reaction, probably involuntary, when he drags his fingers over her skin, pulling the dress away from her body. He stretches the fabric until it finally comes loose.

But she doesn't have to know that yet.

"Come closer. I can't see it."

He wraps his arms around her waist and hauls her onto his lap, her back to his chest.

"Rayaan."

The hitch in her voice belies her irritation at being late to the party.

Smoothly, he reaches one hand up, grasping her full breast and giving it a squeeze. The other hand travels down her thigh, searching for the hem of the full tea-length skirt. Continuing to squeeze and giving an added pinch to her breast, his fingers graze her skin, dragging up her thigh.

"I hadn't considered this as an option," Andi admits with a sigh. She drops her head back against his shoulder. It makes a faint cracking sound, releasing all the tension she's carried for days, wanting to make the party perfect. She begins to grind on his lap as his fingers push her panties to the side-

"Dad! Andi!" A fist pounds on the door. "Are you ready? Gramma Sarah can't find the punch bowl!"

"Gotta love kids," Rayaan huffs as he swipes his finger over her wet opening before pulling away. "Out in a minute, kiddo. I think Andi went down the backstairs. Check the kitchen," he shouts to the closed door.

"For Andi, or the bowl?" Elias says loudly.

"Both!" Rayaan yells. Adjusting her panties back in place, he breathes easier hearing the pre-teen boy's shoes retreat down the hall. Tickling her thigh, he bumps his head against hers. "Thank you for not wanting another one. I think I'm too old," he chuckles.

"Yeah, you're right," she teases, yelping as he bites her exposed neck.

"You're so funny." He fakes a laugh and pats her hip. "Stand up. I guess I have to help you put this dress on after all. Though I'd rather be taking it off."

"Later, King. The party won't last all night."

Andi rises, still straddling his thigh. He lifts his leg, giving her another slight tease. Kissing her exposed back, he pulls the zipper up, latching the little clasp. "They invited the Tomlinsons. You know how they are."

Andi turns to face her husband. "Fine. The more grown-up grown-ups can party all night, and we can sneak off and find a make out spot."

Rayaan squints his eyes, enjoying his wife's playful mood. "Third floor linen closet, midnight?"

Leaning down, she caresses his beard, kissing the dimple to the side of his cheek. "It's a date." She reaches for his hand and pulls. "Come on, we need to go find a punch bowl."

Rayaan turns to the sound of his brother's voice. "The renovations look great. Turning the third garage bay into a home gym was brilliant. Did you guys end up taking the upstairs room, or give it to Elias?"

The changes needed to turn the lake rental house into

their actual home had been a bit more challenging than Rayaan and Andi had anticipated. The owner told them after they had rented it out for their wedding weekend that he was planning to sell. Seeing how so many of their shared memories of their childhood had been on the lake and their new life together had started right there, purchasing the property was the obvious choice.

"We took the upstairs room, and we're remodeling the bathroom. Elias picked the rooms with the Jack and Jill bath on the second floor. He sleeps in one room and has the other one set up for gaming. He had a friend over last weekend, and they played games till nearly two am."

Arin nods. "It all worked out for you, *bhai*. I'm really happy for you both."

Rayaan claps his hand to the back of his brother's neck. "I know you are, and that really means a lot to us." He looks around. "Where's your movie star girlf-"

"I'm here alone. That's all I wanna say." Arin takes a sip from the beer bottle in his hand. "She asked me not to make any videos about it, and out of respect, I won't."

"Hell, man! Does that mean you've grown, as a person?"

The two brothers joke and continue to banter back and forth as the party hits its second wind. Servers run in and out of the house, carrying food to the rented tent set up in the driveway. Tables with beautiful bouquets of flowers scatter around the edges, and white lights sparkle everywhere. Their parents' friends mingle and catch up, as though they haven't seen each other in years. While in reality they most likely played golf or lunched together just last week.

But forty-five years of marriage is an amazing accomplishment. Something to celebrate.

Rayaan plans to have all their luck this time around.

"If I could have everyone's attention!" The DJ's voice booms over the mic and echoes through the chilly night air. "The anniversary couple wanted to invite their oldest son and his new wife to have their first official dance! I'm told they simply ran off and married in a small ceremony, with close friends and family only." He clears his throat. "If you're here now, and weren't invited, take it up with them. I'm just the messenger."

The crowd laughs and begins looking around the tented space for the younger couple.

Rayaan bounces on the balls of his feet, full of nervous energy as Andi walks forward. He holds up his hand, motioning for her to wait there. Andi tilts her head in curiosity. She mouths, "Did you know about this?"

As the crowd quiets, Rayaan looks around to all the faces of their friends and family. Prisha and Sarah stand proudly together, eyes filled with happy tears. Stephen holds a squirming Jackson, who is trying to get away to chase one of the hundreds of balloons on the dance floor. His father nods stoically, sending a jolt of pride through him. Arin, Logan, and Lauren stand together near the dessert table, beaming with joy.

"You got this, Dad," Elias says, patting his father on the shoulder before stepping away from the limelight.

The melody begins, the delicate sounds of a piano keyboard filling the space. He slowly moves towards his lovely bride. He can spot the moment she remembers. That night many, many years ago. Her hands fly to her face, covering her mouth and nose, trying to keep herself from crying as tears fight to spill over.

His heart fills with merriment as the whispered words around him reach his ears.

"She's so beautiful!"

"Her dress is lovely!"

"Look how happy they are!"

"Such a good-looking couple."

His own tears flood his eyes, and he does his best to blink them away, so he can burn this moment into his memory as well. Taking her hand, he twirls her towards him, her skirt swirling around their legs.

Settling against him, Andi smiles. "Good song." She tugs his beard. "You talked your mom into this, didn't you?"

He chuckles, sniffling. "It's always been our song," he says

324

with a shrug.

"Oh, has it?"

"Well, maybe that moment wasn't so special to you." He feigns a hurt look as she taps his chest in fake anger. "But never in my life have I heard it without thinking of you. I mean, you did sing it to me."

Andi pulls back and looks at him, unsure. "I did not. I don't sing."

"You did. You had your head rested on my shoulder and you quietly sang. Listen to the words... You'll remember."

The pair lock eyes as they listen, moving confidently around the dance floor.

Her eyes widen with the memory. "Our song." She agrees. "Since forever."

Author's Note:

A special thanks to my amazing writing team! I couldn't have put this labor of love together without you. I was beginning to think after losing Mom, I'd never write again. But these wonderful women (and handsome Muses!) kept pushing me forward. I wouldn't have made it through the last three years without you. 'Thank you' just isn't enough...

Lisa Andrew
Devika Fernando
Jules Dizon
Liz Shepherd
DJ Siciliano
Mia Epsilon
Fayrouz Naji
Rosemary Rey

And a warm welcome to Mina Dot! I'm so honored to feature her artwork on my cover, depicting Rayaan and Andi just like I pictured them! This is her debut cover- with her amazing talents, she will go far!

About the Author: Cass Michaels

A displaced Southern Belle growing up in the Midwest, Cass Michaels always was an avid reader. At a young age, she was caught more than once sneaking off with her mother's steamy romance novels and gossip tabloids, quickly developing a taste for the rich and famous lifestyles. She was often heard to say after reading a story, "I could write that!"

So one day, she did.

Taking her love of Hollywood glamour and movie star gossip, she slowly built her way up as a popular blogger, sharing short stories and reaching over 48,000 readers under a nom de plume. Like the characters in her stories, she prefers to keep a low profile and wishes to maintain her secret identity.

With the strong support of a group of writers and readers Cass lovingly calls her "girls," she began writing her first novel. This is Cass's sixth published novel.

So devoted to her writing spot, she ruined the family couch and had to get a new one. It's not as comfortable. But most days, she can still be found with her cat cuddled at her side, while she works on her signature theme - sassy, independent women looking for men who need rescuing. Her talent as a writer shines brightest when she takes an everyday situation and adds humor and sex appeal to something as simple as a haircut or baking brownies.

www.writercassmichaels.com

www.twitter.com/WriterCMichaels

About the Artist: Mina Dot

Mina currently attends Rhode Island School of Design, pursuing her degree in illustration with a concentration in Drawing.

This is Mina's cover art debut.

www.minadot.art

Other Books by Cass Michaels

Sweet Thing Brewing
Chasing Winter
Beautiful Design

The Thalia Series, co-written with Gisela Grey
Book 1: Educating Thalia
Book 2: Becoming Thalia

Made in United States
North Haven, CT
14 May 2023

36580157R00183